A very Merry Christmas

To Teresa Marie

1996

Love Always

Grandma Rush

JACK WEYLAND

Deseret Book Company
Salt Lake City, Utah

Library of Congress Cataloging-in-Publication Data

Weyland, Jack, 1940–
    Lean on Me / Jack Weyland.
        p.   cm.
    Summary: Five Mormon teenagers form an a cappella singing group in their senior year of high school and help each other deal with family problems, moral dilemmas, and changing personal relationships.
    ISBN 1-57345-214-9 (hardcover)
    [1. Mormons—Fiction. 2. Conduct of life—Fiction.
    3. Interpersonal relations—Fiction. 4. Friendship—Fiction.]
    I. Title.
    PZ7.W538Le   1996
    [Fic]—dc20   96-27284
                                                                       CIP
                                                                        AC

Printed in the United States of America

10 9   8   7   6   5   4   3   2   1

To friends everywhere who,
as we grow up,
help us hold fast to the truths of the gospel.

This novel is loosely based on a true story. In 1991, five high school students from Rexburg, Idaho, started an a cappella singing group. That group today is called TIME, which stands for *Taking Inspirational Music Everywhere.* Some parts of their story are included in this book, but the rest of the story is fiction. One should not make any inferences about the lives of these talented musicians from reading this book.

1

December 1995

There's a story about a guy who falls asleep for years, and when he wakes up, everything's changed. That was what it seemed like after I got back from my mission.

I'd been home less than a day when my mom sent me to the store. This was at nine o'clock at night during a major snowstorm. The reason it couldn't wait until morning was that, while I'd been gone on my mission, my mom had taken in a stray cat, and that night she'd run out of cat food. Before I left for the store, I asked my mom, "Isn't a cat supposed to catch mice? So why do we have to feed him?"

It was useless to argue. She told me to get Nine Lives Gourmet Chicken and Liver Dinner. I asked what I should do if I couldn't find that exact kind. She told me to go from store to store until I found it. "Even if it takes all night?" I asked.

"Sylvester won't eat anything else," she said. (That's right, my mom named the cat *Sylvester.* See what happens when I go away?)

"He'd eat something else eventually," I said. "I mean if it were either that or else starve to death."

"Greg, how can you even think something so cruel?" she asked.

1

Actually, it was easy. I've never liked cats.

A few minutes later, in front of the cat food display at Albertson's, I finally found Sylvester's food. I grabbed six cans, went down an aisle, turned to go to the checkout counter, and nearly knocked over Jennifer Whittaker.

Jennifer is Amber's younger sister. In high school, Amber and I, with three of our friends, were in a singing group called Fast Forward. By the time I returned from my mission, Amber had graduated from Ricks and transferred to BYU. While at the Y, she'd met someone and got engaged. End of story.

New story. "Greg, is that you?" Jennifer asked.

"Oh, my gosh! I can't believe this! Let me get a look at you. You look so . . . so grown up." We did a quick post-mission hug.

Actually, the first thought that came to mind when I saw Jennifer was not *grown up*. It was *beautiful*. I could have said that, but in high school I'd always thought of Jennifer as just Amber's kid sister. She sure didn't look like a kid now, though. This was going to take some getting used to.

Jennifer is two years younger than Amber. Both have the same dark brown hair and eyes the color of black olives. They look a lot alike, except Jennifer isn't as tall as Amber.

"Do you want to help me find some things?" she asked.

"Yeah, sure. Here, let me push the cart for you," I said.

"No, thanks." She took off without me.

I caught up with her. "Why would you want to push the cart when I'm here?"

"I'm not helpless, you know. I can push my own cart."

"Is this some kind of a self-assertiveness thing?"

She smiled. "Yeah, pretty much."

After we picked up eggs, bread, cereal, nachos, and salsa, I asked, "Is Amber home from the Y yet?" I tried to say it the same way I might ask about the weather.

Jennifer nodded. "She had her last final late yesterday

afternoon, so she didn't get home until around two this morning."

"How's she doing?" I asked.

"Real good." A short pause. "She's engaged, you know."

"Yeah, I heard she was," I said. "I'm real happy for her."

Jennifer glanced at me, probably trying to decide if I really meant it. I wasn't sure myself.

We paid for our groceries and started to leave but stopped at the entrance to get up enough courage to go into the raging storm.

I still couldn't get over how much Jennifer had changed during my mission.

She noticed me watching her. "Looks like I caught up with you, didn't I?" she asked.

"Looks that way."

"I always knew I would," she said almost smugly. "I took a couple of classes last summer, so I'm nearly a sophomore now. Let's see, Greg, you'll be a first-semester freshman, right?"

"Well, yeah, that's right," I stammered.

She was loving this. "Look, if you need any help getting used to college life, just call me, okay?"

It was then I realized that at Ricks I'd be surrounded by the little sisters of the girls I'd gone to high school with. In the two years I'd been gone on my mission, most of the girls from my graduating class had already finished at Ricks.

We left the store. "Let me help you," I said, grabbing her sack of groceries as we started through the snow. "Tell me about the guy Amber's engaged to."

"His name's Michael Dupree. He's really nice. His dad owns some banks in California. His folks are building a house for Michael and Amber right next door to where they live. Michael called this afternoon to ask if Amber wanted a shower with multiple heads—you know, the kind where you don't have to turn around to get your other side wet."

"Is turning around in a shower that much of a bother?" I asked.

"I totally agree."

"Besides, how do you know what to wash if the water is hitting you from all sides?"

"Gosh, I don't know," she said. "We'll have to ask Amber that after they're married." Snow was already beginning to collect on our coats. "Do you want to sit in the car and talk?" she asked.

It was either that or turn into snowmen, so we got in her car. She started the engine and turned on the heater. "So, how's college life?" I asked.

"Great. I love it," she said, and then she enthusiastically told me about Ricks.

While she was talking, I couldn't help thinking about Amber. I didn't envy Michael all that much. I was sure that after he and Amber were married, she'd have him whipped into shape in a few weeks, and then for the rest of his life he'd be hanging the towels in their bathroom exactly the way Amber wanted. Poor guy. It was better this way. For me, I mean.

Jennifer probably regretted asking me about my mission because, once I got started, there was no stopping me. The snow began to cover the windshield like a curtain.

"This is *so* interesting," she said. "Why don't we go to Frontier Pies and have some hot chocolate and talk some more?"

"All right, but I've got to get this cat food home before our cat eats my parents."

"I need to run these things home too. Could you come by the house in maybe half an hour?" she asked.

The thought of Amber watching me drop by for her little sister was too much. "Maybe some other time, okay? I probably should get home."

4

"Are you worried about Amber seeing us together?" she asked.

"Well, yeah, I guess I am."

"Look, you won't even have to come in the house. Just pull into the driveway, and I'll come right out. I really would like to hear more about your mission."

"All right," I said, wondering how I was going to handle being alone with a girl for the first time in two years.

A few minutes later, when I entered our house, Sylvester the Cat met me at the door. He has this way of getting underfoot when he wants attention. As I climbed the four stairs from our entrance to the main floor of our house, he walked ahead of me, leading the way into the kitchen. *He must think I'm so stupid that he has to lead me around to get me to do what he wants,* I thought.

I opened the can and plopped one-third of it onto a paper plate. Sylvester showed his lack of patience by extending himself on the cabinet door. The first time I'd fed him, I had set the blob of cat food on the paper plate on the floor. My mom had caught me and made me take a fork and break the chunks into little cat-mouth pieces. I was beginning to see that if Sylvester was not happy, my mom was not happy.

With the cat taken care of, I went to my room. I couldn't decide whether to shave or not. Shaving before spending time with a girl is almost a serious commitment.

This is crazy, I thought. *What am I doing? Jennifer's way too young for me.*

But on the other hand, Jennifer was now as old as Amber had been when I left on my mission. Also, she was probably the only girl I'd know when I started at Ricks in January. Besides, she was really beautiful and she liked me, which isn't a bad combination. My final justification was that taking Jennifer out for hot chocolate might be a good way to let Amber know I really didn't care that she was engaged.

If I did decide to shave, I didn't want to use my electric

razor because, although my folks were already in bed, the sound might cause my mom to get up and ask me what was going on. If I were to tell her I'd seen Jennifer Whittaker at the store and that we were going out for hot chocolate, my fear was that she'd say, *"You mean Amber's little sister?"*

In spite of the risks involved, I shaved. But I used shaving cream and a razor to keep the noise down. When I finished, I put on a clean shirt.

My mind was playing cruel tricks on me. I thought about going to a store and picking up a yo-yo for Jennifer. I had given her one long ago when she had a stay in the hospital. She had liked the yo-yo because it helped her pass the time.

The last thing I did before leaving the house was to change into cowboy boots because they made me a little taller. Most of the way through high school, Amber had been taller than I was. So tonight, if Amber happened to see me with Jennifer, at least she'd see me walk out of her life looking tall.

I'm so vain, I thought as I walked out to my dad's pickup. *But at least now it's a taller vain.*

True to her word, Jennifer came out as soon as I pulled into her driveway. But she didn't get in. "My mom and dad can't believe you'd come here without seeing them. It's been two years. They'd really like you to come in and say hello."

I'm not sure what worried me the most about going inside—dealing with Mr. Whittaker or having to face the very happily engaged Amber.

Mr. Whittaker was a large man, maybe six-foot-three, easily over two hundred pounds, bald except for a crow's nest growth around the sides. He had a low voice and a perpetual scowl. When I was in high school and hanging around the Whittakers a lot, I could never decide if he liked me or not. Amber kept telling me it was just his way of teasing and that I shouldn't take him seriously.

The first thing Mr. Whittaker said when I walked into the

house was, "I thought we got rid of you." Although it didn't sound like a very warm greeting, he got up from his favorite chair, came over, and firmly shook my hand. But then he turned to his wife. "For two years I've been telling you we needed to move, but would you do it? No. And now it's too late, because Greg's back."

"Dad, don't be such a tease," Jennifer said.

Mrs. Whittaker, probably trying to make up for her husband's teasing, came over and gave me a hug. "We're so glad to see you again, Greg. My, what a fine young man you've become."

"Be careful; don't encourage him," Mr. Whittaker whispered confidentially to his wife, but, of course, loud enough for me to overhear. "We still have one daughter left."

Jennifer was not at all amused by her dad. "We're going now," she announced.

Amber was in the kitchen, talking on the phone with Michael in California. She came partway into the living room, waved at me, and said over the phone, "There's a guy here for Jennifer. I knew him in high school. He just got off his mission, so I need to say hello to him before he leaves. How about if I turn you over to Jennifer?"

Amber came into the living room as Jennifer went into the kitchen to talk to Michael on the phone. Amber looked unbelievably good—not just more beautiful. It was much more than that. She seemed very confident and self-assured.

It was a little unsettling to see her, and at first I didn't know what to do—shake hands or give her a hug. We'd been plenty close enough in high school for a hug, especially after two years of being apart. But, on the other hand, she was engaged now, and I'd just returned from a mission, so maybe a hug would be too much. Also, Jennifer and Mr. and Mrs. Whittaker were watching us.

In high school there were times when Amber and I had been just best friends and that was okay with both of us.

And then there were times when I had wanted it to be more than that, but she wasn't ready for anything more serious. Near the end of our senior year, she changed and wanted us to be more than friends, but by that time I was going with Camille, a girl who had gotten married just before I returned from my mission.

I finally decided that after all that Amber and I had gone through in high school, I couldn't just settle for a polite nod or a handshake. If I were to go to her wedding reception, I'd give her a hug in front of the groom, so why not in front of her parents? After all, we'd been best friends in high school, and it had been two years since we'd last seen each other. So I decided to go for a hug. Perfectly acceptable.

Hug and release. That was the plan. And that's what I did, except the release part was a little delayed. When I finally released, I was blushing, blaming myself for not letting go sooner.

Amber, though, didn't seem to be concerned about the length of our hug.

After two years, I wanted to be witty and charming and very clever, but the best I could come up with was, "So . . . you're engaged, huh?"

"That's right."

"That's real good. I'm happy for you."

"Thank you. I know I should have written and told you, but I was so busy last semester. I had nineteen credits, plus I was working fifteen hours a week."

"My gosh," Mr. Whittaker said privately to his wife, "did you notice how long he held on to her? That's not right, is it?"

Amber started laughing. She has one of the best laughs I've ever heard. In high school she even worked with me on my laugh. "Dad, isn't there something you need to go fix?"

"Are you kidding? I wouldn't miss this for the world."

Mrs. Whittaker took her husband by the hand. "We'll be in the kitchen," she said.

They left, leaving me and Amber alone together for the first time in two years, except for Jennifer, who was keeping a wary eye on us from the kitchen.

"So, how was your mission?" she asked.

"Great. I learned a lot."

"I bet you were a good missionary," Amber said.

"I tried to be."

I couldn't believe how safe we were playing this.

When I first met Amber, in our junior year when we started Fast Forward, she used way too much makeup around her eyes, so when you looked at her all you saw were EYES. We did a lot of back-and-forth advice-giving back then, so one time she asked my opinion, and I suggested she back off a little on the eye makeup. She did and it helped. At least I thought it did.

In high school her hair kept getting longer and longer until it threatened to take over the world; but now it was just down to the neck of her BYU sweatshirt. It looked much better. I would have told her so too, but I thought, *Why waste a good compliment on someone who's engaged?*

What I'm trying to say is I'd never seen her look better.

Most of the way through high school she'd been taller than me. Not bigger, just taller. I've always been a big kid, the kind of guy you ask to move a piano or bust through the line and take out the quarterback. Maybe it was because she was taller that she pretty much wrote me off as anything but a friend. I'd just as soon go on thinking that was the reason. At least that's something I had no control over. But now, standing beside her in her living room, with my cowboy boots on, I was pretty sure I was at least two inches taller than she was.

"So, you and Jennifer are going out tonight, huh?" Amber asked, trying not to break into a cheesy grin.

9

"It's just for hot chocolate. She asked me to tell her about my mission."

Amber put up her hands like she was surrendering. "Hey, you don't have to explain anything to me. I think it's great. Let's see, as I remember it, Greg, you were the one who taught her how to tie her shoes, right?" The grin she'd been holding back now burst across her face. It was such a cheap shot, and, of course, it wasn't true, but I wasn't surprised she'd said it. We had a history of teasing each other.

"Sorry," she said. "I promised myself I wasn't going to do that. Actually, if you want to know the truth, I think it's terrific." She leaned toward me confidentially like a much older and wiser person. "There is one thing, though." She pointed her index finger at me to emphasize the importance of her advice. "I just hope you two kids will always remember who you are." She gave me that same silly grin she had used on me all through high school.

"Are you finished yet?" I asked.

Big smile. "Yeah, I think so."

"Fine, let's move on then. Do you see Brooke much?"

"Not really. You know she's going to ISU, don't you?" Amber asked.

"Yeah, she wrote me almost every month," I said. "That's better than some people I can name."

Amber shrugged her shoulders. "I was pretty good about writing you until I met Michael. Let's see—Ryan gets back in March and Jonathan in April. Have I got that right?"

I nodded my head. "When they get back, we'll have to get together and see if we can still sing."

"Maybe so, but we'll have to hurry. Michael and I are talking about getting married in June, and then we'll be moving to California."

"Do you ever listen to the tape we made?" I asked.

"I used to listen to it all the time, but now, not much.

Actually, Jennifer asked me for it. I think she listens to it a lot now."

I could see the two sisters—Amber, a respectful three feet away, and Jennifer in the kitchen talking to Michael. They had almost the same color hair. Amber had poutier lips and darker eyebrows than her sister. I used to think that Amber looked better on stage than anywhere else. She had this thing about performing. While the rest of us got nervous, she got energized.

If they'd been hot sauces, Jennifer would have been mild, but Amber would be hot with lots of Tabasco sauce, the kind that makes your forehead sweat and causes you to grab for a pitcher of water. Or at least that's the way she affected me in high school.

"Are you singing much these days?" I asked.

"Not really."

"Does Michael sing?"

"No." She paused. "Michael is more into making money."

I felt foolish. "Money is good too."

Jennifer called out from the kitchen, "I'm all done talking to Michael."

Amber started back to the kitchen. "Nice to see you, Greg. I expect Fast Forward to sing at my wedding reception."

"We'll need someone to take your place."

"What about Jennifer? She's a pretty good singer. And she's been taking lessons. Why don't you take her to the stairwell at the Manwaring Center tonight and see how she sounds. I could work with her over the next few days and teach her some of the songs we used to sing. I'll be here until the day after Christmas, and then I'm flying out to be with Michael and his family for the rest of the holidays."

Jennifer must have felt bad she'd put me through all this. She grabbed my sleeve, announced to the whole family that we were leaving, and before her dad could make it into the living room for one last put-down, she hustled me outside.

As we pulled out of her driveway, she said, "I'm sorry about my dad and Amber, and that everything took so long."

"That's okay. Whose idea was it to have me come in and see your parents?"

"It was my dad's idea."

"Really? He likes me then, huh?" I asked.

"Of course he does. Is that a surprise?"

"Before my mission, I was never sure if he did or not."

"He talked about you a lot while you were gone," Jennifer said.

"That's good to know."

"Is it hard for you to deal with Amber being engaged?" she asked.

I shrugged my shoulders. "Not really."

"It's not bothering you at all?" she asked.

"All right, it bothered me at first. But not because of what you might think. It's mainly because she's not going to sing with us. She was the one who made the rest of us promise we'd get back together after our missions."

We had hot chocolate at Frontier Pies. People kept coming up and talking to Jennifer. She always introduced me as a friend of hers who'd just gotten off a mission. I was glad she did that. I didn't want her to think of me as just Amber's friend. That part of my life was over. It was time to move on.

I was impressed by how good Jennifer was with people. She was lively and fun. I could see why she had so many friends.

"Is there any chance I might be able to sing with you guys?" she asked on our way through the snow to the pickup just before Frontier Pies was about to close.

"That's hard to say until I've heard you sing." I paused. "Do you want to go to the stairwell where we used to practice, so I can listen to you?"

"Sure, why not?" she said.

There were only a few cars outside the Manwaring Center at Ricks College. The snow was eight inches deep in places on the sidewalk.

"It's probably closed," I said.

"Let's just make sure," Jennifer said. We walked to the door and opened it. Some of the lights were on, but the building seemed to be deserted. The stairwell we'd practiced in all the way through high school was not too far from the main desk. "You guys spent a lot of time practicing in here, didn't you?" she asked, once we were inside the enclosed stairwell.

I nodded. "This is where I was the happiest."

"Did you know it would be so painful to grow up?" she asked.

"Painful then, or painful now?"

She didn't answer. Maybe she was afraid I'd talk about Amber. But I wouldn't have. On my mission I'd learned to deal with rejection and disappointment. There had been plenty of people who took four discussions and then said they weren't interested. Amber being engaged wasn't any worse than that. I could deal with it. Sometimes things work out and sometimes they don't. You just have to accept it and go on. I mean, what else is there to do? Besides, I'd already been dumped once on my mission, by Camille. I could deal with this. No problem.

I walked up the stairs to the landing where the stairs reversed direction on their upward climb to the second floor. I turned around. Jennifer was still below me. "As I remember, we sounded better up here."

She came up the stairs. She rested her hand on my shoulder as she sat down next to me. "Does it seem strange to be back here again?" she asked.

I looked around. Everything was the same. "Yeah, it does."

"Are you okay being here alone with me so soon after your mission?" she asked.

"Well, not really, but I'll get used to it."

"I've gotten to know a couple of guys at Ricks who just came home from their missions. We're in the same family home evening group and sort of hang out together. I've tried to help them get adjusted. Maybe I could do that for you too."

"My gosh, Jennifer. How did you get to be older and wiser than me?"

She loved the compliment. "It just happened, that's all."

Looking at her from the side in the dim lighting of the stairwell, she reminded me of Amber. She even smelled like Amber. "Are you wearing perfume?" I asked.

"Yes."

"But you weren't wearing any at Albertson's, were you?"

"No. I put some on after I got home."

"It smells familiar," I said. "Is it something Amber used to wear?"

"Yeah, it is, come to think of it. I don't wear perfume much. Let's see, she gave it to me last summer. She said she'd found something she liked better." She paused. "You don't mind that I'm wearing it, do you?"

I cleared my throat. "No, that's okay, really. No use letting it go to waste."

She touched my cheek with her hand. "While we're examining motives here, I noticed something while we were having hot chocolate. You shaved when you went home, didn't you?"

I felt my face turning red. "Well, yes I did, but . . ." My voice faded away.

"Gosh, you don't have to explain. Fixing up for each other is new for us, isn't it?"

"Yeah, it is," I said.

14

"Greg, do you remember that time when I was so messed up, and you came over to help me?"

"I remember. That was scary."

"I was embarrassed to have you see me like that. But it was also really exciting to have you pay attention to me. It feels a little bit like that right now."

I didn't know exactly what to say, so I just sat there. We were seated side by side on the stairs, and Jennifer looped her arm through mine and leaned her head on my shoulder. We sat like that for a few moments, and then she stood up and took off her parka. "Okay, are you ready to hear me sing? I've been taking voice lessons, so I have a couple of songs. This one is in Italian."

She started singing. It wasn't that bad actually. When she finished, I said, "That was really good."

"Not really, but I'll get better. You'll see. I'm a fast learner. I've listened to your tape so much I practically have it memorized."

She sang "Stand by Me" just the way Amber had sung it on our demo tape. It was crazy. If I closed my eyes, I couldn't tell the difference. She must have practiced a long time to match Amber's every inflection. But, even so, for me it wasn't the same because it wasn't Amber.

She plopped her baseball cap on my head. "Stand up and sing with me, Greg."

"I haven't sung any of these songs for two years."

"I know, but that's okay. Please. I just want to see what it's like to sing with you."

We sang one of the songs Fast Forward had done on the tape. I made more mistakes than she did.

"Okay, I'm happy," she said. "Take me home now."

By the time we stepped into the lobby of the building, all the lights had been turned off. While we'd been talking, someone had also locked up the building for the night. We had to push the crash bar on the front door to get out.

15

We were outside walking toward the pickup when a police car pulled up. A policeman got out of the car and walked toward us. "Did you two just come out of there?" he asked.

I turned around to look at the building. Our fresh tracks in the snow showed what had happened.

"Yes, we did. Why, is there some problem?" I asked.

"What were you doing in the building after it had been locked up for the night?"

"Nobody told us to leave. Whoever locked up must not have seen us."

"Why would that be?" the officer said. "Were you two hiding?"

"No, of course not," Jennifer said.

"Where were you then?"

After a pause, I said, "Well, actually, we were in a stairwell."

"I see. What were you doing in a stairwell?"

"Singing," I said.

"If you were singing, wouldn't the person locking up the building have heard you?"

"Well, we weren't singing all the time," Jennifer said.

"Yes, I bet you weren't," the police officer said, flashing a cynical grin that Jennifer and I found insulting.

"You have no worries there, believe me," Jennifer said. "Greg here, just got off a mission."

"What were you doing in a stairwell with him then?"

"Like I told you before. We were singing . . . and talking."

We were glad when he asked us for ID and then let us go.

As we drove into her driveway, Jennifer asked if I wanted to come in. That was the last thing I wanted to do. I told her I needed to get home.

The next day I telephoned the Whittaker's house.

Jennifer answered. She sounded excited until I asked to talk to Amber. I knew this would cause problems, but I couldn't help it. I had to talk to Amber.

When Amber came on the line, she wasn't happy with me. "Jennifer says you wanted to talk to me," she said, trying to be as businesslike as possible.

"I was wondering if you'd like to get together and sing a few songs," I said.

"I really think it'd be better for you to start singing with Jennifer."

"It's not the same," I said, hoping that Jennifer wasn't listening in on another phone.

"I don't think it'd be right for me to spend time with you now, do you?"

"Oh, my gosh, Amber. Do you think this is about us? It isn't. It never was. We both know that. This is about music. This is about the dream we had in high school to make decent music that'd lift people up instead of bringing them down."

"People change. And dreams change too."

"Just think about it, okay? That's all I'm asking," I said.

"I've got a lot of things on my mind right now. For one thing, I need to plan a wedding."

"I know that, but, c'mon, this was your dream. How come you gave it up so easily?"

"Greg, look, let me give you some advice. You can't spend your whole life trying to redo high school. It's over. It's time to move on. That's what I've done."

"You know what? I really feel sorry for you. Good-bye."

"Wait, don't hang up—Jennifer wants to talk to you," Amber said.

"Tell her I'll call her sometime."

"Greg, listen to me, she really is interested in—"

I hung up on her.

17

I did feel sorry for Amber because she'd given up on her dream. But, also, I felt sorry for myself.

It looked like our dream that began in high school had finally come to an end.

But, oh, what a dream it had been.

2

February 1992

Fast Forward began in late February of our junior year. The reason we got together in the first place was that all five of us were in Bel Cantos, the most selective choir at school. There was Jonathan Briggs, Ryan McAllister, Brooke Samuelson, Amber Whittaker, and me, Greg Foster.

Jonathan and I had been best friends since fourth grade. With his blond hair, blue eyes, and quick smile, Jonathan was the poster child for Agreeability. One time I heard him thank a teacher for "writing up such a good test." That's how extreme he got.

It's not surprising that Jonathan was one of the most popular guys in school. He did it all—he played football, sang in choir, had major parts in school plays, and was involved big-time in seminary. Jonathan always did his best. And, of course, he was an Eagle Scout. I was too, but mainly because of a very good Scout leader and a mom who hounded me until I finished all the requirements. Jonathan, though, did it mostly by himself.

Jonathan was really good for me. Looking back on it now, I can see that when I was in high school, especially during my sophomore year and the first part of my junior year, I intimidated girls. Not because I was any real threat, but in those days I didn't smile much. I probably got that from my dad. If the crop was bad, my dad frowned because of all the money we would lose. If the crop was good and the prices were good, then my dad frowned because next year was bound to be bad.

Even though I wasn't much sought after by girls then, all I had to do to improve my image was to hang around with Jonathan. Everyone liked Jonathan. He had enough charm for ten guys like me. When Jonathan and I were out with two girls, the less I said the better it was. If I let Jonathan do the talking, all I had to do was nod my head and smile. But sometimes that didn't work either because some girls thought my smile was more like a sneer. Well, actually, with some girls, it was a sneer.

Most people at school didn't realize it, but Jonathan's junior year had been tough on him. That was when his dad had left home and his parents got divorced. Jonathan felt betrayed by his father's leaving, but he tried his best to be upbeat around his two younger sisters and in school. He didn't talk much about his family life.

Brooke and Amber were good friends too. They'd grown up together and had been in the same ward all their lives.

This is how Fast Forward came to be. One day, Mr. Aldrich, our choir leader, showed us the video called "Spike Lee and Company Do It A Cappella," featuring groups doing songs like "Lean on Me." Jonathan and I decided to try to imitate some of the songs. After we'd practiced a couple of days after school in the choir room, Mr. Aldrich kicked us out. We ended up harmonizing in the boys rest room just down the hall from the choir room. The place has great acoustics, and if you open a window, it's not that bad. By the time we got there, it was already half an hour after school, so the building was pretty much deserted anyway.

People who sing a cappella have this thing about

practicing where they sound the best. Besides, if you don't need a piano, you can practice anywhere you want.

We'd been singing for about fifteen minutes when there was a knock on the door. "Hello?" It was Amber, but of course, with the door closed, I didn't know that.

"What?" I asked.

"Can we come in?"

"I'm not sure we should do this," Brooke said privately to Amber.

"Don't worry, it'll be okay," Amber assured her, and then she spoke to us. "This is Amber. Brooke and I could hear you guys down the hall. We were wondering if we can come in and sing with you."

"In here?" I asked.

"You're just singing, right?" Brooke asked through the door.

"Yeah," I said.

"Then is it okay if we come in?" Amber asked.

"Yeah, sure, I guess so," I said.

They walked in. Brooke looked around the room. "I've never been in here before."

"Actually, that's the way it's supposed to be," I said.

Brooke smiled at me. "I know that." That was a typical Brooke comment. She was too true-blue to even recognize when I was being sarcastic.

"Look, can we just skip the bathroom humor and sing?" Amber said.

One thing I'd noticed from being in Bel Cantos with Amber was that she always said what was on her mind.

I don't think we were prepared for how good we sounded. For me it was the most exciting musical experience of my life. I will never forget it. It was like I'd gone my whole life in a kind of stupor and our singing together finally snapped me out of it.

To be truthful, though, I'm not really sure how good we

sounded that first time. For one thing, we hadn't really worked that much on harmony. Mainly we were just trying to mimic the sound of one of the groups on the Spike Lee video. But, even so, it was tremendously exciting to be creating this music all by ourselves.

When we finished that first song, we just looked at each other in silent amazement. Finally Brooke said what the rest of us were thinking. "Guys, we are *so* good!" That's the way Brooke talks. Besides, it was true.

In November our school had done the play *Peter Pan,* and Brooke had played the title role. She was made for the part. First of all for her size. She was five-foot-two, full of energy, and really upbeat and happy.

I've always loved Brooke's smile. It wasn't just her mouth. It was her eyes, too, that got into the act. Her pixie face put her in the category of being forever cute.

Brooke was born to be the cheerleader for the world. She was always in good spirits, and always concerned about other people. She was the kind of girl you'd like to take home to your parents, just to prove you're not totally hopeless.

Brooke was good all the way through. Not like me. I was grumpy a lot and got mad when things didn't go my way. Also, Brooke was easy to talk to. Which seems strange because she and her dad could never communicate about anything. Actually that was one thing she and I had in common. My dad and I didn't get along either.

That first time we sang together, I remember looking at us in the mirror of the rest room. Appearance-wise, we were a strange combination. Amber, too tall, Brooke, too short. Me, big and hulking, looking like I was trying to decide who to get mad at, and Jonathan almost too upbeat and smiley.

From that first day, Amber seemed totally unaware of the effect she had on me. I think she pretty much just wanted to be one of the boys—which in a way seemed appropriate, considering where we were practicing—but for me it never worked that way. No matter how much I tried, and I did try, I could never get totally used to being with her because I was so distracted by her every move. But, at the same time, I was mad at myself for being so fascinated by her. I tried to tell myself she wasn't that great looking, that she was too tall, that her hair was all over the place, that she used too much eye makeup, and that her lips were too full. Also, just by looking at her you could tell how conceited she was just because she'd played on the team that took the state basketball tournament. I figured she thought she was this big-time star athlete, and that everyone should fall down and worship her. Fat chance.

Some girls in high school acted as though their whole life depended on what others thought about them. Amber wasn't like that, though. She gave the impression that she thought so well of herself that it really didn't matter what anyone else thought.

Much later I learned that she'd had a tough time in seventh and eighth grade. The boys had made fun of her because she was taller than anyone else in her grade, and being teased had really bothered her.

She went through a really hard time when she felt very insecure about herself. And that'd made her stronger. But, also, it gave her a look that said, *I don't care what you think about me.* She wasn't the tallest girl in school anymore, though. It was just that she had hit her growth spurt earlier than most everyone else.

Because of the get-out-of-my-face attitude Amber still carried with her, I'd never heard any guy in school express any interest in her. But, even so, I couldn't get her out of my mind.

In some ways we were a lot alike. I intimidated girls, and she intimidated guys.

After a few days of practicing, we realized that to get an

23

even better sound we needed one more guy to sing with us. The reason was that with me setting down a beat and Jonathan singing high tenor, we needed a guy to sing mid-range. We talked about it after we finished practicing one day.

"I know someone who's got a really good voice," Brooke said. "We were friends up until fifth grade, and then his family moved across town. I didn't see him much after that."

"What's his name?" Amber asked.

"He's got kind of a bad reputation, but he's always been nice to me," Brooke said.

"Just tell us who it is, okay?" I said.

"Ryan McAllister."

There was a shocked silence in the room. I couldn't believe Brooke even knew Ryan. "You're kidding, right?" I said.

"I know he's got a bad reputation, but if he sang with us, maybe he'd change."

"Forget it," I said. "There's got to be somebody else we can get."

"He's got a wonderful singing voice," Brooke said.

"So what?" I said. "You've heard all the stories going around about him, haven't you?"

"Well, yes, but . . ."

"So how can you even think of having him sing with us?" Amber asked.

"We might be able to help him," Brooke said.

"He smokes and he drinks and he gets into fights," I said.

"I know that, but maybe he could stop. Look, let me ask him to come tomorrow, just to sing with us one time, you know, just to see how it goes, and then we can talk some more about it after that."

"*Sing* with him?" Amber complained. "I don't even want to be in the same room with him."

"Why not?"

"Because he's totally out of control," I answered for Amber.

Brooke wouldn't give up. "I know that, but when we were kids, he wasn't. Back then he was as good as anybody. When we were in Primary, he and I sang at a baptism once. We sang 'I'm Trying to Be like Jesus.' I asked him if he really did want to be like Jesus, and he said he did."

"I wanted to be a fireman once, too," I said, "but that doesn't mean I want to be one now."

"Maybe we could help him change," Brooke said.

"Forget it. People like him don't change," I said. "The way I see it, the less we have to do with him the better."

"You don't even want to try?" Brooke asked.

"That's right," I said.

"Is that what Jesus would do?" Brooke asked.

This was Brooke's big gun. She didn't use it very often, but when she did, it always made me look bad. There was no way I could answer the question honestly and defend my position at the same time.

"Brooke, listen. I think Greg has a point," Amber said. "Ryan's always on the verge of being kicked out of school. He'll miss practices. If we ever perform, we'll never know if he's coming or not. Or if he'll show up totally wasted. Besides that, he smells like a smokestack. If he wanted to sing with us for good, he'd need to understand that he'd have to quit drinking and smoking. I mean, not just when he's with us, but all the time."

"I think he could do that," Brooke said, "but he won't do it until he's had a chance to sing with us. He might like it so much he'd be willing to quit. Why don't we have him come and see if this is something he'd enjoy. And then we can worry about those other things later. Is it okay if I invite him to sing with us tomorrow after school?"

"Jonathan, what do you think?" Amber asked.

"I think Brooke's right. People can change. Like my dad. I know he's going to come back some day."

Poor Jonathan. When he said things like that, about his dad's coming back, it made me realize how messed up he really was. The way I saw it, there was no chance Jonathan's dad was ever going to come back. In a way, we were exact opposites. I saw only the dark side of life; Jonathan saw only the bright side. And we were both wrong.

Brooke finally convinced us we should at least give Ryan a try.

Up to then I'd never had much to do with Ryan. Except one time we had a run-in. It was at a school dance after a football game. Jonathan and I were leaving with two girls who were both in love with Jonathan. I was there just to provide them a socially acceptable excuse to be with him.

We'd left the dance and were heading toward my mom's minivan. There was a group of guys standing around a Ford pickup. Ryan was trying to pick a fight with someone. "What are you doing with my girl?" he asked Jason Winters. I was pretty sure by how loud Ryan was talking that he'd been drinking.

"I'm not your girl, Ryan," the girl said. I didn't really know her, but I think she was from Rigby.

"Sure you are. You just don't know it yet." Ryan turned to Jason and shoved him backward. "C'mon, Jason, fight me. The one who wins gets to take Amanda home."

"I don't want to fight you, Ryan," Jason said.

"Why not? If you don't fight me, then I'll just beat you up anyway and take Amanda with me."

"I don't want to go with you," Amanda said.

"Hey, I don't care what you want," Ryan threatened. "If I say you're coming with me, then you're coming with me."

I couldn't let this go on. I turned to Jonathan. "I'll be right back."

"Do you need any help?" Jonathan asked.

"Not if it's just Ryan."

I walked over to where Ryan and his friends were tormenting Jason and Amanda. "Leave Jason and Amanda alone, Ryan."

"You going to stop me?" Ryan challenged.

"Yeah, sure, if I have to."

"You think you're man enough?" Ryan asked.

"Yeah, I think so." I turned to Jason and Amanda. "It might be best if you two left now."

"Wait a minute," Ryan said. "I've got some friends here. You think you can fight us all?"

I looked over at three other guys who were at least as out of it as Ryan. "Yeah, pretty much."

"How come you think that?"

"Because you and your friends are all drunk, Ryan. I could take on fifty like you. No problem."

Jason and Amanda got in their car and drove away.

"So what's it going to be, Ryan?" I asked. I could see the answer in his eyes. He was afraid of me. He had reason to be. I outweighed him maybe forty pounds. And because it was football season, I was in good shape.

I knew there was a ceremonial retreat coming. Ryan had to get out of this so he wouldn't look bad. I decided to let him back out because I really didn't want to fight him and his friends. For one thing, my mom would be mad if I got arrested for fighting.

"I don't want to hurt you," he said, "because the football team will need you for the game next week. So I'm not going to fight you—this time."

It was over. "I really appreciate that." I turned and started to walk away.

"I'll wait until after football season is over."

I turned and backed away from him. "Talk about school spirit. I didn't know you were such a sports fan. Thanks a lot, Ryan." And then Jonathan and I left with our dates.

I was never sure if Ryan even remembered that night. He'd been pretty much out of it. At least if he remembered it, he never mentioned it to me.

And then there was the time at a school dance when Ryan had shown up drunk and tried to get in. He ended up trying to start a fight with a chaperon. Eventually he was arrested by the off-duty policeman they always have at the dances. Ryan was taken away in handcuffs, swearing at the top of his voice.

It was so weird trying to think of Ryan singing "I'm Trying to Be like Jesus" with Brooke when they were little kids. Apparently, along the way, Ryan had given up on that dream.

What was Brooke thinking of anyway? Why did she think she had to rescue every lost creature in the entire world?

I figured this thing with Ryan would last one day, max.

"You all know Ryan, don't you?" Brooke said the next day after school as she brought him into the boys rest room where we practiced every day after school.

We nodded our heads and said hello, but you could tell our hearts weren't in it.

Ryan wasn't one of us. As much as we might talk in church about how we should leave the ninety and nine to go back to look for the one lost sheep, it was not something we ever actually did. Basically there were two groups in school—the preppies and the cowboys. Not that they were actually cowboys, of course. We just called them that. They were the ones who hung out in the school parking lot, smoking and smirking at the rest of us. Ryan was one of the leaders of the cowboys.

Jonathan, Brooke, Amber, and I were in the preppie group. We worried about grades. We went out for teams and we sang in choir and we took seminary. We planned to go to college. We took ACT exams every year just for practice.

We went to church and served in quorum and class presidencies.

The preppies and the cowboys didn't have anything to do with one another. And while we might have lessons once in a while about fellowshipping people who didn't come to church, for the most part, all that meant was that every so often we'd drop by and invite the inactives to something we knew they'd never come to. In a way, it was a game we all played. I can't remember any good coming from our half-hearted efforts to turn the inactives into actives. None of it worked. They stayed the same, and we stayed the same. That's just the way it was.

I'm not sure why Brooke was so different from the rest of us. Somehow she'd taken to heart all the lessons we'd ever had about loving your neighbor. It made her a misfit in school sometimes. Every once in a while I'd catch her in the hall talking to someone the rest of us would go out of our way to ignore. She didn't seem to have very good judgment about things like that. To Brooke, every person was a gem. I tried to tell her differently, but she never caught on.

So, because of Brooke, we had Ryan to sing with us on a trial basis. I'm not sure who was the most uncomfortable—Ryan or Amber and me. But I do know that if it hadn't been for Brooke, we wouldn't have lasted two minutes together. She was the bridge between Ryan and the rest of us.

It's one thing to talk about trying to fellowship someone, but when it comes right down to it, there are a lot of things that keep something like that from happening. Little things like the fact that because of the crowd Ryan usually ran around with, he could hardly get through a sentence without swearing. He knew that would never work around Brooke, so he really tried not to swear. But that meant he had to filter everything, which meant he couldn't say much.

At that first practice Amber always kept at least one person between herself and Ryan, but I didn't have that luxury.

29

Ryan ended up in the middle with me on one side and Jonathan on the other.

Ryan had black hair and a dark complexion that made him look tanned all year round. I found out later his mom had been born in Brazil. She and his dad had met at BYU.

Ryan had a mischievous boy's face that made it hard to get mad at him. He knew how attractive he was to girls. I can't say if he did this or not, but I can picture him in ninth grade standing in front of a bathroom mirror practicing this thing he does with his eyebrows when he smiles at a girl.

When it wouldn't be too obvious, I got a little closer to Ryan and sniffed, expecting to smell cigarettes and maybe even beer on him, but there was nothing. I knew he hadn't quit smoking. In fact, I'd seen him lighting up in the parking lot with his friends that morning when I'd come to school.

And then I realized what must have happened. Ryan had gone home before school was over and taken a shower for us. I could even smell the shampoo he'd used. It didn't make sense. Why should he do that? I was sure that Brooke hadn't said anything. She would never suggest he had to do anything to be accepted by us. His clothes didn't smell either, which meant he'd also changed before he'd come to the practice.

The only explanation I could come up with as to why he'd taken a shower and changed his clothes was he'd done it for Brooke. But why? He couldn't have thought he had any chance of getting anything started with her. Brooke was nice to him, but she was nice to everybody. Maybe that was it. Brooke had been the only preppie at school to treat him the way she treated everyone else. And for that, Ryan had taken a shower and changed his clothes.

While Brooke and Jonathan were helping Ryan with his part to "Lean on Me," I took Amber out into the hall. "Ryan doesn't smell like cigarettes. I think he took a shower before he came here."

"Yeah, so?"

"I don't know. It's just weird, that's all. It's like he's trying hard to fit in."

"He'll never change," Amber said. "You know that, don't you? Guys like him never do."

"I know that, but just the same . . . ," I said.

"What?" Amber asked.

"He's really trying."

"He's trying to con us," Amber said. "That's what guys like him do."

Jonathan called us in and we tried "Lean on Me" for the first time together. We did sound better with Ryan. Amber and I didn't want to admit it because we didn't want him to sing with us. Brooke and Jonathan were on the other side, cheering Ryan on. And he was on his best behavior. You could tell that. Except for one time he messed up on a song and swore under his breath.

"We don't appreciate that kind of talk around here," Amber said.

"I know. Sorry."

We worked on "Lean on Me" for half an hour. The school was nearly deserted. Suddenly the assistant principal barged into the rest room and asked, "What are you people doing in here?"

Talk about an obvious question. "We're singing," Brooke said without a hint of sarcasm in her voice.

The assistant principal glared at Amber and Brooke. "This is the boys rest room. You have no business being in here."

"Most everybody's gone home by now, haven't they?" Brooke asked. "So there's probably nobody around who'd even want to use this as a rest room now."

"That is not the issue here," the assistant principal lectured.

"So, what *is* the issue?" Ryan asked, taking one step

31

toward the assistant principal. Challenging authority was what Ryan did best.

I'm sure the assistant principal had a thick folder on Ryan and the problems he'd caused. "The issue is, I want all of you out of here before I have you all expelled."

Ryan couldn't let it go. "Let me get this straight. You're going to kick us out of school—for singing?"

"You heard what I said."

"Yeah, sure, I heard what you said. I just can't believe you'd be stupid enough to say it. What is your problem, anyway?"

"You're my problem, McAllister," the assistant principal shot back.

Brooke tried to head off trouble. "Guys, look. It's okay. We can practice somewhere else. It doesn't have to be here." She started out the door. Amber followed, turned back, and looked at us. "Are you guys coming?"

So Brooke, the Pied Piper of Rexburg, led us away. As we started down the hall, she and Amber began singing their parts to "Lean on Me." We followed them. It probably saved us from being expelled. It wasn't the last time Brooke kept us out of trouble.

We ended up practicing in the main entrance to the high school. There was a set of doors, a small alcove, and then another set of doors leading into the school. The acoustics in the alcove were even better than those in the rest room.

When we quit that day, Brooke asked, "What would you think if we practiced every day after school?"

Amber and I glanced at each other. A single act of charity for Ryan was okay, but there was no reason to go overboard. As far as I was concerned, it was time to dump Ryan.

Amber must have felt the same way. "I don't want to be in any group where there's drinking and smoking," she said, staring directly at Ryan.

"I won't do any of that around you guys," Ryan said.

"I don't see why you have to do it at all," Amber said.

"I don't *have* to. It's just something I do."

"Why?"

"There's nothing else to do," Ryan said.

"Really? None of the rest of us have trouble finding things to do," Amber said.

"You want me to totally quit?" Ryan asked.

"Yes, that's what I want," Amber said. "If we ever get good enough to sing for an audience, I don't want people thinking you're a friend of mine and that I agree with smoking and drinking."

Ryan must have decided to try out his charm on Amber. "If you want, I'll wear a T-shirt that says 'Amber hates me,'" he said with that smile he used to soften people up and get his own way.

His attempt at charm and humor had no effect on Amber. "I don't hate you, Ryan. I just don't respect you."

Way to go, Amber, I thought.

"What did I ever do to you?" Ryan asked Amber.

"Nothing to me personally, but I've heard all the stories going around about you."

"Most of what people say about me isn't true," Ryan said.

"But some of it is, right?" Amber said.

"I really don't know what you've heard."

Amber wouldn't budge an inch. "I'm sorry, I didn't know I was supposed to take notes. The point is, Ryan, if you want to sing with us, you have to quit everything."

"It'd be really hard to quit everything all at once."

Amber shrugged her shoulders. "Hey, that's up to you."

"But, Ryan, we need you," Brooke said. "I mean we really do. Maybe you could quit gradually. I'll help you. I'll bring cookies every day to school, and whenever you get an urge to have a cigarette, you can just have a cookie instead. And if you'll hang out with us on the weekends, maybe it'll be easier to quit drinking too. I mean it's worth a try, isn't it?

I really think this can be something wonderful for all of us. Please, Ryan, won't you at least try?"

"I guess I could try," Ryan said, "but it might take awhile."

"We'll give you some time," Brooke said.

Amber wasn't impressed. "How much time do you need to quit?" she asked. "A week? Ten days? Two weeks? A month certainly ought to do it, shouldn't it? I mean, this isn't going to drag on forever, is it? If you can't quit, then fine, just tell us and we'll look for someone else to take your place. Some people can't quit drinking no matter how hard they try. Maybe you're one of them."

"Are you saying I'm some kind of hopeless alcoholic?" Ryan asked.

"I don't know. You tell me," Amber said. "When's the last time you went more than a week without getting drunk?"

That made Ryan mad. "I can quit anytime. Two weeks will be fine." His jaws were clenched as he said it.

"Really?" Amber said. "You think you can quit everything in two weeks? Cigarettes? Beer? And whatever else you've been taking? Well, if you can do it, I'll be impressed. But I'm not holding my breath."

"Look, do we have to make such a big deal out of this?" Brooke said. "Okay, Ryan has a few things he needs to work on. And he will too. I'm sure of it. But until then, can't we just practice and see where this takes us?"

"No, Brooke, we can't just sweep this under the rug and pretend it doesn't exist," Amber said. "Ryan, if you're going to sing with us, you have to quit for good. Of course if you can't do that, then just continue on being the school clown. I mean it's up to you."

The rest of us stared at Amber. Nobody talked to Ryan that way. I was worried for her safety if she kept hammering away at him.

"The school clown? Is that what you think I am?" Ryan asked.

"What do you call it?" Amber said. "No one I run around with has any respect for you at all. Isn't it about time you grew up?"

"I've got to get out of here for a minute." Ryan left the alcove and went into the main part of the school to get a drink of water.

"I think you were way too hard on him," Brooke said to Amber.

"Maybe I was, but it's better for him to know right away that I won't have anything to do with him if he's drinking or smoking."

A few minutes later, Ryan came back. "If you guys will let me sing with you, I'll quit . . . everything. I just want you to know, that it's not going to be easy."

"So what are we talking here, three weeks?" Amber pressed.

Ryan looked like he wanted to come over and hit Amber. But he didn't. "All right, three weeks."

"I'm not sure you can quit," Amber said, "but if you can, then I guess I'll agree to let you practice with us, starting now."

After he left, we voted. Ryan got in, provided he quit.

Why did Ryan ever agree to quit? It must have been because Brooke believed in him so much, and then, also, because of the way we sounded singing. The truth is that Ryan has a better voice than either Jonathan or me.

Privately, Amber and I agreed he'd never do it. And we prided ourselves on never being wrong about things like that.

*   *   *   *

Sometimes I wonder what it would have been like for me to quit smoking or drinking, if I'd ever started. I'm not sure I could. It's so hard for me to make any kind of change in my life. I used to set New Year's resolutions, but by March I had always abandoned them all. It's not easy to change.

Ryan must have realized, or else Brooke convinced him, that if he was going to quit smoking, he couldn't hang around before school out in the parking lot with guys who were there to smoke and brag about how much they'd drunk on the weekend.

On Monday I didn't see him with the cowboys. I found out later he came to school with Brooke, who gave him a sack of cookies to help him get through the day.

Everyone should have a friend like Brooke in their life.

*   *   *   *

We practiced every day after school. In two weeks we had three songs that were good enough to sing in front of an audience. Jonathan was a class officer, so he knew how to get things done. He made arrangements for us to sing at a school dance the next Friday.

The night before, at a practice, we tried to come up with the name of our group. We couldn't agree on anything. We were recording ourselves so we could hear how we sounded. Jonathan was running the tape machine. As he worked the controls, he suddenly looked up and said, "How about Fast Forward for the name of our group?"

It had a nice feel to it. And the more we thought about it, the better it seemed. That's how we chose our name.

At the dance the next night I remember how nervous we were before we went on. They had a DJ playing music. We were scheduled to sing during a break.

The guy introducing us gave us the worst possible introduction: "We've got some entertainment for you guys tonight. It's a singing group. This is the first time they have ever performed, so I don't know how it's going to be. The name of their group is . . . is . . . I can't remember. Anyway, here they are."

We were about to start when Amber noticed something about Jonathan. She leaned over to him and whispered. Unfortunately, her microphone picked it up and everybody heard Amber say the word *zipper*. Everybody started laughing. Jonathan, red-faced, left the gym.

We waited for what seemed like forever. I wasn't sure if Jonathan would ever come back, but he finally did. His face was still red. Poor Jonathan. I was embarrassed for him.

Groups like ours, who don't use a piano, need to have some way to find the starting note. We didn't have a pitch pipe yet, but before we'd been introduced we'd found a piano in a storeroom and used it to get our beginning pitch. But because of the delay with Jonathan, that had been a long time before.

Amber started us out too high, so by the middle of the song, it was way out of Ryan and Jonathan's range. They sounded like they were screaming.

I gestured for everyone to stop. "This is awful."

The crowd roared its agreement. Things were basically out of control. People were calling out one-liners to get their own laughs. All at our expense.

"Let's just get out of here," Amber said. "I don't need this."

"No, we're going to get through this," Jonathan said. "We'll just start it again."

Jonathan went off stage to the piano and came back with the starting note.

We got through it, but I'm not sure anyone was listening. By that time they'd lost all respect for us. The polite ones just ignored us. The others were mocking us.

One guy in front was being especially obnoxious. When he started making fun of Brooke, Ryan yelled at him and told him to shut up.

Yelling at your audience is not the best way to win them over. We did our second song, but by that time, because of what Ryan had done, people were booing us.

By the time we finished, I never wanted to sing in public again. "Let's just get out of here," I said.

"No, let's sing our third song," Jonathan said.

"Forget it, Jonathan," I said. "I'm not going to go through this again. They hate us."

"Let me talk to them," Jonathan said. He went to the microphone. "Could I have your attention please? That first part was a joke. That's why I walked out here the way I did and why we started the song too high. You guys were perfect the way you reacted. That's just what we wanted from you. Way to go." He paused. "But now we want to do it the right way. Amber, you want to go to the piano and get us our starting note for our last song?"

Amber left.

Jonathan continued. "I can't believe we started that first song so high. You guys are never going to let us forget this, are you?" he asked with a smile.

"I liked it!" a guy called out in a high falsetto voice.

Everybody started laughing.

"Hey, that was good!" Jonathan said. "You want to come sing bass for us? Next week we're going to do a concert. The only ones who'll be able to hear it will be dogs. That's almost the way it was tonight, wasn't it? Oh, well, I'm sure we'll laugh about this someday."

Amber returned.

"Okay, I guess we're ready now," Jonathan said. "We're just starting out, so we've got a few rough spots, and we could really use your support. The next song we're going to sing is kind of the way we think of you guys. It's called 'Lean on Me.'"

We started the song. This time it sounded more like what we'd practiced. The response was better than before. Don't get me wrong—the kids in the audience weren't out of their minds with ecstasy, but they weren't booing us either. Jonathan had won some of them over.

When it was finally over, we were glad just to get out of there. We escaped to Ryan's house. His mom was so glad Ryan was spending time with us, instead of with his drinking buddies, she'd gone out of her way to fix us something to eat. We went downstairs. The McAllisters had a big-screen TV and a big comfortable couch with a high back. We watched a movie and talked.

A while later I went upstairs to use the bathroom. Ryan's mom and dad were in the kitchen. For some reason it got to me that Ryan's dad was grating cheese. He was this successful businessman, but there he was grating cheese because his son had people over who were halfway decent.

"I need to use the bathroom," I said.

"Down the hall, first door on the right," Ryan's dad said.

I passed Jamie's room. She was Ryan's fourteen-year-old sister and a nice kid. Like Ryan, she always looked like she had a tan. She was talking on the phone. I waved, but either she didn't see me or else she purposely ignored me.

As I passed through the kitchen on my way back downstairs, Ryan's mom said, "We appreciate all you're doing to help Ryan."

"We're not really doing that much."

"We've seen a big change in him. He seems much happier now."

"Could your group sing for sacrament meeting sometime?" Ryan's dad asked.

"I suppose so."

"It might be a way we could get Ryan going to church again," Ryan's mom said.

I went back downstairs. Just talking to his mom and dad made me think about Ryan differently. I'd gotten so used to thinking of him as a complete loser, but he wasn't that way in their eyes. I remember thinking that Ryan's mom and dad probably prayed for him. *Maybe we're the answer to their prayers,* I thought.

It was something to think about.

*   *   *   *

One night after school the next week, as we were practicing, Mrs. Ferguson, one of the history teachers, stopped to listen to us. "You guys sound great!" she said when we finished.

"Thanks," Brooke said.

"I'm the Young Women president in my stake. We're having a dance a week from Friday. Would you want to come and sing to us for ten or fifteen minutes?"

"Sure we would," Jonathan said.

"All right then. I'll expect you. Brooke, I'll give you all the details in class tomorrow. Keep up the good work."

We watched her go. As soon as she drove away, Brooke made a fist and shouted, "All right!"

*   *   *   *

Sister Ferguson nervously cleared her throat and tapped the microphone. It didn't seem to be working, but she went ahead anyway. "May I have your attention, please. Are you all enjoying the dance tonight?"

Because nobody could hear her, the audience didn't pay much attention. One girl near the front of the cultural hall asked, "What did she say?" The boy next to her called out, "Turn up the microphone."

Someone cranked up the volume. "Right now—" Because the volume was now too high, there was a loud, ear-shattering screech.

The person controlling the volume turned it way back down again. "Right now . . ." Sister Ferguson could tell she wasn't being heard, so she decided to talk loud. "Right now we're going to have some entertainment. We have with us tonight five young people who have formed their own singing group. They call themselves Fast Forward. Let's give them a big welcome!"

From behind the curtain, Amber called out, "Wait! Don't open the curtain yet—my mike's not working."

"We're not ready!" I called to Sister Ferguson.

The same helper who had controlled the sound system now enthusiastically pulled the curtain open and there we were, in front of the worst critics we could ever face—three hundred people our age.

"What do we do?" Amber whispered to me. I was the one who took care of our sound system.

"It's probably just the mixer," I said. "I'll go see if I can fix it."

I left. The rest of them stood there, embarrassed they weren't singing.

"Hold on a minute. We just need to check a mike before we start," Jonathan announced.

"Amber, give me a sound check," I called from offstage.

"One . . . two . . . three . . ."

I fought the feeling of panic that threatened to overwhelm me as I frantically tried to get the sound system working again. The people at the dance were getting restless, and I was really perspiring. We would have to start soon, whether or not Amber's mike was working.

It was the first time we'd ever used a mixer. I had borrowed it and the five microphones from a friend of mine. It wasn't Amber's mike that was at fault because when I switched the leads between Amber's mike and Jonathan's mike, then it was Jonathan's mike that wasn't working.

I should be able to fix this, I thought.

Sister Ferguson came over. "Is there anything we can do to help you?" she asked gently.

Just then, I spotted a switch on the mixer over each

41

channel. The others were on, but Amber's had been turned off by mistake. I moved the switch and asked Amber to say something. Her voice came over the sound system.

"Let's go," I said, walking onstage.

"You fixed it?" Amber asked.

"Yeah, sure."

"Thanks."

I pulled a pitch pipe from my pocket and sounded our starting note. Amber hummed it to make sure she got it.

Our first song was "Under the Boardwalk."

We sang it and three other songs that night: "Lean on Me," followed by "Stand by Me." Our last song was "Chain Gang."

That night, for the first time, I saw Amber come alive onstage. I'm not sure how to explain it. For the rest of us, being in front of people wasn't easy, but because we loved to sing together, we would do it. For Amber, the bigger the audience, the more relaxed she was onstage. For Brooke, Jonathan, Ryan, and me it was just the opposite.

The response of the audience depended on how far they were from the stage. The ones near the front were very enthusiastic. In the back they didn't seem to care what was going on. All they wanted to do was talk and mill around.

When we made it offstage, a girl rushed up to Jonathan and handed him a piece of paper. "Here's my name and phone number. Call me sometime and maybe we can go out. You're hot!"

"Wow, thank you!" Jonathan looked at the name written on the piece of paper. "Kristen, right? Thanks a lot."

After the girl left, Jonathan turned to me. "I'm hot," he said, still savoring the moment.

I wasn't impressed. "Drink some water then," I said.

Ryan had a way of flirting with an entire audience when he sang. His dark eyes went from one girl to another—a smile here, a nod there, and before long they were all sure he was in love with them. And so Ryan had the biggest group of girls around him. He made the most of it. He was made to play the part of a celebrity, being witty and charming, while the rest of us carted sound equipment out to the car.

Amber and Brooke helped me finish packing up.

When we were ready to go, I looked around and asked, "Where's Ryan?"

"Still inside, I guess," Amber said.

"Go tell him we're leaving," I said.

Later Amber told me what happened. When she went inside, she saw Ryan talking to one girl.

"Ryan, we're leaving now," Amber said.

"Just a minute."

"No, now. You didn't even help us pack up. Come now or walk home. We'd like to get out of here sometime this week, if that's all right with you."

"Just give me a minute," Ryan asked.

"No way, Ryan."

Ryan shrugged his shoulders and said to the girl. "I'd better go."

"Call me," the girl said.

"You know I will," Ryan said, and then he walked out with Amber.

While we were piling into the car, Brooke was still pumped up from the concert. "Guys, we did so good! They loved us. Aren't you all hungry now? Let's go get something to eat."

"I don't have any money," Jonathan confessed.

I got in the driver's seat. "We've got money. Sister Ferguson gave me fifteen dollars for singing tonight."

"Let's go then," Brooke called out.

We found a McDonald's. We decided to go in and eat instead of doing takeout.

We were all so jazzed by the experience of performing

43

in front of a live audience that we talked for an hour and a half. It was nearly midnight before we finally left to go home.

That night I remember not being able to sleep because I was so excited.

We were all hooked. From that day on we became Fast Forward.

3

I think we all started to feel good about having Ryan sing with us. We were fairly certain he'd quit partying like he'd promised. If he hadn't, we'd have heard about it. Rexburg is a small town, and it's not that hard to find out what's going on.

When we first started singing together, Amber was our featured soloist, but as time went on, because Ryan was so good, we started to do some songs where he could take the melody. That kind of variety went over well with our audiences.

Word was starting to catch on about us. That was good because it gave us more chances to perform. More than half the time, like for church activities, we didn't charge anything. We did it for fun and for the experience.

In April, about six weeks after Fast Forward began, we were the entertainment for a ward supper. It wasn't for any of the wards we belonged to, so ordinarily I wouldn't remember it. But because of what happened that night, I'll never forget it.

After we'd finished singing, Jonathan, Brooke, and Amber got sidetracked talking to some friends from school who went to that ward. As Ryan and I were packing up to move our sound system out to the van, Nicole Darby came up to Ryan. I knew her because, when her family lived in our ward a couple of years before, my dad and I had been the Darbys' home teachers. She was only fourteen, but she looked older than that. She was a good-looking girl, with long, copper-tinted hair, blue eyes, and a great smile.

She walked up to Ryan like he was an old friend. "Hi, Ryan. Good show," she said with a big smile.

Ryan looked embarrassed and didn't say anything.

"It's all right—my mom and dad have already left," Nicole said.

Ryan glared at Nicole and then turned to me and said, "I'll be in the van." And then he left.

Nicole hung around for a minute, for my sake I guess, and then she followed after him. I was curious about what was going on, so I grabbed one of our speakers and carried it outside.

In that building most people use the side door that leads directly to the parking lot. I went out the front door, hoping that if I took a different route, I might not be noticed by Ryan and Nicole.

I stopped just at the corner of the building where I wouldn't be seen. I could hear Ryan and Nicole, who were standing by the van. "I don't see why you're so mad," Nicole said.

"What were you thinking, talking to me back there? If you can't accept my rules, then as far as I'm concerned, it's all over."

"I didn't think it'd do any harm," Nicole said.

"Well, you were wrong then, weren't you? I don't want people to see us together and start asking questions."

"I know, Ryan, but it's been a week since I've seen you."
"So?"

"I've missed you."

"Look, either we do this my way or not at all. Take your pick. It doesn't matter to me."

"You don't have to be so mean, do you?" she asked in a pleading voice.

"Look, just get out of here before the others show up."

"Are you coming tonight?" she asked.

"No, forget it. I was going to, but I'm not now—not after this. Face it, Nicole, you messed up big-time."

"Why can't I talk to you in public?" she asked. "Are you that ashamed of being seen with me?"

"Just go now, okay? We'll talk about this later."

"Tonight?"

"No, not tonight."

"Why not?" she asked.

"Because you need to be taught a lesson for what you did tonight. Greg saw you talking to me."

"All I did was say I liked the show. What's so wrong with that?"

"Look, when I want to see you, I'll come by. Other than that, just stay away from me."

Just then Ryan spotted me standing in the shadows by the corner of the building. He must have realized I'd heard everything. He turned on Nicole. "You want to talk? Fine, let's take a walk and get this taken care of once and for all." He took her arm and ushered her to the far edge of the parking lot.

I carried the speaker to the van and waited for the others. A few minutes later Amber came out of the building. She noticed me watching Ryan and Nicole. "Is that Nicole Darby with Ryan?" she asked. "What's going on?"

"I'm not sure. Do you know her?"

"Nicole? Oh, sure. I used to baby-sit her. Why is Ryan talking to her?"

"I think maybe he's been seeing her," I said.

"Why would he do that? She's way too young for him."

"I know, but something's been going on between them."

"How do you know?" she asked.

47

"I heard them talking."

We could hear Nicole's voice from across the parking lot. She was upset. "Ryan, that's not fair."

Jonathan and Brooke finally showed up. Jonathan had our other speaker. After one more trip back into the building to get our equipment, the four of us ended up in the van waiting for Ryan.

A few minutes later he came back. "Let's get out of here."

Nicole was sitting on the curb, holding her face in her hands.

"Are you going to tell us what this is all about?" Amber asked.

"It's nothing. Let's just go."

"How do you know Nicole?" Amber asked.

"She's a friend of my little sister, so I see her once in a while. That's it."

"It looks like there's more to it than that," I said.

"Why is Nicole crying?" Amber asked.

"How should I know? Let's just go," Ryan said.

"We can't just leave her," Amber said. "I'm going to go talk to her."

"Don't waste your time," Ryan said.

"I'll be right back," Amber said.

Ryan muttered something under his breath.

Fifteen minutes later both Amber and Nicole returned. "I told Nicole we'd take her home," Amber said.

We rode in an awkward silence. When we got to Nicole's house, Amber walked her to the door, then came back and got in the van. From the way she slammed the sliding door of the van when she got in, I could tell she was mad. "Okay, Ryan. You want to tell us what's been going on between you and Nicole?" She said it in a tight-lipped manner, her anger barely under control.

"Nothing," Ryan said.

"Nicole told me everything."

There was a long pause. And then Ryan said, "It's not that big of a deal."

"Just quit stalling and tell us," Amber said.

Ryan sighed. "All right. Well, okay, about a month ago, I came home late from practicing with you guys. My sister Jamie had some of her friends over for a sleep-over. They were supposed to be watching a movie downstairs, but it was so late they'd all fallen asleep in front of the TV. I was in the kitchen having something to eat. Nicole came upstairs to use the bathroom, and when she came out, she saw me in the kitchen. We talked for a while. I guess she'd heard stories about how wild I used to be, so she asked me to get her some beer because she wanted to know what it tasted like. I tried to talk her out of it, but she kept at me, so finally I gave in and we went to my car. I still had a couple of cans hidden away, so I gave her a taste. Basically that's about it."

"You make it sound like the whole thing was Nicole's idea," Amber said. "She says you were waiting for her when she came out of the bathroom and that you were the one who brought up the subject of drinking. You tried to talk her into going out to your car to drink with you. She didn't want to at first, but you asked her how she was ever going to know if she liked it or not unless she tried it. So finally she went with you. The two of you sat in your car and drank beer until three in the morning. How could you *do* that?"

"I didn't force her to go out to my car with me. She could've said no."

"She's fourteen, Ryan."

"I know how old she is, okay?"

"That would've been bad enough, but it didn't end with that, did it?" Amber said. "You saw her several times after that, didn't you?"

"Look, it wasn't *my* idea. The next morning she cornered me and told me she'd thought of a way we could see each other Friday and Saturday nights without anyone knowing about it. She said if I came after midnight and stopped on the street behind her house, she'd be able to see my car through a vacant lot. She said she'd come out as soon as she saw me. She said nobody would ever know."

"So that's what you did?" I asked.

After a long pause. "A few times is all."

"Why would you want to have anything to do with someone so young?" I asked.

"I can think of a reason," Amber said sarcastically.

"It wasn't that. It was never that," Ryan answered.

"What was it then?" I asked.

Ryan shrugged his shoulders. "I don't know."

"If you were going to start drinking again, why not just go back to your old friends?" Jonathan asked.

"Because if I did, I knew that sooner or later I'd get drunk and get in a fight or do something dumb. And then you guys would hear about it and kick me out of the group. I didn't want that to happen. Having a beer with Nicole was better for me because I only brought one six-pack, so it wasn't like I could get out of control. Besides, nobody needed to know about it. I made her promise not to tell anyone about what we were doing. It was just us, and we never saw each other all week."

Amber couldn't resist. "Let's see, Ryan. The reason you didn't see each other all week must have been because Nicole is in the eighth grade at junior high and you're a junior in high school. That's the reason, isn't it?"

"Whatever you say, Amber," Ryan shot back.

"Did she ever ask you for help with her homework?" Amber asked sarcastically.

"Back off, okay? I know how old she is. You don't have to keep bringing it up."

"How many times did you see her?" Jonathan asked.

"I don't know. Four or five, I guess."

50

"Did you ever consider what this was doing to her?" Amber asked.

"What do you want me to say, that it was a mistake for me to be with her? All right, fine. I admit it. I messed up. But now it's all over. I won't be seeing her anymore. So it's over and done with."

"You think you can just dump her and be done with it?" Amber asked. "Well, forget it. I'm not going to let you get away with that."

All the time we had been talking, Brooke hadn't said anything. It was like she was stunned. Finally, she said, "You were doing so good, Ryan. Why did you do this?"

I think Brooke's question hurt him the most because she had trusted him so much.

Ryan hesitated and then said quietly, "I hated having to drink alone."

"So you never really quit?" Brooke asked.

"I quit partying with my friends, but I was still drinking— alone most of the time. I tried to quit, but it was too hard. I'm sorry, Brooke. I really am. At first, on the weekends, after we finished practicing, I used to drive out of town and sit in my car and have a few beers and then go home. Look, I'm not like you guys and I never will be. It doesn't matter how many times I go to church. I still never feel like I belong."

"We tried to make you feel like you belonged," Brooke said.

"I know. You were great, Brooke. I mean that."

"Why did you ask Nicole to drink with you?" Brooke asked.

"There's something really pathetic about drinking alone. It got so I hated it. Being with someone is always better. That's what this was all about. I couldn't go back to my old friends because I knew that sooner or later, you guys would find out. I couldn't let that happen because being in Fast Forward is the best thing that's ever happened to me." He paused. "With Nicole it was better. At least I had somebody to talk to."

"What else did you two do?" Amber asked.

"Look, nothing happened between us."

That set Amber off. "What do you mean, nothing happened? I think a lot of things happened. Who was the one who got her started drinking and smoking? Who was the one who got her to sneak out of her house late at night? Who was the one who made her sit by her window until two or three in the morning waiting for you to show up? Do you call all that nothing?"

Ryan didn't answer.

Amber continued. "This was so convenient for you, wasn't it? You drive by and she jumps in your car. She said you told her that if she ever phoned you, you'd quit seeing her. She wasn't even supposed to talk to you in public. It sounds to me like you were calling all the shots. You are such a loser, Ryan."

Amber turned to talk to Jonathan and Brooke. "It's obvious to me that Ryan has no business in our group. Do we really want people seeing us onstage thinking he might be a friend of ours? I don't know about you guys, but I sure don't."

Ryan sounded desperate. "Wait, give me another chance. I have changed since I've been with you guys. I've quit going to parties and getting into fights. And except for smoking with Nicole, I've quit smoking too. Okay, so I messed up with Nicole, but that's all over now. I'll never see her again. I promise."

Amber couldn't let that go unchallenged. "It wasn't that hard to break up with her, was it, Ryan? Because you never really cared about her anyway. All you did was use her. Do you really think you can just walk away? If you really want to make things right, then go and apologize to her."

After a long pause, Ryan said, "If I do that, and if I never drink or smoke again, can I stay in the group?"

That was not what Amber wanted to hear. "Not after what you've done. It's all over, Ryan. You're finished with us."

"Even if he apologizes to Nicole and promises not to mess up again?" I asked.

Amber was getting mad. "When we first started singing together, he promised he'd quit drinking and smoking, but he hasn't. So what good are his promises?"

"But he's better than he was. You'll have to admit that," I said.

"I'd expect you to take his side, Greg." Amber said.

"Why?"

"Because you're a guy. You probably don't see anything wrong with what he did."

"That's not true," I said. "If you want, I'll go with Ryan when he apologizes to her to make sure he does it."

Amber shook her head. "No way. If you two do it, Ryan will mumble some two-word apology and you'll both come back and tell us it's taken care of. I want to be there too, to make sure he really apologizes."

"If he apologizes and promises never to drink or smoke again, will you let him stay in the group?" Brooke asked.

"Look, it doesn't matter what he promises," Amber said. "Guys like him can never be trusted."

"I'll do whatever it takes to stay in the group," Ryan said.

"You apologize to Nicole first and then I'll tell you if I've changed my mind," Amber said. "Why don't you just admit you can't change, Ryan? That'd be the simplest and most honest thing you could do."

Ryan didn't say anything for a long time and then he said softly, "Maybe I can change."

"I think we should at least give him one more chance," Jonathan said.

"Me too," Brooke said.

"All right, fine," Amber muttered. "I guess we'll find out what you're made of, won't we, Ryan? Just don't expect me to cut you any slack."

*   *   *   *

The next morning, which was a Saturday, I drove past the place where Nicole lived. There were no cars in the driveway. I stopped and went to the door and knocked.

Nicole opened the door.

"Are your folks home?" I asked.

"No, they'll be home this afternoon."

"I need to talk to you," I said.

"What for?"

"Ryan asked me to see you. He feels bad about what happened. He wants to come by and apologize."

"Does he want us to get together again?" she asked.

"No, but he does feel bad about the way he's treated you. Can I bring him and Amber by this afternoon so he can apologize to you?"

Nicole nodded. "All right. You guys can come by, but it'll have to be before four. That's when my mom and dad said they'd be home."

When we got there at three-thirty, there was a car in the driveway. "I think her folks are home now," I said as we slowed down.

"Let's stop anyway. I think we can arrange to talk to Nicole privately. Besides, it might be good for Ryan to meet Nicole's mom and dad," Amber said.

"You never said I'd have to meet her folks," Ryan said.

"Well, you do, but, hey, if you want to back out of this, that's fine with me," Amber said.

"No, I'll do it."

"Let's go then," she said, getting out of the car and starting up the front sidewalk.

We followed her. Amber knocked, and Mrs. Darby came to the door. She was a slender woman, almost too thin, with short red hair. She worked in the admissions office at the college and was always getting phone calls from angry parents about why their son or daughter had not been accepted.

"Amber and Greg, what brings you here?" she asked.

Amber took charge. "Well, we were driving by, and I was telling Ryan and Greg about Nicole's playhouse. Greg is thinking about building one for his cousin. We were hoping we could have Nicole give us a tour."

"Well, of course. Come in."

"Oh, this is Ryan. He's one of Greg's friends."

"Nice to meet you," Mrs. Darby said.

Once inside, Amber made sure Ryan met Mr. Darby. He was almost totally bald and several inches shorter than Ryan.

"I'll go get Nicole," her mom said. "I think she's in her room."

When Nicole came into the living room, I could tell she'd gone to a lot of work to look good for Ryan. She'd braided her hair in back and put on eye makeup since I saw her that morning. She looked lots older than fourteen.

We said our hellos, and then Amber said, "I told your mom we wanted a tour of your playhouse. Can you take us out there?"

The playhouse was near the back fence. It was a miniature, two-story house, painted white with green shutters—just right for a little girl to play in.

"We'll have to bend over to get in, but I think we can manage it," Amber said.

Inside, it was obvious how much time and effort Nicole's dad had put into this playhouse. Every detail was perfect. In the center of the room was a small white table and four chairs. We sat down. Amber said, "I remember that summer I used to baby-sit you. We would come in here and have little parties with orange juice and cookies. You were such a cute little girl." Amber was trying to make this as hard as possible on Ryan.

Ryan cleared his throat. "Nicole, it was wrong of me to get you started drinking and smoking. I'm trying to turn my life around. I'm quitting everything for good."

She looked over at Ryan, smiled, and said, "Yeah, right. Sure you are, Ryan. You'll come back to me. I know you will. It's just a matter of time."

I looked through the playhouse window and saw Mrs. Darby carrying a tray toward us. "Nicole, your mom's coming."

Mrs. Darby poked her head in the door. "Anybody home? I brought you some milk and cookies."

It was strange in a way because Mrs. Darby looked so frail and thin and yet there she was bringing cookies. I could remember her saying once, when my dad and I were there home teaching, that she had a condition and couldn't gain weight no matter how much she ate. My dad said it sounded like a good deal to him, but she said it wasn't all that great. She told us she could die of starvation even though she was eating normally.

Amber stepped to the door and took the tray. "This is so nice. Thank you very much."

Mrs. Darby looked in. "I can't believe you're all in here. Nicole hasn't been in the playhouse for a long time."

"Well, she should," Amber said, glancing in Ryan's direction. "She's still young enough to enjoy it." Amber said that just to make Ryan feel worse.

"If you need any more cookies, there are plenty inside," Mrs. Darby said. "Just come and get 'em."

"Thanks for everything."

Mrs. Darby looked again at us. "Is everything all right?"

"Yeah, sure. Why?" Nicole asked.

"You all look so serious."

"We're okay, really," Nicole said.

Mrs. Darby left. Amber set the tray on the tiny table. She poured us each a glass of milk and passed around the plate of cookies. "I think we need to have some of this. Nicole's mom went to a lot of trouble to fix it for us."

We passed the plate without anyone taking anything. None of us were in the mood for cookies and milk.

"Let's just go," Ryan said, standing up. "Nicole, I am really sorry for what I did. It was wrong. I can see that now."

"You'll be back."

"No, I won't."

She looked up at him and smiled. "I've been reading all about boys in a magazine I bought. I know what boys want now."

Ryan looked like he might get sick. "I don't want anything." He turned to Amber. "Can we go?"

"All right," Amber said. "Everyone take a cookie and a drink of milk, and then we'll go."

A minute later, the three of us stepped outside. Nicole stayed in the playhouse. On our way out we decided to take the gate instead of having to go through the house again. We were walking across the front lawn to the car when Mr. Darby came out of the house and called after us, "Wait a minute." He was short, but he was a powerfully built man. And he looked unhappy.

We stopped. He came over to talk to Amber. "Why did you come here? My wife says that when she took the tray out to you she had the feeling that something was wrong. What's going on here? I think I have a right to know."

Amber looked at Ryan. If any explanations were going to be given, Ryan would be the one to give them.

Ryan cleared his throat. "I came to apologize to Nicole," Ryan said.

"Apologize for what?"

Ryan wouldn't look at Mr. Darby. He stared at the ground and said, "My sister Jamie is friends with Nicole. One time when Nicole was spending the night at our house . . . I let Nicole have a taste of beer."

"You *what!* Why would you do a thing like that?"

"She said she wanted to know what it tasted like."

I knew that wasn't the complete truth, but I couldn't blame Ryan for hedging. It would be very hard to admit to Nicole's dad that he'd purposely set out to talk Nicole into drinking with him. I started to wonder why he'd chosen Nicole. Maybe she was physically more mature than his sister's other friends. Or maybe he could tell she was more vulnerable. He might have even singled her out weeks earlier. How could he admit that to any of us? It would turn this from being just a dumb mistake to something sinister and evil.

"Did anything else happen?" Mr. Darby asked, his face already red.

"No, nothing happened," Ryan said, but then shot a glance at Amber to see if she'd let it go at that.

"You'd better tell him everything," Amber said quietly to Ryan.

"Well, okay, after that, once in a while, we'd go out and drink and talk."

"How come I didn't know about it?" Mr. Darby asked.

"It was always late at night, after you and your wife had gone to bed."

"How old are you?"

"Seventeen."

"What business do you have with my daughter? I think you'd all better come in the house. I'll get Nicole. We need to get to the bottom of this."

There was no escaping. We all returned to their house.

"Go get Nicole," Nicole's dad said grimly to his wife. "Tell her I want to see her."

He turned to us. "Sit down." It was not an invitation.

Nicole came in the living room and sat on the floor.

58

"You've been sneaking out at night to drink beer with him?" her dad asked, glancing in Ryan's direction.

"A couple of times, but that's all. But I'm never going to do it again."

"What else happened?" her father asked Ryan.

"Nothing."

"I don't understand. How did this start?" Nicole's mom asked.

Ryan had to tell it all over again. "My sister Jamie is a friend of Nicole's. One time Nicole spent the night over at our house. After everyone else was asleep downstairs in front of the TV, Nicole came upstairs. I was in the kitchen. We started talking about drinking. We went out to my car, and I gave her a taste of beer." Ryan sighed. "After that, we saw each other four or five other times."

"Does your sister know this has been happening?" Nicole's mom asked Ryan.

"No. She doesn't know anything," Ryan said.

"Are you going to tell her?" Nicole's mom asked.

Ryan winced. "I don't know."

"I think you'd better. Jamie needs to know that if she ever has some of her friends over to your house, they are at risk of being corrupted by you."

"It won't ever happen again," Ryan said, his head down.

"No, it most certainly will not. Nicole will never go to your house again. And I'm going to talk to all the parents with daughters Nicole's age and warn them about you. How could you have done this? We trusted our daughter with your family, and you betrayed that trust."

"I'm really sorry."

"Not as sorry as you're going to be," Nicole's mom said. "Let me make sure I understand what happened. Did you ever have sexual relations with my daughter?"

Ryan gulped. "No."

"Did you ever touch her where you shouldn't have?"

"No, never."

"Nicole, I want to hear it from you."

"All we did was talk. I only drank maybe one can of beer each time we were together. And we were together only three or four times. That's all that happened."

Mrs. Darby turned to Amber. "How do you fit into all this?"

"I found out about this from Nicole last night. We told Ryan he needed to come and apologize for what he did."

Mrs. Darby's expression softened. "Thank you for that. As bad as it is, I'd rather know what happened than to be left in the dark."

Nicole's head was down. "I'm really sorry. It won't ever happen again. I've learned my lesson not to trust boys."

Mr. Darby got up and moved in Ryan's direction. His fists were clenched. "I want you out of my house right now. And don't ever come back."

"Oh, Daddy, I'm sorry," Nicole said. She ran into her father's arms. They stood there rocking back and forth, his hand patting her back like she was a little girl who'd skinned her knee on the sidewalk.

"We'd better go," Amber said to me.

Ryan was the first one out the door, and then Amber.

"Can I say good-bye to them, Daddy?" Nicole said, just as I was leaving their house.

"No."

"Please. I need to thank Amber for her help. And Greg too. They've really helped me. Can't I at least thank them?"

"They have been good to get that boy to come and apologize," Mrs. Darby said.

"I guess so," her father said to Nicole.

Nicole and I walked to the car together. She wiped her eyes, turned to look at me and smiled. "I should get an acting award for that, shouldn't I?"

By then Nicole and I were by the van. Ryan was in the

front seat. Nicole walked up to him, opened his door, and with a smile asked, "So, Ryan, you want to get together sometime soon? Maybe during school. My folks won't be expecting that."

"You told them you weren't ever going to do that anymore," Amber said.

"That was just an act. I can't go back to the way I was. I'll be waiting for you, Ryan."

"I won't be seeing you anymore."

I will never forget the smile that crept across Nicole's face. "Well, if you don't, I'm pretty sure I can get someone else to take your place."

We got in the van and drove away. Nicole stood by the curb and watched us go.

*　　*　　*　　*

We drove around town. Ryan sat quietly, staring out the van door window.

"I don't know how you got through that," Amber said.

"Me either." He sighed. "But it's not over yet. Can you guys wait for me while I tell my folks and Jamie what happened?"

"Where do you want us to wait?" Amber asked.

"Downstairs in our TV room. You could watch a movie or something. It shouldn't take long. I just need some support, that's all."

"Yeah, sure, no problem," Amber said. She seemed more supportive of Ryan now. I was too.

Ryan didn't want his parents fussing over us, so he led us down the stairs without his parents knowing we were around. He pulled out some movies for us to watch, brought us something to drink and some nachos, and then sat down on the couch next to us and stared at the floor. "This is going to be really tough."

᠃"They're going to hear about it anyway," Amber said. "It's probably better if they hear it from you."

He nodded his head. "Is this ever going to end?"

"It will, eventually."

"The more I try to turn my life around, the harder it gets. When I was partying all the time and getting into fights, at least Jamie was on my side. She never wrote me off. But now that's going to change, and I won't have anyone on my side."

"You've got us," Amber said.

"Really?"

"If you really want to change, we'll be behind you all the way," Amber said.

Ryan paused. "That's just it. I'm not sure I can change."

"Sure you can."

"Jamie is my only sister." There was nothing we could say. He had betrayed his sister's trust.

Ryan shrugged his shoulders. "I'd better go." And then he left.

Amber and I were sitting in front of their large TV. The room was cold, but there was a comforter on the back of the couch. I grabbed it and draped it over Amber and me. "You want to see a movie?" I asked.

"Not right now."

We sat side by side, our shoulders touching, our arms folded, our heads resting on the back of the couch, not admitting it to each other, but each of us straining to hear what was happening upstairs.

"I feel like I've spent the afternoon cleaning out a sewer," Amber said.

"I know. Me too. It's been rough."

"Could you do what Ryan has to do now—tell your little sister that you tried to seduce her best friend?" Amber asked.

I was surprised at her use of that word. "Is that what was going on?"

"Seduction doesn't always have to be sexual, does it?" Amber asked.

"I don't know. I thought it did."

She shook her head. "I don't think so. We could look it up in the dictionary."

We were both too exhausted. "I'll just take your word for it."

"Can I ask you a question?" she said.

"Sure."

"Was I too hard on Ryan?" she asked.

"Not really. He had it coming."

"I have a cousin who started drinking when she was thirteen because of a guy she was seeing. Her life has been messed up ever since. Now she's into drugs. The thought of Ryan dragging Nicole into that kind of life really made me mad. That's why I jumped all over him."

"You handled it just right."

"Really?"

"Absolutely. You were just trying to look out for Nicole, that's all. I'm proud of you for that. Last night all of us could hear her crying, but you were the only one who went to see what was wrong. I think that really shows what kind of a person you are."

"Thanks, Greg. That means a lot to me to have you say that."

"I mean it."

"I know you do." She turned to me. "Can I ask you another question? My mom says I come on too strong sometimes and that if I'm not careful I'll end up scaring people away. I've only been on one date in my life. And he never called back, so maybe she's right. What do you think?"

"You don't scare me," I said.

She looked over at me and smiled. "Thanks, but nothing scares you, does it?"

"Sure, lots of things," I said.

"I don't believe it."

"Well, maybe not scare, but there are some things that make me uncomfortable."

"Like what?" she asked.

"My dad and I don't get along very well anymore. So it's sometimes kind of hard to spend time with him. I never know what he's thinking."

"Why don't you ask him what he's thinking?" she asked.

"I'm afraid he'll tell me."

"That doesn't make sense, Greg."

"You'd understand it if you knew him better. How about you and your mom and dad?"

"We get along okay, I guess," she said. "It's just that there's never enough money. They've already told me they're not going to be able to help me with college, so if I go, it's up to me to pay for it. I'm already paying for my clothes, so it's hard to save for college too. Sometimes I really get discouraged."

"How do you save anything? You don't even have a job, do you?"

"Not really, but one thing I've got going for me is that I bake bread for people in our neighborhood. It's really good bread. I'll have to give you some. It's so good I can charge a lot for it. That's turning out to be better than if I was working at some fast-food place."

"Good for you. I love homemade bread when it first comes out of the oven."

"Come over sometime and I'll give you some," she said.

"That'd be great."

She sat up and looked at me. "This is so great talking to you. I'm usually a little nervous around guys, but I'm not around you."

"Why's that?" I asked.

"Maybe it's because you and I are just friends."

"I bet that's it, all right."

The furnace turned on, which made it impossible to hear what was going on upstairs. A few minutes later we could hear the sound of water running.

I was beginning to be aware of how close I was to Amber. I thought of trying to hold her hand. But it didn't seem right to be thinking about making some kind of a move on Amber when upstairs Ryan's world and that of his family was about to blow up into a thousand pieces.

Finally, though, I did reach over to take her hand.

She looked at me and moved her hand away. "What's going on?"

"Do you think there's any chance we could be more than just friends?" I asked.

"That's probably not a good idea. If we're both going to sing in the group, I think we need to stay just friends."

"But what if we weren't in the group, what then?" I asked.

"I really don't know how to answer that."

"I just want you to know I really like you. Actually, sometimes I think I could really fall for you."

She moved away and nervously ran her hand through her hair. "I don't know what to say."

"Sorry. It was dumb of me to bring it up."

"No, that's okay. I think it's better to be honest, don't you?"

"You don't feel anything for me, though, do you?" I asked.

"You mean—like romantically?"

"Yeah, right."

"No, sorry." It must have sounded too heartless to her, so she added, "But I do think that you and I might end up being really good friends."

"That's better than nothing, I guess."

"Sure it is. At least this way we'll never break up." She paused. "Greg, this isn't going to be a problem for us, is it?"

"No, not really."

"Because if it is, eventually it'll break up the group. I don't think either one of us wants that, do we?"

"No. Is it because you're taller than I am?" I asked.

"Not really. To tell you the truth, I've never thought about you that way before."

"You mean as being short?"

"No. As a boyfriend."

"I guess there's no reason why you should."

"I mean, you're a nice guy and everything," she said.

"Yeah, sure. I understand."

"When did you first start thinking of me that way?" she asked.

"I don't know. I've always liked to look at you. I think you're beautiful."

"I'm not, though, not really."

"To me, you are," I said.

"Is that why I catch you sometimes staring at me?"

"Yeah, that's why." I didn't know how much more I should tell her. It was risky, especially for me because it was hard for me to express my feelings. But I decided to at least try. I was sitting with my head resting on the back of the couch, looking up at the ceiling. I knew I couldn't say much of anything looking into her eyes, but somehow staring at the ceiling made it easier.

I decided to let it all out. "I watch you all the time. I can't help myself. Everything you do. Even when you yawn. Or when you run your fingers through your hair, I watch that too. I even watch you when you tie your shoes. You always tie the bows too. That's so they never come untied, isn't it? If you ever want me to do anything for you, just tell me, okay? Like, I could shampoo your hair for you sometime if you want."

She stared at me. "You want to shampoo my hair? My

gosh, Greg, that is the weirdest thing I've ever heard a guy say."

"Sorry. Forget that part then, okay?"

"Having you tell me all this is really making me nervous," she said.

"I won't talk about it anymore if you don't want me to."

"I really don't want you to—ever again."

"I won't then."

"Good. That's the way I want it." She noticed me watching her running her fingers through her hair, and that made her even more nervous. "You're really freaking me out."

"Sorry."

We were saved by Ryan coming back downstairs. Actually, I'd forgotten about him. "So, how did it go?" I asked.

"I haven't told them yet," Ryan said.

"How come?" I asked.

"I don't think I can."

"You've got to, though, before they hear about it from someone else," Amber said.

Just then the phone rang. For us it was like a small bomb going off.

"You'd better get up there, Ryan," Amber said. "What if that's Nicole's mom?"

"I can't do it."

"You've got to. Jamie will respect you more if you're the one who tells her," Amber said.

"She'll never respect me, never again. I just want to go away and never come back."

"You can't do that though," Amber said. "You have to face up to what you did."

We knew Ryan had waited too long when we heard Jamie's voice at the top of the stairs. "Ryan, are you downstairs?" she was practically screaming.

"Yes."

She bounded down the stairs. "What did you do to Nicole?"

"Nothing happened."

"That's not what her mom just said. You've been trying to get her drunk, haven't you? How could you have done this to one of my friends?"

"Sorry."

"*Sorry?*" she raged. "Sorry doesn't cut it, Ryan. Because of you, none of my friends are ever going to have anything to do with me again. Thanks a lot. I'm telling Mom and Dad. I hope they throw you out of the house." She ran back upstairs.

We could hear her telling her folks. Ryan sat down next to me on the couch and stared at the floor.

"Make him leave home!" we could hear Jamie shouting upstairs. "I don't want him around here anymore!" We heard footsteps and then a door slamming and then silence.

"I wish I were dead," Ryan said softly.

And then Ryan's dad came to the top of the stairs. "Ryan, we need to talk to you. Now!"

Ryan shrugged his shoulders and went upstairs.

Later, I found out that Jamie answered the phone. Once she realized it was Mrs. Darby, she wouldn't put her mom on the line until she found out what the call was about. Finally, Nichole's mom gave up and told Jamie what Ryan had done.

We tried to listen in on what they were saying, but his mom and dad weren't as loud as Jamie, so we couldn't hear anything.

"You want to watch a movie?" I asked.

"I guess we might as well," Amber said.

We started to watch *Return of the Jedi.* Not that we'd never seen it before. Maybe that's why we watched it, because we knew we could trust it, that it wasn't going to spin us into a world we didn't want to be in. The world we lived in was scary enough.

I felt a little guilty watching a movie when upstairs, Ryan was being humiliated by having to admit what he'd done. But sometimes you can only take so much and then you have to escape. For Amber and me, *Return of the Jedi* was our escape.

Ten minutes passed, and then fifteen. We moved closer together again, mainly because it was so cold in the room. I wondered if Amber had any idea how beautiful she was. She didn't seem to. I wished I could just look at her face while she watched the movie. But every time I glanced at her for more than a couple of seconds, she'd give me this What-are-you-looking-at-me-for? stare.

Now our heads were close enough together that her hair tickled my cheek. That really got to me. I went to put my arm around her shoulder.

She sat forward to get away. "Why does this keep happening?" she asked. "We're watching a movie, and then all of a sudden you come at me from out of nowhere? Why can't you take a simple no?"

"I just thought we'd be more comfortable if my arm was around your shoulder, that's all."

"Yeah, right," she scoffed. "Look, Greg, we can be friends and everything, but keep your hands off me, okay?"

"Fine," I said.

She wasn't done putting me in my place. "Are you cold?" she asked.

"No."

"Good." She yanked the blanket away from me and slid to the other side of the couch.

Within a few minutes I was cold, but I wasn't about to admit it to her.

"I'm sorry," I said. "I won't try anything again. I promise."

She sighed. "Don't worry about it. I probably over-reacted."

Ryan came downstairs. "Let's go."

Amber and I stood up. "How did it go?"

Ryan shook his head. "I can't talk about it now."

We drove to a park and sat in the car. At first Ryan couldn't say anything, and then a little at a time, he began to open up. "My mom and dad say I have to get counseling."

Amber tried to be supportive. "That might not be so bad."

"Why do you say that? Do you think I'm crazy?"

"You don't have to be crazy to get counseling," she said.

"That's just the beginning. Jamie told me she hated me. She says she'll never forgive me for what I did. She says she doesn't trust me anymore and that if any of her friends ever come to our house, she wants me out of the house. I can't even sleep at home if she has friends over for the night. My mom started crying. And my dad asked me if there was any possibility that Nicole was pregnant."

"What did you say?" I asked.

"It's like I told you guys. Nothing happened. We just sat in a car and drank beer and talked. That's all. Nothing else happened." He paused. "My dad wants me to see my bishop tomorrow after church and tell him everything."

"Are you going to do it?" I asked.

"It's kind of scary to think about talking to him, but my mom says it will help if I do it." He paused. "I would like to change my life around, but I'll need some help." He sighed. "You guys are the only friends I have left anymore."

"We'll be here for you, Ryan," Amber said.

"You will?" Ryan asked.

"Absolutely," I said.

*   *   *   *

This was a time of changing for all of us. Of course, Ryan was changing. But I was changing, too, especially in my attitude about people who weren't active in the Church. I started to think that if I had hope for Ryan, and I did, then maybe I ought to have some hope for some of the others I had given up on.

It was fascinating for me to see Ryan change. He agreed to meet with his bishop every week. The idea was that knowing he'd have to report back would make it easier for him to stay on the right track. He agreed to start going to church, too.

*   *   *   *

A week later, on a Friday afternoon, Jonathan and I went over to Ryan's house. He'd written a song and wanted us to help him on it.

As we walked in the house and into the kitchen, his sister, Jamie, came into the room. "You can't be here," she announced.

"Why not?" he said.

"I have a friend here."

"We won't be long," Ryan said.

"No, Ryan, you have to leave. That's what we agreed on. You can't be around when my friends are here."

I could tell it was embarrassing for Ryan to have us watch his little sister order him around. "How about if we stay in the kitchen and you and your friends stay in your room?" he suggested.

"No, you can't be in the house. I don't want you around any of my friends ever again. You have to go now, Ryan. And my friend is going to stay the night. So you'll have to stay with Greg tonight. Do you want me to call Mom?"

We went over to my house and worked on Ryan's new song. Around midnight I took Jonathan home. Ryan stayed the night. He slept on the floor on a mattress we hauled in from the garage.

We'd just turned out the light when Ryan said, "The first time, when we were in my car and I gave Nicole a taste of beer, I remember thinking, *This doesn't count.* Have you ever felt that way? That you knew something you were doing was

71

wrong, but you kept thinking that it didn't count or that it didn't matter or that it wasn't really that important?"

I had felt that way just a few weeks before when I'd cheated on a quiz. I'd never told anybody about it, and I'd never got caught. I remember thinking it wasn't important because it was only a quiz. But it was cheating.

"I've felt that way before," I said.

"Everything counts. That's one thing I've learned. I'd give anything if I could go back to that night Nicole and I first talked in the kitchen." He paused. "Jamie's never going to trust me again, is she?"

"She will . . . sometime." I'm not sure I believed it myself.

"Do you think there's any hope for me?" he asked.

"Sure there is. You're trying hard to change your life. That's really good."

"Thanks."

We didn't talk anymore that night. I had a hard time sleeping, though. I was surprised I'd forgotten about cheating on that quiz. Maybe it was because I'd talked myself into thinking it wasn't important. I felt bad, too, that I'd been so negative about Ryan at first. And now Ryan was ahead of me. He'd gone to his bishop and talked about the things he'd done that were wrong. That night as I lay in my bed and went over my own life, I came up with some other things I'd done that weren't right. I'd never talked to my bishop about them, either, because I'd talked myself into thinking they weren't important.

I knew I needed to talk to that teacher on Monday. And then I needed to talk to my bishop. I didn't want to admit to either of them that I'd messed up. But I didn't see how I could be encouraging Ryan to straighten out his life if I wasn't willing to do the same with my own.

I'm sure Ryan didn't mean to, but he had taught me an important lesson.

Everything counts.

4

Amber had made it clear enough that she wanted us to be *just friends*. Once I accepted that, things were better between us. I started going over to her house Saturday mornings and hanging around while she baked bread. Most of the time it was just Amber, her sister Jennifer, and me. Her mom and dad worked almost every Saturday. They'd usually get home around two-thirty in the afternoon, just about the time we were delivering the bread around the neighborhood.

I couldn't stay there every Saturday because sometimes my dad needed me to do chores around the farm. But after a while, even when I knew he wanted me to lend him a hand, I'd get up early and sneak over to Amber's place.

At first Amber wouldn't trust me to do anything to help her with the bread. But after I swallowed my pride and showed that I could follow her instructions exactly, she relaxed and let me work in the kitchen with her. It was interesting to be working with her as my boss. It was not something I let too many people know about. Actually, just Jonathan.

If I got there around seven-thirty in the morning, we'd have two or three hours to be alone before Jennifer got up. Not that anything was going on. It was just easier to talk when we were alone.

About that time I found out something, almost by accident, that ended up bringing us closer. The one thing Amber didn't want was for me to tell her how much she meant to me. Any move in that direction always made her pull away. But if I was dating other girls, then Amber relaxed and let me get closer to her as a friend.

It sounds crazy, but it worked. Once or twice a month Jonathan and I would take two girls to something that didn't cost much. And then when I got with Amber, I'd tell her what a great time I'd had, and that I was definitely going to see this girl again. After a couple more dates, I'd tell Amber it hadn't worked out. By that time, I'd find another girl to take out.

Amber was going out with other guys, too. And nothing seemed to work out with any of them either, but, unlike me, that wasn't part of Amber's plan. It was just the way it was. I wasn't surprised, though. She was a little intimidating to most guys. First of all, she was tall and athletic looking. I personally like that in a girl, but I know some guys don't.

Another reason why she might have intimidated guys was she had a voice that carried well. Not only that, but she always said exactly what was on her mind.

I remember once in Bel Cantos we were sight-reading some songs from the old-time musical *Carousel*. I think Mr. Aldrich was thinking of doing a musical the next year and wanted us to run through the music. Anyway, we came to a solo that he asked Amber to sing. In this song a girl is saying that it's okay if a guy wants to hit her. Amber stopped singing halfway through the song and said, "I'm not going to sing this."

"Why not?"

"Because it encourages physical abuse. I'm surprised you'd have us sing something like this."

At first I thought Mr. Aldrich was going to take her head

off. He doesn't like people questioning his authority. I don't blame him. "You have to take it in context," he said.

"I see. And in what context is physical abuse of women acceptable?" Amber asked.

I'd never heard it so quiet in choir.

"I agree with Amber," Brooke finally said.

With Brooke on Amber's side, Mr. Aldrich knew he had no chance. We never sang any more songs from *Carousel* again.

I admired Amber for speaking up, but I also knew that some guys shy away from girls who speak their mind.

I think Amber realized she needed a little help knowing how to deal with guys. And since I was around anyway, she started asking me questions.

I remember her first question. "If I'm out with a guy and he asks, 'Where would you like to eat?' what should I say?"

"What do you usually say?" I asked.

"I usually tell him where I'd like to eat. I mean, if he didn't want to know, why did he ask me?"

I shook my head. "Big mistake."

"Why? What should I say?" she asked.

"Tell him it really doesn't matter to you. And then he'll suggest a place, and you say, 'Sounds good.'"

"But what if he keeps insisting that I pick the place I want?" she asked.

"Then you can pick the place, but never before your first 'it doesn't matter.'"

"I'm glad I asked," she said. "This is a little tricky."

"Tell me about it. I have a question maybe you can answer. What do I do when I'm out with a girl and she asks me to call her the next day, but I really don't want to."

"What have you been doing?" Amber asked.

"I usually just say, 'Yeah, sure.' But then I don't call her. Should I say, 'No, I'm not going to call you tomorrow. In fact, I may never call you again.'"

"Of course not. That's too cruel."

"So what should I do?" I asked.

"Is it going to kill you to call her the next day?"

"What would I say?" I asked.

"Tell her you had a nice time."

"If I said that the night before, shouldn't that be enough? I mean, how many times do I have to keep saying the same thing over and over again?"

Amber had the answer. "Just because you say it when you tell her good night doesn't mean you still feel the same way the next day. That's why she needs you to call her."

"And say the same thing all over again?" I asked.

"Sure, why not?" she asked.

"If I said it once, that should be enough."

"It isn't, though. She won't know for sure how it went unless you call her the next day. Try it and let me know if it works. Okay?"

I tried it once and it worked. In fact, the girl brought me cookies at school the next Monday. So after that, I always called girls the next day.

Amber asked lots of questions about guys, and I answered every one. Sometimes I felt like a spy, giving away important secrets to the enemy.

I gave her so much good information about guys—things she'd never learn anywhere else. Like, if she was with a guy and he was trying to repair something and she noticed he was doing something wrong, I told her never to say anything because guys don't like suggestions from girls when they're fixing something. The best thing for a girl to say is something like, "I'm sure you'll figure it out."

At first Amber acted insulted by my advice. "I'm not going to act like I'm some airhead just to satisfy some guy's ego."

"You'll make him mad if you start giving him suggestions.

Fixing things is supposed to be what guys do well. So back off."

"That is so lame," she complained.

"I'm just telling you the way it is."

"Well, I'm not going to do it," she said defiantly.

"It's up to you, but don't say I didn't warn you."

She paused. "All right. I'll think about it."

A few days later, Fast Forward was on our way back from performing and the car died. I couldn't get it started again. After ten minutes of Ryan, Jonathan, and me trying to find what was wrong, Amber got out of the minivan, put her hand on my shoulder, and said, "I'm sure you guys will figure it out."

It made me feel so good when she said it. I felt like she trusted me to fix the problem. And we did get it fixed eventually.

It wasn't until the next day when I realized that she'd just followed my advice. When I confronted her with it, she just smiled and said, "It does work, doesn't it?"

Amber tried to help me, too, mainly by asking questions after I'd been out with a girl. The first time she did it, I didn't do very well. "You were out with Melissa last night, right? What color eyes does she have?"

"I don't know," I muttered. "She has eyes, though. I'm pretty sure of that."

"I can't believe you, Greg. Give me one reason why you wouldn't want to know the color of a girl's eyes," Amber said.

"What difference does it make?"

"Here, I'll show you how it works." She came close to me. "My gosh, Greg, you have the most fascinating eyes. How would you describe their color?"

We were staring into each other's eyes. "Brown," I said, swallowing hard.

"Just calling them brown doesn't do them justice." She had me in her spell.

"Your eyes get to me, too," I said, quite honestly.

Suddenly, school was over. "Good, Greg. Okay, let's move on. After you've been on a date, I want a complete report from you on the color of her eyes, the color of her hair, three things about her that you complimented her on, what her hobbies are, and the names of her brothers and sisters."

"What for?"

"Your job is to find out what's wonderful about the girl you're with."

"What if there's nothing wonderful about her?" I asked.

"There's something wonderful about every person."

"What's wonderful about me?"

She looked at me strangely. "Don't you know?"

"Not really." I paused. "Well, I know I'm good at some things, but I've never been that confident about my physical appearance. If it weren't for the fact that I hang around with Jonathan, no girl would ever look at me."

"That's not true at all."

"It is, though."

"You really think that?" she asked.

"Yeah, I do."

"Hold still while I get a good look at you to see what there is to work with . . . Hmmm . . . strong features . . . brown hair . . . dark brown eyes . . . strong jaw . . . kind of a charismatic charm. You have no reason to worry about the way you look, Greg, no reason at all."

"Then why do I scare girls?"

She thought about it while we worked on the bread. "Laugh for me, Greg," she finally said.

"I don't laugh much."

"I know, but if you were to laugh, how would it sound?"

I tried it. It sounded like something from a horror movie.

"Is that the best you can do?" she asked.

"Yes."

"You have to work on your laugh, that's all there is to it. Laughing is like singing. Here, laugh with me."

For the rest of the morning we practiced laughing. The trick is to do it the way you'd sing, with lots of support from the gut. It sounds a little phony at first, but if you work on it, it begins to sound more natural.

"Is this really that important?" I asked.

"Are you kidding? Of course it's important. Think about 'jolly old Saint Nicholas.' How do people know he's jolly? It's because of his laugh. I mean, without the laugh, he's this really old guy who comes down peoples' chimneys and eats their cookies. Without the laugh, he's very possibly a psychopath."

I scowled. "I know this will be a shock to you, but I really don't want to be mistaken for Santa Claus."

"You have to learn to laugh, Greg. People will like you a lot better if you have an infectious laugh. Trust me on this one. It's just what you need. Now let's practice it some more."

Jennifer came in the kitchen while we were practicing. "What's so funny?"

"Nothing. We're just practicing laughing."

"You two are the weirdest people I've ever known," Jennifer said on her way out again.

We laughed as she left. Big breath, lots of stomach support, cascade down in pitch with either an Oh or a Ha. Amber was right. People love a good laugh. If a person can learn to sing, he can learn to laugh in such a way that it puts people at ease.

Amber helped me develop the kind of laugh that makes people want to tell a joke just so they can hear you laugh. She called my perfected laugh the "young Santa Claus laugh." Not that it sounded like Santa Claus, but it did put people at ease when they heard it. The more I laughed, the less scared girls became of me.

* * * *

Before Amber and I started helping each other, I think we were both too intimidating for the opposite sex to be comfortable with us. But the more we worked together, the more popular we became.

Guys started asking Amber out. After every date, we'd talk about how it could have gone better.

The more popular Amber became, the worse my chances with her became.

Like it or not, Amber and I were stuck in Friendship Land.

* * * *

During those Saturday morning bread-making sessions, once Jennifer woke up and came in the kitchen to be with us, things changed. I'm not sure why. Amber turned into the Older Sister. For one thing, she talked down to Jennifer. It must have been from having to baby-sit her when Jennifer was little.

Sometimes I'd go in the living room and sit on their couch and watch TV with Jennifer. It wasn't very long before I realized Jennifer had a crush on me. One day she sat close to me and put her head on my shoulder.

"Jennifer, quit crowding Greg," Amber said.

"I'm not crowding him. Am I, Greg?" Jennifer answered.

"She's okay."

A sexy model in a swimming suit appeared in a commercial. "What would you do if I looked like that?" Jennifer asked me.

"Wow, I don't know. Go crazy, I guess."

Jennifer smiled. "I am going to look like her someday."

"How do you know that?"

"I'm going to control my weight. I'm not going to be like my mom. She's gained a lot of weight. And not like Amber, either."

"What's wrong with Amber?" I asked.

"She could stand to lose at least ten pounds."

"Really? I've never noticed." I wasn't just being polite. As far as I was concerned, Amber really didn't need to lose any weight.

"You've noticed, but you're just too polite to say anything. What if Amber looked like that girl on TV?"

"I probably wouldn't even know it."

"Why's that?" Jennifer asked.

"Because Amber would never wear what that girl was wearing."

"I bet she would if she looked like that," Jennifer said.

"I don't think so," I said.

"We'll probably never know because Amber's never going to lose any weight. She'd look a lot better, though, if she lost ten pounds. Fifteen would be even better."

"If she weighed ten pounds less, it wouldn't matter to me," I said.

"It would, though. You just don't want to admit it."

"Not really. She looks good already. She doesn't need to do anything."

"How can you say that?" Jennifer asked. "Her stomach has a bulge."

"That's what stomachs do."

"That girl on that commercial had a perfectly flat stomach," Jennifer said.

"Yeah, but the thing is, I've never known a girl who looked like that girl. For all we know, she might have been created with computer graphics. They can do that, you know."

"No, she was real. You really don't think Amber needs to lose any weight? She's as big as a cow."

81

"How can you say that? It's not true. Amber is tall and strong, that's all."

"I'm never going to let myself get like her," Jennifer said. "I'm on a diet right now. I'm going to lose ten pounds."

"You don't have ten pounds to lose."

She held her right arm out horizontally. "See here on the back of my arm? There's a lot of fat there." She brought my hand up to show she could move the bottom part of her arm near her shoulder.

"That's muscle."

"No it isn't. Look—it's flabby."

"Do this," I said, turning my hand over and flexing. "Now feel it. See, it's muscle."

"Well, here then." She stretched her T-shirt tight and then pushed out her stomach so it'd look big.

"Jennifer, what are you doing?" Amber asked.

"Nothing."

"Well, whatever it is, stop it because you're embarrassing Greg. Go get dressed."

"I wasn't doing anything," Jennifer said.

"I'm sure Greg doesn't want to see your stomach," Amber said.

"Well, he sure doesn't want to see yours," Jennifer shot back.

Amber ignored the comment. "Go change. I need you to take some bread around the neighborhood as soon as it comes out of the oven."

"I'm not your slave. Why do I always have to be the one who delivers bread to the neighbors? You never pay me for doing it."

"If you help out today, Greg and I will take you to *Beauty and the Beast*."

"That's for kids."

"You're a kid."

"Not really, but I will let you and Greg take me to *Beauty and the Beast* if I can sit next to Greg," Jennifer said.

"Hey, you can hold hands with him all through the movie for all I care."

"Very funny." As Jennifer got up to go change, she leaned down and whispered in my ear, "I am going to look like that girl on TV someday. You'll see."

Later, I wondered if I could have said anything then to discourage her.

I still don't know.

*   *   *   *

Even though Jonathan and I had been best friends for a long time, he seldom talked about his mom and dad's separation. The trouble with Jonathan was that you never knew when he was hurting because he never really blew up, never started yelling, never walked out in a rage during a practice when things weren't going his way. Like I did.

It was early in May when I suddenly realized how little I knew about what was happening in his life. If I'd been a warm and sensitive person—that is, if I'd been more like Brooke—I'd have sat down with him and just asked him. But I wasn't Brooke, so I did the next best thing. I talked him into going on our ward's Aaronic Priesthood restoration camp-out. It was a fathers and sons' activity, but my dad and I were not that close anymore. Besides, I figured if I asked my dad, he'd tell me he had too much work to do. It would be left unsaid that he blamed me for not helping out more than I did.

So I didn't ask my dad. I asked Jonathan.

We drove to the campground on a Friday afternoon. We got there about five o'clock. The plan was we'd cook our own supper, but the ward would furnish us breakfast. We got there before most of the others made it. We started a campfire right away because we needed some good hot coals to cook our hobo dinners.

Camping was no problem for us. We were Eagle Scouts. We set up our tent, then threw our sleeping bags in. And then we ate and cleaned up. By that time people were starting to show up. I'd brought a Frisbee, which we threw around until it got dark.

And then they had the program around the campfire. It was the same as all the others since I'd been twelve, except up until I was fifteen, my dad took me. He was the one, when I was twelve, who showed me how to cook a marshmallow and put it between two graham crackers.

When I was twelve, everything seemed possible, even that I'd turn out the way my dad wanted. There didn't seem to be much hope for that now.

*   *   *   *

For one thing, my dad and I didn't talk much anymore. It was better that way. When we did talk, it became even more clear that I wasn't what he wanted for a son. He wanted someone who'd take over his farm someday. But that wasn't going to happen. I didn't want to be held hostage by a few acres of land.

Being in Fast Forward wasn't helping things either. My dad thought it was a waste of time. It took me away from chores he'd set aside for me to do. When I was working with him, I felt trapped. He wanted everything done his way, even when it didn't make any difference.

My going over to Amber's on Saturday was taking me away from chores. I knew that, but I did it anyway. I didn't like being with him anymore. He was too critical of everything I did. He was impossible to work for.

I had become two people. With my friends, either at school or hanging out with Fast Forward, I was relaxed and had a lot of fun. But around my dad, I felt a lot of tension and was much more serious.

It had not always been that way. My dad must have politely put up with my sense of humor when I was younger. But the summer before I entered junior high, while we were working together on the farm, he said something to me that really hurt. Our tractor had broken down, and my dad was trying to fix it, but things were not going well. I was perched alongside him, handing him tools as he requested, trying to keep him and myself amused. Finally my dad looked over at me and said, "Don't you think it's about time you grew up and started to take things seriously?"

I was devastated. It was as though my dad was demanding that an important part of myself be done away with.

"The way you carry on all the time, you sound like a girl," he said as his parting shot.

To a seventh-grade boy, that was the ultimate insult. I had no use for girls then, and I certainly did not want anyone saying I sounded like one. I felt my face turning red. I didn't say anything more to my dad after that except what was absolutely essential. If my dad noticed any change, he didn't say anything.

That was the beginning of a growing separation between him and me. We could talk about machinery, or safety, but from then on I held back when I was around him.

During the summers, I felt smothered working for him. Getting away from the farm was like escaping from a prison camp.

My dad heard Fast Forward perform one time at a ward talent show. It wasn't until the next day that he said anything and that was, "You call what you did last night singing?"

I felt myself getting mad. "What would you call it?"

"The others sang, but it sounded to me that all you did was make strange sounds."

"That's called beat-box. I'm trying to sound like drums or a bass fiddle."

My dad shrugged his shoulders. "Whatever it is, it's not singing. Why don't they just get some drums instead of having you standing there in front of everybody making strange noises."

"That's what groups do these days."

"What kind of groups?"

"In the Spike Lee video, it shows some groups from New York City that sing on street corners."

My dad shook his head. "So you're just going along with what some weird people in New York City do, is that it?"

I felt like the top of my head was about to explode. "That's right." I bit my lip. I didn't know what to say. All the way out to the dry farm, I tried to think of something I could say that would put my dad in his place. But in the end I said nothing. He left me off to spend the rest of the day pulling a rod weeder behind our tractor. That was the day I decided that once I got out of high school, I'd never work for him again.

As I became more distant from my dad, I grew closer to my mom. Shannon Elizabeth Billingsley had been Woman of the Year at Ricks her sophomore year. She'd been active in drama at Ricks. She'd played Blanche in *A Streetcar Named Desire,* and she played the lead role in the musical *Auntie Mame.* Between her freshman and sophomore years she toured with Show Time. They'd gone all over the country to perform, even to Washington, D.C.

During her sophomore year she met the shy young returned missionary who would later become my dad.

My mom always let me use her minivan to travel to our performances. In the beginning she came to hear us sing, but then, when she was called to be Relief Society president in our ward, she had less time for that. But she always supported me in whatever I wanted to do when it came to singing.

At times I thought about asking her why she'd ever married my dad. But I never did because I knew she would allow no negative comments about her husband. She was on his side. Once when I complained about him, her response was, "Your father is under a lot of pressure right now. We need to have a good year or we'll be in trouble."

"What are you talking about?"

"We might lose the farm."

"Good, I hope we do."

"I know you don't mean that," she said.

I wasn't sure if I meant it or not. The best thing I could say about my dad was that my mom seemed to like him.

My dad and I had only one out-and-out argument about my singing with Fast Forward. And it wasn't really an argument because I never fought back. Instead I held everything inside. It was the morning after Fast Forward sang at a stake youth dance in Pocatello. We hadn't gotten home until two-thirty, so I slept in until noon the next day. After I got up, I was lounging at the kitchen table, still in the sweats I wore as pajamas.

My mom had been there to talk to while I ate. She asked me for every detail of the concert. She shared my excitement. Her eyes, her face, the tone of her voice, all told me she was as excited as I was about the way the performance had gone.

In the middle of this, with the sun shining into the kitchen, with everything bright and cheery, with the smell of bacon still in the air, the phone rang, and my mom answered it. Her expression fell as she heard the news that a member of the ward had died in her sleep and had just been found by a neighbor.

"I have to go see the family," she said.

I remember wanting to say how much I admired her. But

87

it was hard for me to express any kind of feelings of tenderness, and there was no time to say anything before she left.

I turned on the TV and thought about getting dressed. It was nearly one o'clock in the afternoon. Fast Forward was going to practice at seven, and I still needed to work on a new song I was writing.

I was so interested in the TV show I didn't hear my dad pull into the driveway. If I had heard, I'd have hurried to my room and gotten dressed and tried to act like I was doing something productive.

My dad walked into the kitchen and saw me sitting at the kitchen table. "Just getting up?" he said with little emotion but plenty of accusation.

"We got in kind of late last night. We sang in Pocatello."

My dad had come home to look for a receipt. He was rifling through a stack of papers in a file folder.

I wanted to say something to justify what I did with my time. I didn't dare talk about how much fun it had been, or what a good reception we'd received from the audience. None of that would have impressed him. The only thing I could brag about was money. "We got paid for singing."

"How much?" my dad asked without looking up from the stack of papers.

"We each got twenty dollars."

"What time did you leave here for Pocatello?" my dad asked.

"Four o'clock."

"What time did you get back last night?" he asked.

"About two o'clock."

"Ten hours for twenty dollars. That's two dollars an hour . . . not even minimum wage. If you'll let me pay you that, I can keep you busy all day. And you'll even get a good night's sleep."

I had had it with him.

My dad found the piece of paper he was looking for. "I'd better go. Some of us have to work for a living."

He didn't even look back for what my reaction might be. He went out the door and got into his pickup, and then he was gone.

I couldn't stand it anymore. I wanted to smash the front window, but I didn't. I wanted to set the house on fire, but I didn't. I wanted to run away, but I didn't.

I didn't do anything but let it fester.

*   *   *   *

Back to the fathers and sons' outing.

When we were both twelve years old, Jonathan and I went to our first fathers and sons' camp-out with our dads. And now at seventeen, Jonathan's dad had left him, and my dad and I weren't even speaking.

I'm not sure why, but during the program I couldn't help but watch the deacons with their dads. Those dads thought their boys would turn out just the way they'd always hoped. And the boys thought their dads would always be their best friend.

That hope for Jonathan and me was gone. Jonathan and I were two extremes. My dad was disappointed in me, and Jonathan was disappointed in his dad.

After the program, Jonathan and I stayed by the fire and drank hot chocolate and ate some Fig Newtons that one of the dads had brought and left for us when he and his son went to their tent.

"Do you ever get discouraged?" I asked Jonathan.

I expected Jonathan's quick and easy smile and a no. That's all I ever got from him.

He looked like he was ashamed to admit it, but he said, "Sometimes."

"Really?"

"Does that surprise you?" he asked.

"Yeah, it does. How come you never let anyone know when you're feeling bad?"

"That's just the way I am," he said.

"You know, if you ever need to talk to someone, or if I can ever do anything . . ." It was very awkward for me to say anything, but I felt like I had to because if I didn't then, maybe I never would.

"I know. Thanks."

"I mean it," I said.

"I know you do. I'm okay. Really."

I thought it was over and that we'd said enough. Maybe I didn't really want to go any deeper. I might have felt it'd be a sign of weakness. Men should be above that sort of thing.

But we did go deeper. A few minutes later Jonathan said, "When I first realized my parents weren't getting along, I tried to be a good son so my dad wouldn't leave. I guess I'm still trying to do that. It doesn't seem to be doing much good, though. He's still gone."

"My dad might as well be gone. We never talk anymore. What happened between us and our dads?" I asked.

"We're not cute anymore." Jonathan smiled. "Well, at least you're not."

I took another bite of a Fig Newton and looked down at what was left. "I don't even know why I'm eating these things."

"My dad is seeing someone now. Another woman."

"Oh."

"I guess it's serious. They might get married. So I guess that means he's not coming back. I used to think he was, but now I can see he isn't. So that's it."

I had no words of wisdom for Jonathan, no golden gems of thought that would suddenly make everything better. I couldn't do it for myself, so there wasn't much hope I could do it for him. "All right, so you don't have your dad around anymore. My dad is still around, and believe me, it's not that great. We never talk anymore."

"Do you ever wonder if you'll turn out just like your dad?" Jonathan asked.

"Never," I said quickly.

"I do sometimes. And I could see how it could happen. I'll get married and everything will be fine. And then we'll have children. And then when my kids are in their teens, I'll just walk off and abandon my kids and tell them if they want to go to college, it's up to them because I never really cared for them in the first place. I could do that. I'm sure I could do that." He had tears in his eyes.

"You'll never do that."

"How do you know what I'll do?"

"I know you, Jonathan. You're not like that."

"What if it's like wisdom teeth, though, and doesn't show up until I have a couple of kids and a wife who's starting to look like she's not in her twenties anymore. What if I wake up one day and decide to walk away from it all?"

"You're not your dad. And I'm not my dad. We're totally different from them. We'll make mistakes, but they won't be the same mistakes our dads made."

"I don't want to make any mistakes," Jonathan said.

"All we can do is to try to do the best we can."

"And what if that isn't good enough?" Jonathan asked.

I shrugged my shoulders. "I don't know. I guess we try harder."

"But what if I get to a place where no matter how hard I try it isn't good enough?" he asked. "What do I do then?"

"You can always ask me to help you."

"You won't always be around," he said.

"I'll always be somewhere. All you've got to do is call and I'll come."

"What if it's when you're married and have kids of your own and a job?" he asked.

"It won't matter. If you call me, I'll still come, no matter what."

"You would, wouldn't you?" He was getting emotional. I didn't want to embarrass him by letting him know I'd seen it, so I looked away.

"Of course I would. Anytime. It wouldn't matter when it was either."

"I'd come for you, too," he said.

"Good. It's settled then. We don't need dads. We'll help each other out."

We sat for a long time just watching the fire die away to nothing.

"Well, we'd better get some sleep if we're going to get an early start in the morning," I said. It made me feel sad to say that, because it reminded me of my dad. He was always saying things that were obvious.

I wondered if my dad knew that this was the night of the fathers and sons' camp-out. I wondered if he knew how important these camp-outs had been to me when I was younger. I wondered if he ever wished we were close like we used to be. I wondered if he would've come with me if I'd asked him. And if he had come with me, I wondered what we'd have talked about.

I also wondered if he knew that I was seventeen and had only one more fathers and sons' camp-out, and then I'd be on my mission, and that would be the end of fathers and sons' camp-outs for us. I wondered if, at that moment, he was asleep or if he couldn't sleep, like me. I wondered what was so important that he couldn't take an afternoon and part of a Saturday morning to be with me. Was he so mad at me that he couldn't stand to be with me for a few hours? I wondered if it was wrong that I could relate with my mom better than my dad.

My dad and I had both been in priesthood meeting when they announced the fathers and sons' camp-out. Why didn't he say anything to me about it? Not even one word. Was it because he's given up on me, that he doesn't care about me anymore because I'm not there to help him all the time.

Well, so what if he has written me off? I don't need him. I have my friends. I have Jonathan, Ryan, Amber, and Brooke. That's all I need. I don't need anyone else. Jonathan doesn't need anyone else either. We'll get by just fine.

Nobody needs to worry about us.

At eleven-thirty that night, long after everyone else was asleep, Jonathan and I washed up in the campground rest room. It had a cement floor and one light bulb that gave a depressing kind of light. The water was cold and there was a cricket in one of the corners. It was chirping when we first went in but then quieted down when it heard us. When I went over to kill it, I couldn't find it. Jonathan said for me to just leave it.

It would have been hard making our way back to our tent in the dark, but I had a flashlight that helped. We walked past other tents. Boys and their fathers were sleeping. We could hear one of the dads snoring as we passed one tent. My dad snores too.

We got to our tent. I put the flashlight on the floor of the tent so we'd have some light to get ready for bed. I slept in my underwear because I never got cold, but Jonathan, being smaller, put on sweats. I got in my sleeping bag. It was cold at first. A few minutes later I realized I needed a pillow, so I grabbed my jeans and folded them over and put them under my head.

Jonathan turned the flashlight off, but I couldn't hear him get into his sleeping bag. It was quiet. Without even looking, I knew he was on his knees saying his prayers. It made me feel a little guilty. I thought about getting out of bed and saying my prayers too, but I didn't want to get out of a warm sleeping bag, so I just thought a prayer and then tried to fall asleep.

I couldn't sleep, though. I started thinking how things never seem to change, and then, all of a sudden, you realize they've changed so much you can't believe it. Like with the fathers and sons' camp-out. It's always the same. We always come to the same camp. We always have a program by the fire. And someone always talks about how we should honor the priesthood and never do anything that would bring dishonor to it. And the next morning we have pancakes and hot chocolate, and later we play softball on a field that is full of rocks and holes. The fathers let the younger boys get ten strikes. And then just before noon we pack up and leave until the next year.

The fathers and sons' camp-out never changes. And so you think that nothing is ever going to change. But then one night you realize things have changed, and you can't ever go back to the way they used to be.

I thought back to the way it used to be when I was twelve. I'd have given anything to go back to that time.

*   *   *   *

The next day at the fathers and sons' softball game, Jonathan and I were the stars. We were much better than any of the dads. I hit a home run every time I batted. A home run was if you hit into the deep weeds in center field. Jonathan did almost as well, except one time he grounded out.

I think we were both glad we'd gone to the fathers and sons' camp-out. It wasn't so much the things we said, although we said more than we usually did, but just being together had been good for both of us.

*   *   *   *

The next Friday night, Fast Forward got together at my house to watch some movies.

We started one movie, but within a few minutes there was the beginning of a bedroom scene.

Brooke stood up. "Guys, I can't watch this."

I hit the remote to stop the movie. I'd seen the movie before. "It's not that bad," I said. "I mean, all we see is the back of her when she walks away."

"With clothes or without clothes?" Amber asked.

"Without clothes," I said, "but it's just for an instant."

"So we see her backside?" Brooke asked.

"Well, yeah, but it's just for a few seconds," I said.

"I don't really care to see that," Brooke said.

"Me either," Amber said.

"Amber and I will be in the kitchen," Brooke said. They left.

Now it was just Ryan, Jonathan, and me.

"It's not that bad," I said. "I mean, it's no worse than you see on TV all the time. And the thing is, it goes by so fast, you probably won't even notice it," I said.

Ryan wasn't convinced. He stood up. "I'll be with the girls," he said, walking out. And then Jonathan left.

So I was left alone. I should've joined the others, but I was too stubborn. I'd paid good money to rent this movie. It wasn't R-rated, but even so, that one scene was messing up the rest of the movie. But was that my fault? I didn't rent it just for that one scene. The rest of the movie is good. It's just that one part.

Sometimes I'm too stubborn for my own good. I watched the rest of the scene just to prove my point. When the scene was over, a few minutes later, I went in the kitchen.

"So, Greg, did you get a good look?" Amber asked sarcastically.

"You make it sound like I'm some kind of pervert."

"You can make your own decision about that," Amber said, "but the fact is you're the only one of us who watched it."

"How come you knew that part was coming?" Brooke asked.

"I'd seen the movie before."

"Really? How many times?" Amber said, trying to push me into a corner, the way she usually did when I didn't agree with her.

"Back off, okay? You're not perfect either, you know," I said to Amber.

"I never said I was."

"Look, the movie wasn't even R-rated," I said.

"It doesn't matter what the rating is," Brooke said. "I always know when I shouldn't be watching something. It's when I start to feel guilty."

"You mean the way Greg is feeling now?" Amber said. It was like after stabbing me, she had to turn the knife.

Sometimes I really couldn't stand Amber. "Just back off, okay?"

She gave me her famous twisted smile. "Sure, whatever you say, Video Man."

I slammed my fist down on the table. "I said knock it off! I really don't need you hassling me all the time, Amber! So just lay off, okay?"

I was so mad at her I had to go outside to cool off.

A few minutes later Amber came out to see me. She walked over and stood next to me without saying anything for a few moments. "Greg, I'm sorry for being so mean to you. I really am."

At first I just stared straight ahead, but then she touched my chin and turned my head so I'd look at her. "I don't know why I'm such a witch sometimes. I'll try to do better, okay? Just give me another chance. Please."

I shrugged my shoulders. "Don't worry about it. I had it coming."

She cuddled closer to me. I put my arm around her

shoulder. "What should I do about the movies I rented?" I asked.

"Whatever you think best. I know you'll do the right thing."

It was my advice to her about dealing with guys. But I appreciated that she trusted me.

"I think I'll just take the movies back to the video store," I said.

"Let me come with you, okay?"

As we drove to the video store, she sat close to me. "You know that, except for Brooke, you're my best friend, don't you?" she said.

"Yeah, I know that. And, except for Jonathan, you're my best friend."

"I would never hurt you intentionally," she said. "It's just that sometimes, when I start teasing you, I don't know when to stop. I'm really sorry, Greg. From now on, I'll do better. I promise."

"It's okay," I said. "Don't worry about it." I paused. "Besides, you were right. I had no business watching that."

When we got back, everyone was in the backyard. Brooke was lying on her back on the trampoline, and Ryan and Jonathan were standing on either side of her, jumping on the trampoline, trying to time it so they could launch her as high as possible.

Amber and I soon got in on the fun.

* * * *

It's true that Amber and I didn't always get along. I'm sure that some people, seeing us together, sometimes wondered if we even liked each other. The one thing that people might overlook is that we always tried to be totally honest with each other. I didn't hold anything from her, and she was the same way with me.

She and I never talked to others in the blunt manner we

sometimes used in talking to each other. If she thought I was being a jerk, she told me so. And I did the same with her. Once in a while we got mad at each other, but most of the time we ended up paying attention to what the other said.

Most people won't tell you when you're wrong. They might think it, but they won't say anything because they're afraid of hurting your feelings. Amber and I were close enough that we could be totally honest with each other. We came to depend on each other a great deal.

I don't think you ever forget the person who helps you grow up.

5

In June, with school out, I ended up working for my dad on the farm, mainly because I couldn't find anything else that paid as well. We reached a truce. He gave me a job to do and then left me alone to finish it. If I needed any help, I'd call him on our cellular phone. Otherwise, I'd just do it. It kept us from getting on each other's nerves.

That summer Fast Forward practiced three or four nights a week. In addition to that, we performed at wedding receptions, family reunions, and youth conferences. We put on a few firesides too. So we kept busy. It meant we were together a lot.

On the second Friday in June, after one of our practices, we decided to go to the sand dunes for a cookout. We went to a store and bought hot dogs and buns, then went to Brooke's home. While she was raiding her refrigerator for mustard and drinks, Ryan and I hauled wood from a pile on the side of her garage to my minivan.

It takes about half an hour to get to the sand dunes. We parked and hauled everything over a couple of sand ridges so we'd be alone. At the bottom of a sloping hill we made a fire. There we were, the five of us sharing a campfire, cooking hot dogs until they were black and crispy, drinking lukewarm diet something, and talking.

"What kind of hot dogs did you get?" Jonathan asked.

"They're just hot dogs. Why?" I asked.

"My mom always gets the kind made from turkey."

"If you're worried about what's in 'em," I said, "just put a lot of mustard on 'em. That'll kill anything."

"That's not true," Jonathan said.

"Maybe not, but Brooke believed it," I said.

Brooke smiled and threw a marshmallow at me. "Take that."

I fell over like I was dead. Brooke came over and knelt down beside me. "Gosh, guys, I think I killed Greg."

"Can I have his hot dog?" Ryan asked.

Brooke folded my arms across my chest. "Those who live by the marshmallow, die by the marshmallow," she said.

"You mean look like a marshmallow, don't you?" Amber teased. "Since he's dead anyway, do you think it'd be all right to make a little mustard mustache on him?"

"Well, I don't know," Brooke said. "It doesn't seem very respectful."

"We'll do it very respectfully then," Amber said, with that wicked little laugh she uses when she's about to do mischief.

"Well, I suppose that'd be okay," Brooke said.

Brooke and Amber got the jar of mustard and a plastic spoon and put a line of mustard above my upper lip.

"Actually, I think it's an improvement," Amber said, looking at their artistic creation.

"You know, I think you're right," Brooke said.

"I wonder what he'd look like if his eyebrows were mustard colored?" Amber said. "Or maybe his nose? Whataya think?"

That was enough. I reached out to grab Brooke and Amber, but they jumped away. I stood up and roared.

"Oh no! It's Mustard Man!" Amber shrieked.

I chased them up a sand dune. The sound of their giggling was music to my ears. They were too fast for me, so

I gave up and came back and wiped the mustard off my face.

All this time Jonathan had been studying the hot dog label. "What does *assorted pork by-products* mean?"

"It means whatever's left on the cutting floor at the end of the day," Ryan said.

Brooke and Amber came over the ridge. "Greg," Brooke asked sweetly, "you're not really mad at us, are you?"

If it'd been Amber who asked, I would have faked being mad, but Brooke was too nice a girl to mess with. "Not really."

"And you won't put mustard in our hair, will you?" Amber asked.

"No, not in your hair," I answered.

Brooke had to make sure. "And not anywhere else, right?" she asked.

"I won't do anything. C'mon back."

They returned to the fire.

"Maybe I'll just have a hot dog bun and some mustard," Jonathan said.

"Don't be such a baby," I said. "Pork by-products will grow hair on your chest."

"Or in your mouth," Ryan added.

"Guys, when we were singing tonight, I didn't want it to end," Brooke said. "We're getting so good."

"Want a hot dog?" Ryan asked Amber. "I'll cook one for you."

"Yeah, sure," Amber said.

"Do your folks ever give you a hard time about us being together so much?" Brooke asked us.

"Mine don't," Ryan said. "They can't say enough good things about you guys."

"My dad does," I said. "He thinks the whole thing is a waste of time."

"My dad is the same way," Brooke said. "He's always

101

asking, 'Now are you sure singing in that group is what you really want to do?' And I go, 'Yes, I am. Thanks for asking, though.' One time he said, 'I'm curious—what do you think it does for you?' And I said, 'Well, for one thing it gives me a purpose in life.' And he looks at me like I'm stupid and goes, 'Really? I would think the gospel would do that.' So I tried to tell him what it means to me to sing with you guys. And it's like he's not even listening. He goes, 'My concern is that this may not get you where you want to go.' Like he knows where I want to go. I mean, isn't that my choice?

"One time I asked him if I had any say in how my life turned out, and he goes, 'Well, of course. You have your free agency.' But the thing is, he only lets me have free agency when I do what he wants me to do. He's never happy with anything I want to do. He'll say things like 'Someday you'll thank me for making you buckle down and make something of your life.' I swear he makes me crazy sometimes. I mean, shouldn't I be the one to decide what direction my life takes?"

It was unusual to hear Brooke talk like that. She was the original Miss Positive, and we had never heard her complain about her family.

"Sure you should. It's your life, not his," I said.

"I don't think you should be so critical of your dad," Jonathan said to Brooke. "I'm sure he's doing the best he can."

"How are things at home for you?" Brooke asked Jonathan.

"Good," Jonathan said with his usual cheery smile.

"That's not true," I said. "Tell them the truth, Jonathan. They're also your friends."

"Well, it has been hard, but I try not to let it show."

"When you're hurting, you've got to let us know," Brooke said. "Guys, we have to stick together, no matter what. We have to be here for each other. Okay?"

The rest of us nodded.

"This is great being here together," Jonathan said.

"My mom and dad think it's cool that I'm spending time with you guys," Ryan said. "They know you have been good for me." He paused and his hopeful expression caved into despair. "Of course, Jamie is just glad it keeps me away from home. She still won't have anything to do with me. When I walk into a room, she walks out. The only time she talks to me is to tell me some of the things people are saying about Nicole. Nicole's running around at night, like I used to. Jamie says it's all my fault."

"How can Jamie blame you for what Nicole's doing now?" I asked.

"I got her started."

We didn't say anything. I guess that even though we were on Ryan's side now, we all still felt he was at least partly responsible for the way Nicole was turning out.

"I thought it was supposed to get easier," Ryan said. "I did everything you said. I went to Nicole and her mom and dad and apologized. I went to my bishop and told him everything. But sometimes I wonder if all this is just make-believe. I mean, what if there is no God? What if it doesn't matter what we do?"

"There is a God, though," Brooke said.

"How do you know that? Have you ever seen him or heard his voice?" Ryan asked.

"No."

"So what if he doesn't even exist?" Ryan asked. "What if it's all a lie? What if it doesn't matter what I do?"

"If you did harm to somebody, even if there wasn't a God, it would still be wrong," Brooke said.

"But what if I lived all alone on top of a mountain, and I never even saw any other person? Then it wouldn't matter what I did, would it?"

"You don't live on a mountain, so quit trying to justify your actions," Amber said.

"I'm not."

"You are too, Ryan," Amber said. "You want us to say it doesn't matter what you do. You got that from the crowd you used to hang around with, but you won't get it from us."

Ryan was getting worked up, and he threw up his hands. "You all act like you've got this private pipeline to God. Well, you don't. Nobody does, so why not just admit you're as clueless as I am? I go to church, but I don't feel anything."

"You've never felt the Spirit?" Brooke asked.

"Never."

"You will, though," Brooke said.

"I don't think so. People say how much they felt the Spirit in a meeting. I never feel anything. And that's not all. I've never had a prayer answered either."

"You have," Brooke said. "You just didn't recognize it."

"Do you pray much?" Amber asked.

"Not anymore," Ryan said. "Do you guys pray by yourself at night in your room?"

"Most of the time," Amber said.

"Me too," Brooke said.

"I do too," I said.

"My mom makes sure we have family prayer," Jonathan said.

"Every night?" Ryan asked.

"Yeah, pretty much," Amber said.

"Will you pray tonight after you get home?" Ryan asked.

"Probably," Brooke said.

"What will you pray for?"

"I don't know—just the usual," Brooke said.

"Like what?" Ryan asked.

"I usually ask Heavenly Father to bless the sick and the needy," Brooke said.

"The sick and the needy in the whole world?" Ryan asked.

"Yeah, sure. Why not?"

Ryan smirked. "You think he answers that? I mean, do you really think that someday you'll turn on the news and the announcer will say, 'Guess what? Today nobody's sick or needy. We don't know how it happened, but that's the way it is.' Is that what you think is going to happen?"

"Not really. There will always be the sick and the needy," Brooke said.

"Then why pray for them?" Ryan asked.

"Because it shows I care."

"Does it?" Ryan said. "I think if you really cared about 'em, you'd do more than just pray. Like maybe donate a can of food to some charity that'd feed 'em. Do you ever do that?"

"My mom does."

"But you don't?" Ryan asked.

"Not really," Brooke said.

"So what good does it do for you to pray for the sick and the needy?" Ryan asked.

"Probably not much, but I'm going to keep it up," Brooke said.

"Amber, what do you pray for?" Ryan asked.

"Personal things."

"Like what?" Ryan asked.

"Things I don't want to talk about with you."

"Like what, though?" Ryan pressed.

"Like I said—it's none of your business," Amber said.

"Well, just give me a for instance."

"No," Amber said. "It's between me and God."

Ryan smiled. "Are you hiding something?"

"No."

"Then tell me what I don't know about you. Is it like

some personal weakness you're trying to overcome?" Ryan asked hopefully.

Amber was getting mad. "Knock it off, Ryan. You have no right to ask me that."

"I went too far, didn't I?" Ryan asked.

"Yes, you did, way too far," Amber said.

"Sorry." Ryan sighed.

"How are you doing now, Ryan?" I asked.

"Okay, except for one thing."

"What?" I asked.

Ryan hesitated telling us. "Nicole's been calling me. She keeps asking me to spend some time with her. I keep telling her no, but sometimes I think about it. One time, late at night, I drove by her place, but I didn't stop."

"Seeing her again would be the worst thing you could do," Brooke said.

"I know it would, but sometimes I think about it."

"Call me when you're having a tough time, even if it's late at night," Brooke said.

"I might take you up on that sometime. The last time she called, she said she'd do anything to get me back. She kept saying she knows what boys want."

"What did she mean by that?" Brooke asked.

"Oh, Brooke, you're so naïve," Amber said. "Even I know what that means."

"Really?" Brooke asked, wide-eyed. "What did you say?"

"I told her I wasn't going to see her anymore," Ryan said. "And then I hung up on her."

"Good for you," Jonathan said.

"But sometimes I think about what it'd be like, you know, to see her again. Sometimes it's hard to know what to do."

For a while, no one said anything. We all just sat there, staring into the fire, lost in our own thoughts.

"My mom told me this thing once that kind of helped

me," Brooke said. "It's sort of dumb, I guess, but, anyway, she said that sex is like a game of tennis."

"Really?" Ryan said with a smile.

"If you're going to make fun of this, I'm not going to say anything more," Brooke said. "This is serious."

"Okay, sorry," Ryan said.

Only Brooke could say this and get away with it because she was always so totally sincere. "All right, well, the ways that sex is like a game of tennis is, first of all, if you're going to have a game of tennis, you need to go to a place where there's a tennis court. I mean, you don't play tennis on a football field. So my mom said that sex is like that. It's just for marriage. Just like it's okay to play tennis once you've got the court reserved, it's okay to have sex if you're married, and, of course, if your partner wants to play tennis too."

I shook my head. "This is getting really weird, Brooke."

"I'm almost done. Also, my mom said you can't play tennis if both players are on the same side of the net. Okay, so what that tells us is like if two guys or two girls—"

"We know what you mean, Brooke," Amber said.

Brooke continued. "Okay, good. And then the other thing is you can't play tennis alone, because it's not a game that's meant to be played alone."

We all sat there in a shocked silence. Finally Ryan said, "Your mom told you this?"

"Yes."

"How old were you?" Ryan asked.

"Eleven, I think," Brooke said.

"Having your mom talk to you about this must have delayed puberty at least a couple of years," Ryan said.

"Not really. I was glad she talked to me. At least I knew what was expected of me."

"So basically, it's no tennis until you're married, right?" Ryan asked.

"Is this really news to you?" Amber said.

"Not really," Ryan said. "It's just that the people I used to run around with pretty much wanted all the tennis they could get. That's all they talked about. Tennis . . . tennis . . . tennis."

"You're not with them anymore. You're with us," Brooke said.

He smiled. "I am, aren't I? How smart of me to be with you guys."

On the way back to the car, Amber and I walked together. On one hill she stumbled in the dark. I reached for her hand. She tensed up. "Greg?" She sounded worried.

"Just until we get to the car."

"All right." But her hand was still tense.

"Sometimes I don't know what I'd do without you," I said. "You've helped me so much. I want to thank you for being such a good friend." How could she object to that? She was the one who told me to show appreciation.

"Thanks, Greg. I feel the same way about you—as a friend I mean."

"Of course as a friend," I said. "What else is there?"

With that her hand relaxed.

"You're so much fun to be with," I said. "Even that thing you did with the mustard tonight was fun."

"You were a good sport to let me do it."

"I can't ever remember being happier than I am tonight," I said.

"Me either."

"I really like being able to talk to you the way we do," I said.

"I know. Me too. You're so good for me." She squeezed my hand.

We held hands until we started down the final hill leading to the car. And then she pulled away and ran ahead of me down the hill. I understood. We didn't want the others seeing us holding hands.

On the way home we were all still in a good mood, so we sang. Not songs we performed. Just silly songs. Songs that made us laugh. Amber and I secretly practiced laughing. It sounded so natural that nobody knew what we were doing. Except it made everyone else laugh more too.

Not long after I got home, I climbed into bed. But then I felt guilty because I was pretty sure Amber, Brooke, and Jonathan, and maybe even Ryan, would be kneeling by their beds perhaps at that very instant, saying their prayers.

So I got out of bed and said a quick prayer too.

Mainly I thanked God for my friends.

It had been a great night.

6

It was a week later, on a Saturday morning, when Amber called and asked me to come over right away. She sounded desperate. I told her I'd be right there.

My dad was expecting me to work for him all day, but I told him I needed to go see Amber for a few minutes and that I'd only be gone a little while.

"I need you now," my dad said.

"I know. I'll hurry."

"I can never depend on you anymore," he said.

"What are you talking about? I've worked all week for you."

"We have to work until the job is done, and the job isn't done yet."

"I know, but with you, though, the job is never done. Look, I won't be gone very long."

"Amber calls and you come running. Is that the way it is?" he said.

"Yes, that's the way it is."

When I got to Amber's place, she was in the middle of baking bread. "What do you need me for?" I asked. "My dad is expecting me to work all day."

She looked worried. "Jennifer's locked herself in the bathroom."

"How come?"

"She's mad at me," Amber said.

"Why?"

"I told on her."

I knew that if I didn't get back home soon, my dad would be impossible to work with all day. "What do you want me to do, break the door down?" I asked.

"No," Amber said.

"What then?"

"I tried to get hold of Brooke, but she's not home. My mom and dad are both working. Can you stay with me until they get home?"

I knew what my dad would say, that he could never depend on me for anything anymore, that I should be more responsible and pull my own weight, that he had to do everything all the time. I'd heard it all before. But Amber was my friend, and I couldn't let her down, even if it did make my dad mad. "I'll stay here for as long as you want," I said.

She laid her hand on my arm and kept it there while she said, "Thanks."

"Yeah, sure. So what's the problem with Jennifer?"

"Last night after I went to bed, I heard Jennifer get up and go into the kitchen. We had half a tray of leftover brownies. She must have eaten them all because they were all gone this morning. Anyway, I heard her go into the bathroom. It sounded like she was throwing up. I got up and opened the door and saw her bent over the toilet. I asked her if she was throwing up on purpose, and she said no, she just got sick, that's all. I didn't believe her, so I woke up my mom and told her what she'd done.

"Jennifer just kept saying she had the flu, but if a person has the flu, why would she eat half a tray of brownies? Mom asked Jennifer if she was bulimic. Jennifer said no, that nothing was wrong and that we shouldn't make such a big deal out of her being sick. By that time my dad had gotten up. He

111

came in and asked what was wrong. When I told him what I'd seen, he got real mad at Jennifer and told her we didn't have enough money to waste any of it by eating good food and then throwing it right back up again. He told her he wanted her to put a stop to it immediately. My mom said that sounded easy but that Jennifer might not be able to stop on her own and that she might need some counseling. That really made my dad mad. He goes, 'She's had it too easy, and she's got too much time on her hands anyway!' He said the best thing for her would be to get a job and work after school and on Saturdays and then she'd learn the value of a dollar. When my mom reminded him that Jennifer's only fifteen, he got really mad and said if she's got enough time to throw up good food, she's got enough time to get a job and pay for the food she's wasting. That's the way it ended, with everybody mad at everybody else." She paused. "Now do you see why I need you with me today?"

"What do you want me to do?" I asked.

"Would you quit being the man of action for a minute? I don't want you to *do* anything. I just want you to be with me. I wish Brooke had been home."

"What would she do that I can't do?"

"She'd tell me, 'I'm sorry you've had to go through this. You've really had a bad time.'"

"That's what you want me to do?" I asked.

"Yes."

"I'd rather break down the bathroom door," I said.

"I know, but that's not what I need from you."

"All right, I'll do what I can," I said.

"Thanks. When Jennifer got up, she and I had this big argument, and then she went and locked herself in the bathroom. I'm afraid she might do something to hurt herself."

"You want me to see if I can coax her out?" I asked.

"Well, yeah, sure, if you want to, but I tried and it didn't do any good."

I went with Amber to the bathroom door. "Jennifer, this is Greg. I need you to open the door."

"What for?" she said through the door.

"Amber is worried about you."

"I wish people would just mind their own business," Jennifer said.

"Have you been throwing up after you eat?" I asked.

"Just once, but that was because I had the flu."

"Oh, yeah, right," Amber said sarcastically.

"Oh, just shut up, Amber," Jennifer said. "I don't expect you to understand. At least I'm able to control my weight."

I looked over at Amber. I wondered if all the unkind things people had said to Amber when she was in junior high and towered over all the other girls in her class might be rushing through her mind again.

"Amber?" I said quietly.

"What?"

"You're fine . . ." She seemed confused by what I was talking about, so I added, ". . . you know, in the body department."

I had intended my remark to be a compliment, but it made her blush. I started to blush too. I had never told a girl she had a nice body. I was afraid she might take it wrong. I didn't mean it in a bad way.

Amber and I were both really embarrassed. "Thanks, I guess," she finally said.

Amber spoke again through the bathroom door. "Jennifer, what you're doing isn't right because it does harm to your body."

"So? It's my body, isn't it? I should be able to do with it what I want. At least I have control. That's more than you can say."

"You think you've got control," Amber said, "but what's really happening is you've lost control. But don't worry.

Mom and Dad will get help for you. Even if it means you have to be locked up in a hospital for a year or two."

Jennifer threw something against the door. It landed with a thud.

I didn't see that Amber was helping to calm things down any. "Why don't you let me talk to her?" I said to Amber.

"Fine, she's only my sister," she snapped. Then, fed up with me and Jennifer, she returned to the kitchen.

"She's gone now," I said to Jennifer through the door.

"I hate her," Jennifer said.

"Do you?"

"Yes, totally."

"Are you okay in there?" I asked.

"Yes."

"I'd like it if you would come out so we can talk face to face."

She opened the door. She was wearing an oversized sweatshirt and jeans that looked too baggy. "Here I am."

I looked for signs of any damage her eating disorder had caused. On the surface I couldn't see any, but, of course, she was wearing baggy clothes. I did notice a small outbreak of pimples around her mouth, but I wasn't sure if that was just normal or not. Also, her face seemed paler than usual. Other than that I couldn't see anything. I suppose if it had been obvious, her mom would have recognized that something was wrong.

"You want to have some breakfast?" I asked.

"Not really."

"Would you mind if I had something to eat?"

"No, go ahead."

"Maybe you could keep me company," I said.

"I really don't want to be in the same room with Amber."

"I won't let her get after you."

We went into the kitchen. "Jennifer and I are here for

some breakfast. I promised I wouldn't let you give her a hard time."

"I can't make bread anyplace but here."

"Maybe if you didn't talk to us then," I said. "Okay?"

"Fine," she said, slamming down a glob of bread dough on the counter.

"I hate to bother you, but could you get me something to eat?" I asked Amber.

Amber seemed to be mad at me because I'd gotten Jennifer out of the bathroom when she couldn't. She went to the fridge and took out some milk, then got two bowls and a plastic container of homemade granola out of the cupboards. She scattered everything on the kitchen table and then glared at Jennifer. "Jennifer, if you're going to have anything to eat, go to the bathroom *first*."

Jennifer looked up from the table. "Excuse me?"

"You heard me."

"Now you're telling me when I can go to the bathroom?" Jennifer asked.

"Does that go for me too?" I asked, trying to cut down the tension in the room.

Amber wasn't amused. "Just be quiet, Greg, okay? This is between me and Jennifer. Jennifer, I won't let you go in the bathroom right after you eat."

"Why not?"

"You know why not," Amber said.

"I can't believe this," Jennifer complained. "It's like a prison around here. I can't stand you breathing down my neck all the time."

"Well, get used to it," Amber said. "Mom and Dad are talking about sending you away to a treatment center."

I filled a bowl with homemade granola and poured milk over the cereal and started to eat. Jennifer just sat there.

"Jennifer, quit acting so dumb and eat something," Amber ordered.

"I'm not hungry."

"Oh, yeah, right. You're not hungry now, but as soon as everyone is out of the kitchen, you'll come in here and scarf down everything in sight and then go throw it up!"

"Amber," I said, "back off, okay? You're making things worse."

Amber was near tears. "She's killing herself. You know that, don't you? She's going to die from this if we can't get it stopped. I can't just stand by and let it happen. I really do hate this." She ran to her room and slammed the door.

My simple bowl of granola now seemed as dangerous as a loaded gun.

Amber was in her room crying. Jennifer was crying next to me. There was bread baking in the oven and a timer ticking.

There were two people in the house who needed comforting, but I had no idea what to say or who to start with. I tried to imagine what Brooke would do. She was always helping people, but it was never that she came up with brilliant suggestions that solved somebody's problem. It was just that she showed she cared and that she understood how the other person felt.

I wasn't good at this. I would have given anything then to be working with my dad, enduring his impatient answers to my questions about how he wanted the job done.

And, also, I was hungry. I finished the first bowl of granola and then, even though I felt guilty for eating so much in front of Jennifer, I poured myself another bowl.

Maybe ten minutes later, Amber came back into the kitchen. She looked pretty bad because she'd been crying. "How can you do this to yourself?" she asked Jennifer.

Jennifer just shrugged her shoulders.

"That's why you've been wearing baggy clothes, isn't it? So Mom wouldn't know what you are doing to yourself."

"I was in control."

"Are you in control now?" Amber asked.

"Just leave me alone, okay?"

"All right, but from now on, anytime you want to use the bathroom, you tell me so I can go in there with you," Amber said.

"I don't want you in there with me," Jennifer said.

"Get used to it, Jennifer. If Mom and Dad send you to a treatment program, they'll have a nurse watching you every time you go to the bathroom. Is that what you want—strangers watching you go to the bathroom?"

"No."

"Then stop this nonsense while you still can."

"You're just jealous because you can't lose weight and I can," Jennifer said.

The timer dinged. Amber took the hot bread out of the oven. When she turned to face us again, there were tears streaming down her face. "I've got to get outside for a minute. Greg, can you watch Jennifer for a few minutes?"

"Yeah, sure. No problem."

Amber left.

"Do you ever get scared about what you've been doing to yourself?" I asked.

"No."

"You're sure?"

She hesitated. "Well, sometimes, maybe."

"What scares you?" I asked.

"The way it keeps repeating itself over and over."

"I don't understand," I said.

For a long time she didn't say anything.

"How does it keep repeating itself over and over?" I asked.

"In the morning, when I first wake up, I think, *Okay, today I'm not going to eat anything that'll make me fat.* So I skip breakfast, but then after a while I keep getting more and more hungry, so then I decide to just have a little snack. At

117

first I'm just going to have a bowl of cereal, but then I see some leftover pancakes, so I have one, and then I end up eating them all, with lots of butter and syrup, and then I feel guilty, and I start thinking, *How can I lose weight if I eat like that?* So then I go in the bathroom and throw it all up, and then I feel like I'm back on track again. But then after a while I'm so hungry I can't stand it, so I go back in the kitchen, and I eat some more, and then I go throw it up again . . ."

"You know this will kill you if you keep it up, don't you?"

"No it won't. I've got it under control."

"How much weight have you lost?" I asked.

"Ten pounds."

"When you started, how much weight did you want to lose?"

"Ten pounds."

"So you're done then, right?"

She hesitated. "Not exactly. I'd like to lose another ten pounds."

"It will always be ten pounds, won't it? Even until the day this thing kills you."

"It won't kill me."

"What's going to stop it from killing you?" I asked.

"I'll stop."

"When?"

"After I lose ten more pounds," she said.

"What if you lost a pound today? How many pounds would you have yet to lose?"

"Nine pounds."

"But, see, that doesn't happen. No matter how much you lose, you always have ten pounds more to lose. Don't you see, this is not a diet."

"What is it?"

"I don't know for sure, but, whatever it is, it's not right."

Amber returned to the house. "Jennifer, I'm sorry I yelled at you. Are you okay now?"

"I guess so. I'm kind of hungry."

"What do you want?" Amber asked.

Jennifer hesitated. "I'm afraid to eat anything."

"Why?"

"Because if I eat anything, I know I'll try to throw it up," Jennifer said.

"We have some bananas," Amber said. "Could you eat one?"

"I think so."

Amber cleared away the breakfast dishes and set out a single banana on the table. "It's ready," she said.

"I don't think I'd better eat a whole banana," she said.

Amber cut it in two and peeled it, cut it up into sections and put it on a plate. "Take your time. Take it slowly. Don't rush it."

Jennifer smiled. "You sound like Mom sometimes."

"I suppose I do."

Jennifer took a long time to finish half of the banana. And then she looked up and, almost like she was apologizing, she said, "Sorry, but I think I'm going to throw up."

"No, don't! You've got to keep it down," Amber pleaded.

"I can't help it." Jennifer stood up and quickly moved toward the bathroom. Amber jumped in front of her. "Don't do this, Jennifer. It's only a banana. Keep it down."

Seeing the way blocked by Amber, Jennifer turned toward the kitchen sink. She didn't make it. A small fountain of banana pulp came out of her mouth onto the floor. She wiped her face with a dish towel and looked over at us. "I guess it was too rich. Sometimes I can get celery to stay down." She fell to her knees, bent over, and continued retching, but there wasn't much more that came up.

Amber went to the phone and tried to get her mom at work, but there was no answer. She couldn't reach her dad either. She decided she couldn't wait, so she dialed 911. "I need an ambulance right away. I think my sister is dying. She's bulimic and she can't keep anything down anymore."

Amber gave the information they needed and then hung up.

Jennifer was lying on the kitchen floor, her body pulled up into a fetal position. Her eyes were closed and her face was pale and perspiring.

Her sweatshirt had vomit on it. "Don't let them see me this way," she pleaded.

Amber went into the bathroom and grabbed some towels. First she wiped up the vomit from the floor around where Jennifer was lying, and then she started wiping off what had gotten on Jennifer. It was mostly on her sweatshirt, so she went into their bedroom and got one of her own sweatshirts and came back. "Let's get this off you." I turned away while she helped Jennifer remove her sweatshirt. But then she cried out, "Oh, Jennifer!"

I turned around and saw Jennifer's bare back, but then I turned away.

"It's not that bad," Jennifer said.

"It is though," Amber said. "It's terrible. I can't believe you've done this to yourself."

"Just ten more pounds, and then I'll stop for good."

We could hear the sound of the ambulance first and then the tires hitting the gravel as it came up their driveway.

Amber and I followed the ambulance in the pickup I used when I worked for my dad. Once at the hospital, the hardest part was trying to get Jennifer admitted. Amber didn't know all the details of whatever insurance their family had. Finally, she had to give up and keep trying to get hold of her mother at work.

When she finally reached her mom, she asked her to come to the hospital and help get Jennifer admitted.

The hospital had an eating disorders program that Jennifer was accepted into.

I didn't get home until three in the afternoon. When I drove out to the place where we kept all our machinery, my dad was inside working. He glared at me and said he didn't need my help anymore.

"Don't you want to know what happened?" I said.

"All right, what happened?"

I told him about Jennifer ending up in the hospital.

"What exactly did you do?"

"Amber needed me to stay with her."

"I needed you too, but I guess what I need isn't that important to you. Why is it you can always run off to help somebody else, but you don't have five minutes for me when I need help? It looks to me like everything else in the world is more important to you than your own family."

"I would have helped if this hadn't come up," I said.

"No, you wouldn't. You'd have found some other excuse. I'll tell you something. If you don't want to work with me, just say it straight out and I'll get some hired help."

I felt he was pushing me into something neither one of us wanted. But I didn't have much choice because it was true—I didn't like to work with him. He was too demanding. Nothing was ever good enough for him. "Maybe that would be a good idea—for you to get some hired help."

He glared at me again, then returned with a vengeance to his work.

I moved toward the pickup. He came out after me. "If you aren't going to help out around here, then just leave the pickup and walk back. That vehicle is for work."

"You want me to walk back to town?"

"You heard what I said."

"How are you going to get two pickups to town all by yourself?" I asked.

"Let me worry about that."

"Fine then. Have it your way." I turned and started walking.

Instead of walking home, I thumbed a ride to Jonathan's place and stayed there most of the rest of the day. I should have phoned my mom and told her where I was, but I didn't. When I got home that night, she told me she would have appreciated a phone call. I told her I was sorry.

The next day Amber came over and explained to my mom and dad what had happened and how much she appreciated me being with her.

Amber's visit softened my dad a little. He let me continue working for him. But we still didn't speak to each other except when it was absolutely necessary.

7

I tried to visit Jennifer every day while she was in the hospital, which was almost the entire month of July. I went mostly with Amber, but sometimes when Amber was busy, I'd go by myself. I always tried to bring Jennifer something. I brought her a yo-yo and some funny get-well cards and a glass crystal that, if you held it to the sun, you could see a rainbow. Mostly dumb things. Just to get her mind off of where she was.

Of course, I never brought her food.

One night after Amber and I had visited Jennifer, I pulled into the Whittakers' driveway. Amber didn't get out of the car right away like she usually did. "Jennifer really looks forward to having you come by to see her. You're so good with her. I just wanted to thank you for being such a good friend to both of us. You're so much a part of my life now that I don't know what I'd do anymore without your help and encouragement," she said.

I walked her to the door. "I feel the same way about you."

"I think the way things are going for us now is really good," she said. "Especially the way we can talk to each other about almost anything. Thanks for giving me suggestions, you know, about boys. It's really helped." She noticed my silly grin. "What's going on in that devious mind of yours, Greg?"

"Well, I was just thinking. Since I am your coach with guys, if you ever wanted to practice kissing, I'd be willing to work with you on that, too."

She started laughing. "In your dreams, Greg, in your dreams."

I put my hand to my chest as if I'd been terribly misjudged. "Excuse me, did you think I was suggesting that you and I kiss?" I shook my head. "Believe me, that was the furthest thing from my mind. The offer was strictly a professional one. See, I have these lip exercises you can do with a ripe kiwi. Three sets of ten reps each. I'll show them to you sometime."

That broke her up. "You are out of your mind, Greg. I mean it. Someday I'm going to have you put away."

"No you won't. You need me too much for that."

Her eyes got big. "I need you? How do you figure that?"

"You love this bantering we do every day."

"Bantering? Wow, that's a pretty big word for you, Greg. What happened? Did somebody give you a dictionary?"

"I'm going now. This may be the last time you ever see me."

"Finally," she said with a big grin.

Of course, I knew that's how she'd react. She's so predictable.

I was really happy going home that night because being Amber's best friend was so much fun.

*   *   *   *

When it was just me visiting Jennifer at the hospital, we had some great talks. I could tell she had a crush on me because of the way she looked at me, like I was somebody very wonderful. Nobody else looked at me that way. I knew

I wasn't wonderful, though, but it did feel good to know that someone thought I was.

Near the end of her month in the hospital, especially when it was just the two of us, she would give me a hug when it was time for me to leave.

The day she was released from the hospital, I was invited to have supper with her family to celebrate her coming home.

I was asked to sit between Amber and Jennifer.

Of course, Mr. Whittaker had to have fun teasing me. He looked at me after the blessing on the food and said, "Every time I turn around you're here. You do have a home, don't you?"

I smiled. "I do, but I like it here better."

"Why's that?" he asked.

"Mainly because of your daughters."

"What do you appreciate most about my daughters?" he asked.

"Well, there are lots of things. But one thing I'm most grateful for is that they look more like your wife than they do you."

Both Amber and Jennifer laughed.

"I don't have to put up with that kind of abuse, do I?" Mr. Whittaker complained to his wife.

"I think you do, dear."

"Well, okay." He gave me his best intimidating stare. "Amber and Jennifer don't say too many bad things about you, so I guess we'll let you keep coming around."

"Thanks," I said.

"Just don't eat too much," he said, with just the hint of a smile.

We had spaghetti, garlic bread, a salad, and ice cream for dessert. I'm not sure about everyone else, but I watched each mouthful of food that Jennifer took.

She caught me looking at her. "I'm okay now. Honest."

"Of course you are," I said quickly, looking down to hide my embarrassment.

We finished eating. Amber and I waited to see if Jennifer would head for the bathroom, but she didn't. She seemed content to sit and visit. We all just sat around the kitchen table and relaxed. Everyone was really comfortable.

Amber and I volunteered to do the dishes, but halfway through the job, Amber got a phone call. Jennifer came and filled in for her. She washed while I dried.

"Thanks for coming to visit me so much when I was in the hospital," she said.

"Sure, no problem."

"No other boy came to visit me," she said.

"They probably didn't know."

"Some did. Greg?"

"What?"

"I've had a lot of time to think while I've been in the hospital. When you get off your mission, I'll be nineteen."

"I suppose."

"I know you think of me as too young now, but I won't always be."

"I'll keep that in mind."

"It's hopeless for you and Amber," she said.

"How can you say that? She and I are best friends."

"But it's never going to go beyond that. You know that, don't you?"

I shrugged my shoulders. "Yeah, I guess I do."

"Good. I'm glad you do, because it isn't. You're the nicest guy I've ever known."

I was really embarrassed by all this. "Thanks."

"That phone call Amber got—it was a guy."

"How do you know?" I asked.

"I can always tell when it's a guy she's interested in because her voice changes. She'll probably want you to go home pretty soon so the other guy can come by for her."

126

"You think so?"

"Yeah, I do. Is it hard just being friends with Amber?" Jennifer asked.

"It kind of is sometimes."

"I can see why. I think she's crazy for not paying more attention to you."

"Thanks."

"I'm not sure, but sometimes I think I love you," she said.

I cleared my throat. "Really?"

"Yes."

"Well . . . ," I stammered.

"You don't love me though, do you?" she asked.

"I like you more as a friend."

"That's okay for now. I guess now you know how Amber feels when you talk to her."

"I guess so," I said.

"Don't look so worried. I won't ever bring it up again."

When Amber hung up, she returned to the kitchen. "Greg, I've got to go out in a few minutes. You can stay if you want, but I'm leaving."

"What's his name?" Jennifer asked.

Amber ignored the question. "I need to get ready, so I'll see you tomorrow when we practice." She left the room.

"I told you," Jennifer said softly.

"Yes, you did."

"You can stay here with me after she leaves," Jennifer said.

"No, I'd better go."

"That's okay. I understand."

*　　*　　*　　*

Near the end of June, Jonathan went to California to stay with his dad. A month later, when he came back, all he could talk about was a girl named Alisa he'd met at a stake dance.

"What does she look like?"

"She's kind of a blonde, and she has blue eyes, and she's about this tall." He put his hand to the level of his chin. "She looks like the kind of person who'd play the violin in an orchestra."

"You mean she's always looking off to the side?" I asked.

"Don't make fun of her."

"Sorry. Do you have a picture?" I said.

"Yes." He took it out of his shirt pocket and gave it to me. In a way it was what I would have expected from Jonathan. Alisa was blonde and she had kind of an aristocratic face. She looked smart, too, and maybe a little stuck-up, or maybe that was just me. I don't really care much for girls with faces that make them look like they're some kind of goddess.

"Lookin' good," I said, handing the picture back to him. "You met her at a dance? So did you dance all night with her?"

"No."

"Why not?"

"She wouldn't dance with me," Jonathan said.

"Why not?"

"She didn't trust me," he said.

"Why didn't she trust you?"

"Well, when I met her, I held both her hands and looked into her eyes. It really made her uncomfortable."

"This is great, Jonathan. The first time you meet the girl, she doesn't trust you and won't dance with you. What a great beginning. So what did you do?"

"We went in the hall and talked for two hours," he said.

"What did you talk about?"

"Everything. We're so much alike. It's like we knew each other a long time ago."

"That is so lame," I muttered.

"It's true, though."

"You were in California a long time. So, did you kiss her?" I asked.

"No, it's not that kind of friendship."

"You are so weird, Jonathan. I'm serious."

"I know, but if you met her, you'd understand," Jonathan said.

"So what are you going to do—with her in California and you here?"

"We're going to write, but we're going to still go out with other people. I mean we're just friends." He paused. "Very good friends."

"There're plenty of girls right here in Idaho who won't dance with you and won't let you kiss them. So why go all the way to California for that?"

He didn't even laugh. "It's like I've known Alisa all my life . . . and maybe before that."

"You're crazy. You know that, don't you?"

"I might be . . . but it's wonderful. I'm going to write a song for her."

"If you do, make it so you can insert any girl's name into it," I suggested.

"Why?"

"That way you can use it for every girl you start going out with."

He looked at me like I was a child.

Something had happened to our Jonathan, all right. And I didn't like it.

8

Football practice at our high school began the second week in August, with our first game scheduled for the last Friday in August. Jonathan and I had been on the football team our sophomore and junior years. Not stars, but by the end of the season we were playing a lot. We had every reason to believe we'd both be starters at our positions in our senior year. Except for one thing—our hearts weren't in it anymore.

We finally decided. We could do football or we could do Fast Forward, but we couldn't do both.

After a week of practices, I came home one night, aching and tired, and lay down on my bed and looked at the ceiling. There were tunes going through my mind. I felt like something wonderful was slipping away, that there were songs in me that might never get written or sung if I didn't do something.

High school football in Rexburg is a time-honored tradition. The town is full of men who played for Madison High when they were in high school. To them, what happens each year is very important. It's like the honor of the town is on the line every time there's a football game. I didn't want to be known as someone who'd let the team down.

And yet I knew I'd have only one senior year. I was the

one who had to decide what it would be. I couldn't let someone else decide my future. I went over to Jonathan's and we talked about it and decided to quit football.

Those who went out for football also got to count it as a PE class. Since it was a class, in order to drop it, we needed the coach's signature on the drop card.

The next day we went through the entire practice, trying to find a time when we could be alone with the coach, but it never happened. After practice, Jonathan and I showered and got dressed as fast as we could. Coach Miller had an office just off the locker room. Jonathan and I walked into his office. "We need you to sign these," I said, handing him both of our cards.

The coach looked at the top card. "What's this?"

"We're dropping football," Jonathan said softly.

"You can't drop football now. It's too late. We've got our first game in less than a week. Besides, why would you want to quit anyway? You'll both be starting."

"We're not as interested in it as we were last year," I said.

"Why's that?"

"We're in a singing group," Jonathan said.

"You're in a *what?*" the coach barked. Some of the team members had stopped dressing and were looking at us.

"A singing group."

"Let me get this straight. You two clowns would rather be in some sissy choir than play football?"

Well, there goes my life, I thought. This was going to be all over school by morning.

"Coach, we'd appreciate it if you'd sign the cards," Jonathan said.

"I can't believe you'd walk out on the team like this." He took his baseball cap off and ran his hand through his thinning hair. "Most kids would give their eyeteeth to play on this team. You two need to think about what you're giving up. Come back tomorrow."

131

The coach threw the drop cards on his desk and brushed past us and went in the locker room, mumbling, "Quit football to sing in a choir. I've heard it all now."

We were about to go home when the coach's anger got the best of him. He yelled at the team. "Anybody else around here want to quit so they can sing soprano in some choir?"

Everyone was watching us. We could either give up and play football or else we could stand up for what we wanted. We walked over to where the coach was standing. "I don't need any more time," I said. "I've thought about this a lot, and I won't be playing football this year. I need you to sign the drop card," I said.

"Why should I?"

"Because I don't want to play football anymore," I said.

That set the coach off. "What *you* want? That's all you care about, isn't it? Well, let me tell you something! Why don't you think about this team? When I was a kid, loyalty to a team meant something, but not anymore. If something isn't convenient, kids these days just bail out. I don't want to see either one of you around here ever again." He took each drop card, signed it, then thrust the cards at us. "Now get out of here."

The next few days were rough on Jonathan and me. Guys on the team treated us like traitors. Some would break into high-pitched falsetto singing when Jonathan passed by in the hall. They tried it once with me, but I went over and shoved the guy who'd done it up against the lockers and told him if he ever did that again to either me or Jonathan I'd break his arm. I'm pretty sure he believed me. I'm not sure I'd actually have broken his arm. But, of course, he didn't know that.

That didn't stop it, though. If anything, it made it worse. There wasn't much I could do about it either. I mean, I couldn't fight the whole school.

We didn't go to the first game. It was just as well because we lost.

Amber told her coach she wasn't going to play basketball her senior year. But had an excuse. She had a bad knee from last season. I wished I'd had a bad knee.

My dad didn't say much about me quitting football. But, of course, we really didn't talk much about anything, especially with me in school and spending hours every day practicing with Fast Forward and not helping much around the farm.

Just before school started, my dad came to me. "I'll need you to help me with spud harvest again this year," he said.

"I always do, don't I?"

"I didn't know if you still wanted to do it or not."

"I'll do it."

My dad nodded and walked away.

"You're welcome," I muttered, angry at him all over again.

Amber got after me the next day when I complained about my dad.

"I don't see why you're always so mad at him," she said. "He's always real nice to me when I see him."

"Great. I just need you to stay with me when I'm working for him."

"In some ways you're a lot like him," she said.

I felt like she'd insulted me. "That is not true, Amber. You don't know what you're talking about."

"You *are* like him, Greg. You just can't see it yet."

"So what are you saying, that with your superior insight, you can see things I can't see?"

She smiled. "Yep, that's pretty much it, all right."

"You're on his side then. Is that it?" I asked.

"I didn't know there were sides to this."

"Well, there are. I'm not like him, not at all."

"Most sons become like their fathers," she said.

133

"Yeah, right. Take Darth Vader and Luke Skywalker, for example."

"Give me a hint—which one are you?" she teased.

"Very funny."

"Lighten up, Greg. I hate it when you turn into Mr. Black."

"You try working for that man day after day with him always finding something wrong with everything you do. See how you like it."

"Have you ever told him you appreciate how hard he works?" Amber asked.

"What for? That'd be like telling water you appreciate it for running downhill. I mean, working is all my dad knows."

"Maybe you're not seeing things all that clearly," she said.

"Why do you say that?"

"There's a lot of changes taking place in your body right now. I read all about it in a book I checked out from the library."

I could take a lot of things from Amber, but this time she'd gone too far. "Look, not that it's any of your business, but for your information, I'm all done with those kind of changes, okay?"

"Are you sure?" Amber asked.

"I should know, shouldn't I? I mean, after all, it is my body, right?"

"Maybe so, but I'm the one with the book."

"So that makes you some kind of an expert all of a sudden?" I asked.

"That's right. It's not just changes in your body either. It's psychological too. You probably think you're the only guy in the world who doesn't get along with his dad, but you're not. As far as I can see, you fit the classic mold exactly."

"Who asked you?" I asked.

"I think you should take a clue from your mom. She likes your dad. And she has pretty good judgment, doesn't she? So maybe it's not just him. Maybe it's you too. Maybe you're at least partly at fault for the fact you two can't seem to talk to each other. That's all I'm saying."

"Are you done yet?" I grumbled.

"Yes."

"Fine. I really don't want to talk about this anymore," I said.

"And you complain because your dad is noncommunicative. If you ask me, you're worse than he is."

"I didn't ask you."

"Do you want to read my book when I'm done?" she asked.

"No, I don't read books like that."

"I give up," she said. "You are impossible to talk to sometimes. You know what I think when you're like this?"

"No, what do you think?"

"I think, *Oh, well, maybe he'll be better after his mission.* I had to put up with a lot from Amber.

*   *   *   *

Right after school started in the fall, Brooke wrote a song. She asked me to help her with it. So one day, after I'd eaten supper, I went over to her house.

I never really felt comfortable at Brooke's house, especially if her dad was there. I had the feeling he blamed Fast Forward for turning Brooke from the kind of success his other children had achieved. They had all gotten straight A's and received big-deal scholarships and gone on to great heights in college.

Brooke's dad answered the door. He's not a big man physically, but he commands people's attention by the intensity he brings to everything he does. He works for one of the accounting firms in town. I think he does my dad's taxes. His black, plastic-frame glasses seem to take up most of his face.

135

He has this way of looking at you like you were a bug he's just found trapped in the bathroom sink.

"Is Brooke here?" I asked when he came to the door.

"We're eating," he said.

"I see. Well, can I wait for her?"

"I suppose so. Come in." He made it sound like I'd just ruined all his plans.

He let me in the house and showed me to the living room.

Their house was so formal and old-fashioned that every time I was there it reminded me of the board game Clue. I always felt like saying, "It was Mrs. Peacock in the drawing room with a knife." I could hear the family talking.

"Who was it?" Brooke asked once her dad returned to the dining room.

"Just one of those boys you sing with."

"Which one?"

"I don't know his name. He's a big boy though."

"That's Greg. Can I be excused for a minute?"

"I'm sure he'll wait until you finish your meal."

"I know, but I'll just go say hello," Brooke said. "I'll just be a minute."

"Ask him if he's eaten," her mother said.

I've always liked Brooke's mom. She's the reason Brooke turned out to be so wonderful.

Just seeing Brooke walk in the room made me feel great. "What's up?" she asked.

"I came over to help you with your song."

"Oh, that's great. Can I finish eating first?" she asked.

"Yeah, sure. Go ahead. I can wait."

"You want something to eat?" she asked.

"No, I've eaten. That's okay. You go ahead."

"You're sure?" she asked.

"Really. I'll be fine."

She returned to the dining room. They always ate their

136

evening meal in the dining room. My guess is that it was her dad's idea. I could hear them, but I couldn't see them.

"How are you doing in chemistry?" her dad asked.

The question surprised me because Brooke wasn't taking chemistry.

"Pretty good," she said.

"What are you studying now?" her dad asked.

"It's pretty much just been introduction so far."

"If you need help with problems, I'm always available," he said. He sounded like he was talking to a client instead of to his daughter.

"I'm doing okay now. Mr. Peterson explains things really well. I'm finished eating. May I be excused?"

"You won't be too long with that boy, will you?" her dad asked. "This is a school night."

"I really don't have that much homework," Brooke said.

"You can always review past lessons. Especially in chemistry. I always found that helpful to keep everything fresh in my mind."

I got depressed listening to them. In the first place, I'd never heard Brooke tell a lie before. Also, I wondered if her dad had any idea how wonderful Brooke was. I felt bad that Brooke, the person I admired the most of anybody in school, was made to feel like she didn't live up to her dad's expectations. It wasn't fair.

When Brooke came in the living room, she looked flustered. "Let's go out to your van. We can talk there."

Once we got there, she asked, "Did you hear my dad and me talking about chemistry?"

"Yeah. What's going on?"

"My dad made me sign up for advanced chemistry. I don't even need it for graduation, so after the first day, I dropped it. The only thing is—I didn't tell my folks."

"What are you taking instead?" I asked.

"A business course called Poise and Personality."

137

"Poison personality? Sounds like a course just made for me."

"Actually it's Poise . . . and . . . Personality," she said slowly.

"Whatever. Do you like it?"

"Yes, very much."

"Why didn't you tell your folks you'd dropped chemistry?" I asked.

"My dad would never have let me drop it."

"So every day you're going to make up things about chemistry to tell your dad?"

"I guess so."

"I've never heard you tell a lie before," I said.

"I know. This is my first time."

"I think you should just tell your dad the truth," I said.

"I would, but I'm really afraid his punishment would be to not let me sing with Fast Forward. He already thinks our singing is a waste of time."

"Let me talk to him," I said.

"What would you say?"

"I'd tell him you're the best."

"That wouldn't mean much to him, coming from you. He wants me to be just like my brothers and sister—smart in math and science. But I'm not like that."

Brooke's dad was looking through the front door window at us. He turned on the porch light so we'd know he was around.

"Your dad is worried about you being out here with me," I said.

"He worries about a lot of things," she said.

"He doesn't have a clue how lucky he is to have a daughter like you, does he?"

"Actually . . . I think he's always been—" She choked up. ". . . a little disappointed in me."

"He's crazy then. You're my hero, Brooke. You always have been and you always will be."

"I don't feel like much of a hero now. I don't enjoy lying to my folks, but I have to for a little while more. If I told my dad now, he'd make me sign up for chemistry again next term."

"Couldn't you just tell him no?"

"Someday I'll be able to tell him that . . . but not right now. I'm getting stronger, though, every day. Poise and Personality is really a good course for me. It won't be long before I'll be able to stand up to him."

We went inside and worked on her song in the living room, both of us at the piano. At nine-thirty her dad called out, "Brooke, this is a school night."

"I'd better go," I said.

"I'll walk you outside."

Just before I left, Brooke and I hugged. It felt so good. We both relaxed in each other's arms. We probably would have stayed there longer, but we heard her dad fiddling with the door, so I left before he could come out and say something demeaning to her.

That night I said a prayer for Brooke. I don't know if it did any good, but the way I figured it, it was worth a shot.

*　　*　　*　　*

After school a few days later, we were practicing at Brooke's house. Her mom was out buying groceries. Suddenly her dad burst into the house. "Brooke, I need your friends to leave. You and I need to talk." He wouldn't even look at us, and he talked like his jaw was wired shut.

"We're in the middle of a practice."

"I'm only going to say this once more. End the practice, and send these people home."

"We have a big concert coming up. We need to practice. Why can't we have our talk upstairs?"

"All right then. Come with me. Let's get this taken care of."

Brooke and her dad went upstairs to her room. We could hear them talking through a heat vent. I don't think her dad knew that though. He wouldn't have wanted us to listen in.

"Tell me again about chemistry," he said, speaking even more precisely than usual.

Brooke realized she'd been found out. I guess she figured there was no way out except to tell the truth. "I dropped chemistry after the first day of class."

"I thought we'd agreed you'd take chemistry."

"I signed up for it, but I didn't like it, so I dropped it."

"You should have talked to me first," her dad said.

"If I did that, I knew you'd make me go sign up for it again. Daddy, I know you think I'm just like Samantha and Jared and Scott, but I'm not. I'm different. The things that interested them don't interest me."

"I thought we had agreed on your course of study a long time ago."

"It wasn't exactly an agreement. You told me what to take, and I wrote it down."

"So you dropped chemistry behind my back?" he asked. "And you've been lying to me ever since?"

"Yes. That was the only way I could do what I wanted to do."

"Are you taking anything in its place?" her dad asked.

"Yes. It's a class called Poise and Personality. I really like it."

"It sounds like a totally worthless course to me," he said.

"It's what I want, Daddy. Doesn't that mean anything to you?"

I couldn't see how anyone could talk that way to Brooke. How could she stand to have this dictator ruling with an iron hand at home?

"I'm only thinking of your own good. How do you

140

expect to get into BYU with fluff courses like Poise and Personality?" he demanded.

"There are other places to go. I'm going to try to get into Ricks and go there for two years, and then I'll transfer, maybe to ISU."

"There's no guarantee that Ricks will even let you in," he said. "Especially if they see Poise and Personality on your transcript."

"Fine. Then I'll go somewhere else."

"And what will you major in?" he asked.

"I'm thinking either music or drama."

"You're not serious, are you?" he asked.

"Yes, I'm serious. It is my life, isn't it?"

"I know what this is all about. It's those people you hang around with. You waste so much time with them you never have time for more important things."

"There isn't anything more important to me than singing with my friends. It's the only thing that keeps me going. I don't know what I'd do without those guys."

"I know you can't see it now, but they're not doing you any good. For your own sake, I'm afraid I'm going to have to forbid you from spending time with them anymore. They're taking you away from your studies."

"Why don't you ever listen to me?"

"I could ask the same thing about you."

"Why don't we ask Mom what she thinks about my singing?" Brooke asked her dad. It was the perfect come-back. She knew her mother would never agree to making her stop singing with us.

"I'm the head of this family. And what I say goes. I will not let you waste your time with that group anymore. I'm only trying to do what's best for you."

"What's best for me? How can you say that? You don't even know me. I'm not Samantha, Daddy. Why can't you understand that?"

"Someday you'll thank me for this. Tomorrow I'll get you enrolled in chemistry for next term. Now go downstairs and tell those people they'll have to leave and that you won't be singing with them anymore."

When Brooke came in the room, she looked devastated. "Let's get out of here."

We hurried outside and drove away.

"What are you going to do?" Amber asked Brooke after a few minutes of silence.

"I don't know, but, one thing for sure, I'll never give up being with you guys," she said.

We pooled whatever money we had and went to McDonald's to get something to eat.

"I'm never going back," Brooke said.

"You can stay with me," Amber said.

Brooke nodded her head. "Thanks. Why don't people just leave us alone? I wish we could get on the road and just keep driving. We could get an apartment in California and sing every night and go to the beach during the day and never have to worry about anything."

"Let's do it," Amber said.

"And not graduate?" I asked.

"I'm not learning anything in school," Amber said. "The classes are so boring. I mean, what difference does it make if we graduate or not?"

Ryan thought it was a great idea. He was still having a hard time with his sister, and he had never liked school that much.

Jonathan wasn't sure. "You mean just leave now?" he asked.

"Sure, why not?" Amber said. "You guys mean more to me than anybody else in my life."

The more we talked, the more sense it made. We'd go home like everything was okay, and then after our folks were asleep, we'd secretly pack. I'd come by for each of them after midnight. We'd drive to Salt Lake City, ditch the minivan, then take a bus to California. It was the perfect plan.

We all were back home by nine.

Because I didn't want my mom or dad to suspect anything, I sat at the kitchen table and did my homework. I was so excited, though, at the thought of leaving school behind and starting over.

My mom was working in the kitchen, and my dad was in his little office catching up on paying some bills. I kept stealing glances at them. They were really getting to look old and a little tired. My dad had worked hard all his life, and now it was beginning to show.

The thing I felt the most guilty about was that I would be taking my mom's minivan without her permission. She'd been so good about letting me use it whenever we needed it for a performance. She'd always been supportive of what I wanted to do. Leaving for good, without even saying where I was going, didn't seem like a very nice way to thank her for all she'd done for me.

I didn't want to just walk out on my family, but I'd do it for Amber and Brooke. I'd have done just about anything for them.

I studied until ten-fifteen, and then we had family prayer like always. My mom gave me a hug, and then I went to my room to pack up my things. There wasn't much to take. I remember trying to decide whether or not to take my Sunday clothes. I decided against it because if we went to church it would give us away and they'd find us.

The decision about the Sunday clothes made me realize we would be giving up much more than just graduating from high school. *I might never go on a mission if we go through with this*, I thought. I told myself I'd stay worthy, but in my heart I wasn't sure if I would or not—especially if we weren't going to church. Most of the time church was boring to me,

143

but at least it kept me on track. It was hard to say what would happen if we were off by ourselves.

When it was eleven-thirty and time to leave, I couldn't let my friends down. If they wanted to skip town, I'd go with them.

I drove to Amber's house first. All the lights were off. I parked at the corner and waited. A few minutes later she came out carrying a couple of lawn bags with clothes in them. She came around to my side. "Jennifer knows. She wants to talk to you."

"What for?"

"She didn't say. She doesn't want me around when she talks to you. I'll start walking to Brooke's house. You can pick me up along the way."

Jennifer was still in her pajamas, which made her look more than ever like a little girl. And she was barefoot, which meant she had to try to avoid stepping on gravel as she made her way to the corner where the minivan was parked.

She got inside. "You're running away?" she asked. She sounded as though she couldn't believe it.

"Yeah, I guess so."

"Have I ever told you that you're my hero?" she asked.

"No."

"Well, you are."

I looked over at her. She looked like somebody you would tell a bedtime story to. But even so, she was really a cute kid.

"Take me with you then," she said.

"No."

"Why not?" she asked.

"You're too young."

"Oh, yeah, and you're not?"

"At least I have a driver's license," I said.

"I can do the cooking while you guys are out singing."

"We can't take you with us."

"Why not?" Jennifer asked.

"Your mom and dad would miss you too much."

"They'll miss Amber, too."

"I suppose," I said.

"If you run away, then you won't be my hero anymore."

"I never asked to be your hero, did I?" I said.

"I know. It just happened. Because you came to see me when I was in the hospital. I'll never forget that. I carry your picture with me all the time."

"You'll have to get out of the car now. We need to go," I said.

"Heroes don't run away from their problems. They stay and face them. That's what you should do."

"I don't need you hassling me all the time," I said. "Just get out of the car."

"Don't do this, Greg. It's not right and you know it."

It was embarrassing to have this little girl telling me what to do, especially since I realized she was right. It wasn't that great of an idea for us to run away. It was true we wanted to be treated like adults, but the end of that reasoning is that adults don't usually run away from their problems. They stay to face them.

I leaned my elbows on the steering wheel, and, with my head resting on my hands, I agonized over what we should do.

After not saying anything for a while, I finally admitted, "All right, Jennifer. We won't run away."

"You promise?"

"I promise."

She leaned over and hugged me, then jumped out of the car and, because of the gravel on her bare feet, walked gingerly back home.

There was still Amber to talk to. I drove down the road and caught up with her. I pulled over to the side of the road. She got in.

"We can't do this," I said.

"I know."

"Why did you pack up then?" I asked.

"It seemed like a good idea at first, but the more I thought about it, the more I could see it was a mistake. I knew we'd talk about it and eventually we'd all decide we couldn't go through with it."

Brooke came out but without a suitcase. "I'm not going."

"How come?"

"My mom and dad and I had a talk. My dad is going to let me take the courses I want to take. And they're going to let me sing with you guys. My mom thinks my folks and I ought to get some family counseling. Maybe that will make things better between us."

I took Amber home and then dropped by Jonathan's and Ryan's and told them we weren't going. They had both had second thoughts too.

Fast Forward was back in business again.

*   *   *   *

The next Friday night we sang during the intermission for a dance at Ricks College. The dance was held in the Hart Auditorium. We arrived at four that afternoon to get set up. And then we went home to get dressed. It was a formal affair. The boys were wearing tuxes and the girls wore formals.

We ate something at Ryan's house and warmed up a little and waited until it was time to go. At eight-thirty we gathered in their family room downstairs and closed the door and had a prayer.

This performance was important to us. There would be several hundred people listening to us. We felt a little intimidated because we were still in high school and would be performing for college students.

"Just a minute," Amber said after the prayer. "I just want

146

you guys to know there's nothing I'd rather be doing right now than this."

There was an uncomfortable silence. We usually didn't verbalize how much we meant to each other.

Brooke and Amber hugged each other. We guys just mostly looked uncomfortable.

Standing offstage at the Hart Auditorium, we watched everyone dance and waited for intermission. We were scheduled first on the program, which was good. We wouldn't have extra time to be nervous.

The emcee for the talent show introduced us. "Tonight we have a real treat. We have a singing group from Madison High School. They call themselves Fast Forward. Let's give them a big welcome!"

We hurried onstage. I took out my pitch pipe and softly blew one note. And then we were off. It wasn't an original arrangement. We'd copied it by listening to another group. But that wasn't necessarily a drawback because people loved the song already.

When we finished, the response was enthusiastic and loud. I looked at Amber, Brooke, Jonathan, and Ryan. No drug could duplicate the way we were feeling then. It was great.

Our nervousness was gone now. We were loving every minute. We were in the groove. We were singing our hearts out.

We had been asked to sing three songs. When we finished "Don't Let Your Heart Slip Away from Me," we took a couple of bows and then went offstage, but the applause wouldn't go away.

"Do one more!" the young woman in charge of entertainment told us.

"Listen to them," Brooke said. "They love us!"

"Lean on Me," I said, pulling out my pitch pipe. We went back onstage. We sang that song and then the girl told us we needed to stop even though the audience was still wanting more.

We sat backstage and listened to the rest of the program. We were as good or better than any of the others.

As we were hauling our equipment to the minivan, Brooke's folks walked up to where we were parked. At first it looked like the beginning of an Old West shootout—the five of us in one group, and Brooke's mom and dad facing us.

"We came to hear you tonight," Brooke's dad said. "It was . . . real good." He was doing his best to be positive, but his praise was at best only lukewarm. I knew by the way he talked that this wasn't his idea. I was pretty sure Brooke's mom shamed him into it. The way I see it, most men pretty much do what their wives tell them. Not all the time, of course, but when a woman gets emotional, they do. I was pretty sure this was one of those times.

"Thanks, Daddy."

"Your mother and I had an idea," he continued. "Go ahead and tell her," he said to his wife.

Brooke's mom came and put her arm around Brooke. "This is such a wonderful time in your life. You need to make a good-quality sound tape of your singing, so you'll all have something to remember after you graduate from high school."

"We'll pay for it," Brooke's dad said reluctantly. "Within reason, of course."

"That's so nice of you, Daddy. Thank you."

"We'd like to pay for you to get some pizza too," her dad said, awkwardly placing some money in Brooke's hand.

"Having you both come tonight really means a lot to me." She went to him and gave him a big hug. And then she threw her arms around her mom.

"Well, we'd better be going," her dad said.

"You want to come with us for pizza?" Brooke asked her mom and dad.

"No, that's all right. It's late and we need to get home," her dad said.

They should have come with us. Sleep isn't that important. At least it wasn't to us.

I thought it was really good for Brooke's dad to at least make an attempt to try to get closer to his daughter. That was more than was happening with my dad and me.

9

In October, four days before spud harvest was supposed to begin, there were three nights where the temperature got down to the mid-teens. Farmers feared frost damage to their potatoes, but after inspecting their fields, they decided that with the potatoes still buried several inches in the ground, most of the crop had been spared serious damage.

But then it rained, which postponed spud harvest another three days until the ground dried enough for farmers to get their equipment in the fields.

Every day was critical. How long would we have before the weather turned really bad? Would we be able to get all of the crop out of the fields? Nobody knew.

But then, finally, the weather improved enough for us to get started. After a couple of fourteen-hour days, I once again remembered why I didn't want to be a farmer. The work was hard, monotonous, and never ending. I had the best job, though—driving truck from the fields to my dad's potato cellar. There, a crew sorted the potatoes, tossed out the bad ones, and loaded the others onto a conveyor belt that gently dropped the spuds onto a steadily growing pile.

Everyone managed to finish up before the weather turned bad. But as time went on, it became obvious that the three nights of frost had caused some damage. My dad thought it was a manageable problem because he could control the humidity in the potato cellar. If he blew dry air over the potatoes, it would take the moisture away. But then it rained five days in a row. Because of the high humidity of the air, it was a losing battle to try to dry out the potatoes.

My dad didn't say much at first because he thought he could control the situation, but things quickly went from bad to worse. Water began seeping through the pile of potatoes.

I'll never forget Thanksgiving Day. I slept in late and awoke to the smell of pumpkin pie baking in the oven. I got up, went into the kitchen, grabbed a banana and a box of cereal, and turned on the TV to watch a football game.

A little after one-thirty, my mom said, "I'm worried about your dad. He left this morning to check on things at the potato cellar, and he hasn't come back yet. Could you go see how he's doing?"

"He's all right," I said.

"Greg, please go check on him. I'm worried."

I drove to the potato cellar, five miles from home. It was raining again and threatening to turn to snow. My dad's pickup was there all right. I could hear an engine running. I walked to where I could see what was going on. There was water, three inches deep on the cellar floor. Inside, my dad was driving a front-end loader into the pile, backing up past me, and dumping the rotting potatoes onto a nearby field.

I made my way inside the potato cellar. There was an ammonia stench in the air. I picked up a potato. It was soft and mushy. Because the potatoes had turned mushy, the pile had shrunk down to about a third of its original size.

I stood and watched as my dad made trip after trip, dumping his crop on the ground. He was usually careful about watching gauges, but on that morning the front-end loader ran out of fuel. After the engine sputtered and stopped, Dad just sat there. I climbed up to where he was sitting on the seat. "We lost the crop," he said. I could tell he

151

was trying to keep it matter-of-fact, but he had a tough time even saying the words.

"All of it?" I asked.

"Yes."

"What are you going to do?" I asked.

"There's nothing we can do now."

"Did you run out of gas?" I asked.

He nodded.

"Do you want me to bring some and pour it in so you can get started?"

He didn't answer.

"Mom sent me to find you. She was worried about you."

No response.

"Dad, do you want to go home now?"

He turned to look at me. "What for?"

"It's Thanksgiving."

It was probably the worst thing I could have said. My dad just shook his head.

"We can do this tomorrow, Dad. Or if you want, I can do it for you, but I think you should go home now because Mom is worried."

"We might lose the farm over this."

Suddenly I realized that if my dad lost the farm, he would lose a part of himself. I'd heard stories about farmers who had killed themselves after a bad year. My dad kept a rifle in a locked cabinet in the shop next door. I wondered if it was still there, and I got an awful feeling, imagining what he might be tempted to do.

"Go home, Greg. I'll be along in a while," he said.

"No, I'm staying here with you."

"There's no point in that."

"I've got nothing else to do." I moved one more step up the ladder and awkwardly put my hand on his shoulder. It had been a long time since the two of us had touched each other in any kind of gesture of affection.

"The whole crop," my dad said softly. And then he turned to look at me. "I thought I could get on top of it. If it hadn't been raining I could have dried the frost-damaged potatoes and then things would have been all right, but it kept raining, and it got out of control."

"I didn't know things were so bad."

"I didn't want to worry you or your mother," he said.

"You shouldn't take things on yourself like that. It's too much for you."

"That's the way I was raised," he said.

"Let's go home now, Dad. Mom is baking pumpkin pies."

He smiled slightly. "I'm not sure we can afford the pumpkin."

"C'mon, let's go. We can take care of this tomorrow. It's not going to get any worse, is it?"

"I guess that's one of the advantages of being on the bottom. You can't get any lower."

"You go ahead. I'll lock up," I said.

After he drove away in his pickup, I stayed around to check on the rifle. It was still in the cabinet. I took it and put it in my pickup. If he asked, I'd tell him I needed it for target practice.

I arrived home a few minutes after my dad. By the time I entered the house, he was sitting at the kitchen table. He and my mom were talking.

"We'll get by," she said.

"I'm not so sure, this time."

"We will. You're not the only one this has happened to this year. Tomorrow we'll go to the bank and tell them what happened. They'll help us."

"They can't bail us out every year," he said.

"It's only been the last two years that've been hard. For gosh sakes, there's nobody who works harder than you do. Everybody knows that. They'll give us a loan to get us by until next year. We'll survive this. It takes more than this to stop us."

"I've let you down," he said.

"I won't listen to you talk like this. I love you more than anything in the world, but I won't let anybody, not even you, bad-mouth my husband."

I stood and watched all this. It's strange how little you know about life when you're seventeen. I had grown up thinking that my dad knew everything and didn't need anybody's help. But now he did. Maybe he even needed me.

That night, twenty minutes after we'd had family prayer, I realized I hadn't removed my contacts yet. I opened the door to my bedroom and stepped into the hall. My parents' door was open. I looked in and saw my mother in a beautiful white nightgown that I'd never seen her wear before. She didn't see me. She was brushing her hair. There was music coming from their room, and a candle flickered on their dresser.

I closed the door. At first, the thought was disturbing. I wasn't sure why. My parents had been married for twenty years. It seemed impossible to me they should still want to be physically close.

But then, after a while, I thought maybe that was why God gave us that, so people like my mom and dad, on the day they find out they've lost everything, can hold each other and insulate themselves against the feeling of hopelessness that comes with a crop failure in Idaho.

*   *   *   *

I had planned to get up early the next morning so I could help my dad move the rest of the rotting potatoes out of our cellar. But I must have turned the alarm off. By the time I woke up it was eight-thirty. I jumped out of bed with the intention of getting dressed and then hurrying out to the farm. When I walked into the kitchen, I was surprised to find

154

him still at home, just finishing up breakfast. Wearing her usual slacks and a sweater, my mom was cooking pancakes.

"Greg," she called out, "come have some pancakes with us."

I joined them. I was curious how they'd be. There was nothing to give their secret away, except that once, after dishing out three pancakes onto my plate, as she returned to the skillet, she ran her hand lightly across the back of my dad's neck. He reached out for her hand for an instant and then let go. Otherwise there was no difference.

I found it difficult not to stare at them.

"Is anything wrong?" my mom asked.

"No, nothing. I just . . . wanted to say . . . that these pancakes are really good."

My dad stood up. "Well, Greg and I need to finish up from yesterday."

"When do you want to go to the bank?" she asked.

"Dad, you can go anytime you want," I said. "I can haul the potatoes out by myself."

"How about if we go after lunch?" he said.

"You'll be coming home for lunch?" she asked him.

"Sure will."

She smiled. "How nice for me."

My mouth dropped open. My mom and dad were flirting.

Out at the potato cellar, I tried to do as much of the work as possible because I knew how painful it was for my dad to haul out and dump the crop that would have given us our income for the year. I talked him into sitting in the pickup and calling around to see how other farmers around us were doing. Most of them had also lost their crop.

At noon my dad motioned for me to stop for lunch, but I said I wasn't hungry and for him to just bring me a sandwich when he got back from the bank.

He returned about two o'clock with some sandwiches. We sat in the pickup together while I ate.

"We're down but we're not out," he said. "We've got a loan to keep us going for another year. Maybe we can even learn something from all this."

"What?"

"Potatoes aren't the most important thing in the world." He faced straight ahead. I could tell this was hard for him. "For a long time your mother has been telling me I've been too hard on you. I couldn't see it at first, but now I think that maybe she was right." He looked over at me. "I just want you to know that from now on I'll try to do better."

At first I was stunned and didn't know what to say. It was so unlike my dad to talk about things like this.

"I'll try to do better too," I said.

He nodded his head. I'm not sure who of us was the most embarrassed.

He turned on the radio to listen to the farm news. I finished my sandwiches and then said, "I'll go finish up now. Thanks for lunch."

"You want me to spell you for a while?" he asked.

"No, that's okay. It won't take much longer."

I got out of the truck. He nodded in my direction and drove away.

Our Christmas that year was pretty meager because we had very little money except for the bare necessities. We limited our gifts to no more than ten dollars. But, actually, it wasn't as bad as I thought it'd be. For one thing, my dad and I were closer than we'd been for a long time.

10

Brandon Eliason discovered Amber in January. They were assigned to sit next to each other in one of their classes. Brandon was a nice enough guy, one of the stars on the school basketball team. He was taller than Amber, something I had been unable to accomplish. He had blue eyes and an easy smile. His dad was a rich industrialist from California, who after spending a brief but highly successful career polluting the Los Angeles landscape, escaped to Idaho to become an environmentalist.

Brandon and his family lived in a huge house along a country road. Brandon could have had any car he wanted. His dad drove both a Mustang convertible and a GMC pickup, depending on the occasion. Brandon was offered the use of the Mustang but, out of modesty, chose something older. He had his dad buy him on old Ford pickup, maybe because it fit in with all the other pickups in the high school parking lot.

Amber called me one weekday night around nine. "Brandon said he'd call tonight, but he hasn't yet. What should I do?"

"There's nothing you can do except wait."

"What if he doesn't call?" she asked.

"It's not the end of the world. You'll see him tomorrow. Maybe something came up."

"I can't stand this, Greg. Can you come over and be with me?"

Ten minutes later I pulled into her driveway. Jennifer came out to see me before I made it to the door. "Amber said for me to tell you that Brandon just called. She's talking to him now, so . . ." Jennifer sighed. ". . . she doesn't need you anymore."

I nodded my head. "I guess I'll go home then."

"I'm sorry, Greg," Jennifer said.

The next day I found out that Brandon had asked Amber out for Friday night.

Amber was anxious that everything go well for her first date with Brandon. Thursday night, after we'd practiced in the stairwell at Ricks, I drove her home.

"I'm really nervous about going out with Brandon. Is there anything about me I should change?"

"No, there isn't, not a thing."

"Be honest, Greg. Please. This is very important to me. Anything at all?"

"You're asking the wrong person. I think you're great just the way you are."

"There must be something," she said. "What if Brandon decides he doesn't like me after we go out one time?"

"Then he's an idiot."

"I asked my mom what she thought I could do to improve my appearance, and she suggested I try not going so heavy on eye makeup. Can you come in and give me your opinion while I try a couple of different things?"

"I don't know anything about things like that."

"Please help me. I need a guy's opinion."

"All right."

A short time later we set up shop on her kitchen table. Amber brought in a mirror from her bedroom wall and used books to prop it up so she could use it to put on makeup. She brought in a bunch of makeup tubes and bottles from her bathroom.

It doesn't sound like it'd be much fun, but actually it wasn't that bad. Amber would try something and then ask me what I thought. It meant I had to look very carefully at her face, something I loved doing anyway—with or without makeup.

Two hours later, Mr. Whittaker came in from some church meeting and saw me sitting next to Amber with makeup bottles and tubes scattered all over the kitchen table.

He frowned at us. "Give it up, Amber He's not going to look any better—no matter what you do."

Amber smiled. "You never know, Dad. I haven't tried blush yet."

"Speaking of blush, he should be blushing he's here so late on a school night. You will kick him out of the house soon, won't you? If he spends any more time here, I'm going to start claiming him as a tax deduction."

"We're almost done, Daddy. Good night," Amber said as he left to get ready for bed.

"So, you think blush would help me?" I asked.

She laughed. "You want me to make you up? 'Cause I will if you want me to."

"What if I ended up liking the way I looked when I was made up? That'd probably cause some talk at school."

"You look great just the way you are now."

I loved it when she said things like that.

After another half hour, I ended up agreeing with Amber's mom—it was better for Amber to use a lighter shade of eyeliner and eye shadow and not pile it on so much.

Standing with me at the door on my way out, Amber kissed me on the cheek. "Thanks, Greg. I don't know what I'd ever do without you."

                    *   *   *   *

I'm not sure if it had anything to do with Amber's decision about her eye makeup, but after that first date with
Amber, Brandon started seeing her exclusively.

This was during the middle of basketball season.
Brandon usually led the team in points scored. I was probably the only one in school who wished they wouldn't
make it to state. They did though. Just my luck.

There was very little bad that could be said about Brandon.
I liked the guy, but I was also out of my mind with jealousy.

I still got to be with Amber on Saturday mornings to help
her make bread. She now asked my advice about her and
Brandon. I answered her questions, although I sometimes
felt bad for making her more appealing to him.

Because I was dating too, Amber didn't seem to worry
much about my feelings being hurt because of Brandon. So
she told me everything. She told me about the first time she
went to Brandon's house and met his mom and dad, and
how well they treated her. She told me what they ate. She
told me she loved being seen with Brandon. She told me
that all his friends said how good the two of them looked
together. She also told me she couldn't talk with Brandon as
freely as she could with me.

I knew the reason why Amber and I could talk about
anything. It was because we knew each other's strengths and
weaknesses so well, neither one of us had anything to hide.

Brandon didn't know Amber had a temper because she
kept it hidden around him.

Brandon didn't know that when Amber was in junior
high, people made fun of her because she was so much
taller than the other girls.

Brandon didn't know how devastated Amber had been
when she was eleven and wore a dress to church that her
mother had bought for her at Deseret Industries. The girl

who had owned the dress saw Amber wearing it and made fun of her.

Brandon didn't know that Amber was embarrassed because she lived in such a small house.

Brandon didn't know Amber's biggest fear was that she wouldn't be able to raise enough money for college.

There were a lot of things Brandon didn't know about Amber.

*   *   *   *

In March, Amber and I ended up at the junior prom, Amber with Brandon, I with another girl. Amber looked beautiful and seemed confident and at ease. I knew that in some small way, I'd played a part in that.

I'd changed too. Because of Amber, I'd learned how to be around girls. Amber told me I was the best-looking boy at the prom. It wasn't true, of course, but I appreciated her saying it. Brandon was easily the best-looking guy there. The two of them together stole the show.

Before the dance, Amber had given me the lesson "Talking to Your Date's Parents on the Night of the Prom." I was glad she'd helped me. It worked out well.

Brandon had no clue how much I cared about Amber. I'm sure she told him, "Oh, he's just a friend." *Just a friend.* It sounds so insignificant. But it wasn't. At least it wasn't for me. To me, being Amber's friend was the most important thing in my life.

*   *   *   *

About this time Fast Forward began to work with Addison Thomas. He did all the sound for Ricks concerts, and he had a studio in his home. We went there one Saturday afternoon and recorded four of our songs. He called a few days later and asked us all to come in. After we listened to what he'd recorded, he asked, "Any comments?"

161

"It sounds okay to me," I said.

"It's better than okay," he said. "You guys are better than you should be at your age. I think you should do a professional-quality recording you can send to agents and producers."

I figured he was going to tell us we could be big stars and then offer to work some more with us and when it was over, we'd end up owing him thousands of dollars.

"Sorry, but this is all we can afford right now," I said.

"I'll work with you for free to get you started. You can pay me back later."

"This doesn't make sense," I said. "Why would you do this for us?"

"I believe in you guys."

We sat there stunned. We'd been singing all this time. People had told us we were good, but nobody with any professional credentials had said so.

We agreed to his offer. It was a good opportunity, but also, it was a curse, because suddenly we started thinking that we might go somewhere with this. Our tape couldn't just be good. It had to be excellent.

The pressure nearly did us in. First of all, we didn't have enough songs to do a professional-quality, standard-length recording. We decided to show we had real talent by recording some original songs. Jonathan nearly drove us crazy, bringing a new song every time we practiced. Every song was about Alisa, and also, every song was pretty bad.

Around the sixth time he did this, I'd had it.

"Well, what do you think?" Jonathan asked, bright smile and all.

"It's so sincere," Brooke said. Leave it to Brooke to find some redeeming quality about almost anything.

"Amber, what do you think?" Jonathan asked.

"Well, I don't know. I mean I only heard it the one time. I'd have to think about it."

"Ryan, what do you think?" Jonathan asked.

"Well, gosh. I sure bet Alisa will like it."

"She does," Jonathan said with a big smile.

So it was going to be up to me. I was always the heavy. When Jonathan asked me how I liked it, I said, "Actually, it's pretty bad."

"What part?" Jonathan asked.

"From the beginning to the end."

"The lyrics or the melody?" he asked.

"Both."

"I can work some more on it."

"Don't bother," I said. "I'd be embarrassed if we recorded this song."

Jonathan's smile slowly disappeared. "I'll work on another one then."

"You can try," I said, "but I'm not sure you have what it takes to write a really good song."

Jonathan looked stunned. And then he got angry. "Don't you ever say anything like that to me again!"

It was the first time Jonathan and I had ever had words.

Brooke to the rescue. "Guys, c'mon. We've got to work together."

That was strike one.

A day later came strike two.

I didn't like to be reminded of Amber's relationship with Brandon. And so, the next night when Brandon showed up with Amber for one of our practices, it made me mad. When they walked in together, he had his arm around her waist. I didn't think I could stand watching them make eyes at each other while we tried to practice. I knew I wouldn't be able to concentrate on what we were there for. "Can I talk to you alone?" I asked Amber.

"Yeah, sure. Where?"

"Outside."

We went outside. It was freezing cold on the porch.

163

"Why did you bring him here?" I asked.

"We're going somewhere afterwards. And, besides, he wanted to come."

"He has no business being here. This is a practice."

"He won't get in the way. You won't even know he's here."

"I'll know."

"How will you know?"

I ignored the question. "We're here to work, not play around, and definitely not for you to put on your own little private concert for him. I don't want him here. Tell him to go home. You can call him to come and get you when we're through." It was freezing, so I didn't want this to turn into a long conversation.

"You're being totally unreasonable, Greg."

"If he starts coming, then pretty soon everybody will be here, and we won't get anything done. Is that what you want?"

"I want you to quit being such a total jerk. That's what I want," she said. It was so cold, it hurt our faces.

"All I'm saying is that we're here to work. I don't have time to waste just so you can impress Brandon."

"Why not try it tonight and see how it goes?" she asked.

"No way. If he stays, then I'm out of here."

She threw up her hands. "That's just great. It's either your way or no way. That's the way it always is with you. You make me so mad sometimes." We could see each other's breath as we argued.

"I'm just thinking of the group," I said.

"Don't give me that! You're just thinking of yourself. You are so bullheaded sometimes."

"Bullheaded? How can you say that?" I asked.

"What do you call it?" she said.

"I have a strong personality, that's all."

"Same thing," she said.

"It isn't the same thing."

164

"You are impossible to get along with," she complained.

"Oh, and you're not?"

"Not half as bad as you are," she said.

"I'm sorry, but I can't go through a practice with Brandon and you in the same room," I said.

"Why not?"

"That's my business."

"Is it because you're jealous?" she asked. She had her arms folded, hugging herself in an attempt to stay warm.

"That has nothing to do with it."

She touched my arm with her hand. "Greg, look. Let's not fight. You're my best friend."

That helped a little to calm me down. "I know."

"Do you still want it to be more?" she asked.

I had a little pride left. "I don't have to answer that."

"Poor Greg."

"I don't want your sympathy either," I said.

"I know you don't."

We stood there, stuck in time, and freezing to death.

Finally I said what was really on my mind. "What's wrong with me that you have to go after him?" I asked softly.

"Nothing's wrong with you, Greg. You're my best friend. It's just that . . . Look, I'm not even sure I can explain it . . ."

"Don't try then."

She sighed. "Let's go back. It's too cold to stay out here. I'll tell Brandon to pick me up in two hours."

On our way in, she reached for my hand. It made all the difference in the world that she did that.

*   *   *   *

That night, still feeling sorry for myself, I wrote a song. It was about friends. I called it "So Many Times." The next day I sang it for everybody.

"I really like it," Brooke said.

"Me too," Ryan said. "I definitely think we should put it on our demo tape."

We worked on harmony for the song. I kept looking at Jonathan. I could tell his feelings were hurt because I'd shot down his songs.

"Jonathan, what do you think? Be honest," I said.

He gave me a brave smile. "It's really good. I definitely think we should include it."

"I'm sorry . . . you know . . . ," I said.

"Don't worry about it."

"Are you sure?"

"I'm sure."

"Thanks for being such a good sport," I said.

"It does none of us any good to record something that isn't any good. I don't mind being told when something I've written doesn't work."

That was vintage Jonathan all right.

*   *   *   *

By the first of March we finally finished our demo tape, which we were sure would bring us fame and fortune. We had three hundred copies made. Jonathan worked up a cover that almost looked like something you'd buy in a store.

After that, whenever we performed, we'd take some copies with us to sell. We could usually sell two or three.

Ryan and I spent a lot of time together because when his sister Jamie was having friends over, she still made him leave the house. He stayed the night two or three times a month at my house.

Jamie made sure Ryan knew all the gossip that was going around school about Nicole. The word was that sometimes she'd disappear for a couple of days, and when she would finally come home, she wouldn't tell her folks where she'd been or what she'd been doing.

166

"I hope you're happy now," Jamie would say to Ryan with each new story about Nicole.

Ryan was sorry. He told me that enough times, but he didn't know what he could do to change things. He tried to talk to Nicole once, but as soon as she saw he was trying to talk her into quitting the life she was leading, she just laughed and walked away.

He started reading the Book of Mormon. Brooke and he had an agreement that they'd read it every day. After that, it was almost as if I could see him change day by day.

He also got his patriarchal blessing. That made a big difference for him. Before that, I think he still thought of himself as a rebel and not worth very much.

In a way, it didn't seem fair that Ryan should be able to turn his life around when Nicole was still running wild. And yet the same thing that had helped Ryan was there for Nicole if she'd just let it. Heavenly Father hadn't given up on her. The Savior hadn't given up on her. But she'd given up on herself.

Many people who have messed up big-time seem to have this idea that it will take years to turn their lives around. It seems like such a huge thing that they don't even want to try. Maybe it does take a long time, but it doesn't take long to at least feel like there's hope. Ryan felt a lot better after the first time he went to his bishop and told him everything. That was true for me too. Not that everything was forgiven or anything like that. But at least there was hope that it was possible to turn our lives around and be forgiven and start over again.

That would have worked for Nicole too. She had a bishop. She could have gone to him, even if she was still messing up. He would have tried to help her straighten out her life. But she wouldn't even try. And there was nothing Ryan or any of us could do about it.

167

11

The weather turned warm right after general conference in April. Snow started to melt in the high country. One Friday night, after we'd sung at a family reunion, Brooke suggested we pick up some food at Subway and then drive up to Mesa Falls where we could have a picnic. Everyone agreed to the idea.

As we were getting in the van to go to Mesa Falls, I asked Amber, "Why don't you ride up front with me?"

"Ryan usually rides with you."

"I know, but sometimes a change is good."

"What if we get in a fight?" she asked.

"I'll referee it," Brooke offered.

For some reason, on the way to the falls, we started pretending that Amber and I were the parents and our bratty kids were in the back. "Are we there yet?" Brooke asked, the way children do during a long trip.

"Not yet," Amber said, trying to sound soothing. "Play with your toys."

Brooke complained, "Ryan hit me."

I knew how to sound like a father. "If I hear one more complaint from any of you, I'm stopping the car and coming back there and paddling everyone."

"I didn't do anything," Brooke whined. "It's all Ryan's fault."

"Quiet down," Amber said, "or your father will stop the car."

"I have to go potty," Jonathan complained.

"Can you hold it?" Amber asked. "We're almost there."

"I have to go now."

"Hold it," I ordered.

"He can't hold it if he has to go," Amber explained.

"You coddle him all the time. That's the trouble with him," I said.

Enjoying the challenge, Amber shot back at me, "At least he recognizes me when I come into the room."

"Never mind," Jonathan called out happily. "I don't have to go anymore."

"Jonathan's all wet!" Brooke complained.

"That happened to me once," I said to Amber, briefly coming out of character.

"What did your parents do?"

"My dad pulled into a car wash and hosed me down, and then they put clean clothes on me. I remember it was outside. When I complained about taking my clothes off, my mom said, 'That's all right, dear. We don't know anyone in this town.'"

Amber broke up laughing. "Well, that explains a lot. I hope that was the last time you were seen naked in public."

"Yeah, pretty much," I said.

"Have you guys ever dreamed about being in public with no clothes?" Brooke asked.

"No, we haven't, Brooke," Ryan teased. "But I've heard that if you've ever had a dream like that, it means you're a pervert."

"I've heard that too," Jonathan joined in.

"Never mind then," Brooke said in a sing-song voice.

"Don't believe them," Amber said. "I think everybody has dreamed that at least once in their life."

"You want to know my worst dream?" Jonathan said. "It's that I'm Superman and I can fly and I'm strong. And then, for some reason, I'm in a dark alley at night and these guys are coming in to beat me up. At first I'm not worried, but I can't decide whether to fly away or to use my superpowers to fight them. Finally I decide to fly away. But when I try to take off, for some reason, my superpower isn't working, and they're getting closer and closer. I realize they're going to beat me up, but there's nothing I can do about it. And then I wake up."

"That is really sad," Amber said.

"It is. I have that dream almost once a month."

By the time we had each told our worst dreams, we'd arrived at Upper Mesa Falls. It's one of my favorite places. The falls are really huge, especially in the spring when the water is running high. To keep tourists from falling to their deaths, the state had constructed a fenced walkway that permitted visitors to get close to the river without falling in.

By the time we got there, it was almost eleven o'clock. We might not have been able to see a thing except for a full moon. The parking lot was deserted as we pulled in. Even if there had been anyone nearby, the roar of the falls would drown out any noise we might make.

At the first overlook, I shouted out, "I've got a great idea for a prank, okay? Amber, you be my date. Okay, so I bring this girl I've been going with up here, and I have this jewelry box, okay? And I bring it out, and I say to her, 'I've been planning to give you this for a long time, but I wanted to wait until we could be here.' As I go to hand her the box, my hand hits the railing, and I drop the box over the falls. And then I say, 'You know, I really think this was the sign I was looking for. So, never mind.'"

"That is so cruel," Amber shouted above the roar of the falls.

"You don't think it's funny?" I yelled.

"I do, sort of," Ryan shouted, but then he was stared down by Brooke. "Well, not really, I guess."

"So what would you do then?" Brooke yelled. "Have the ring in the car?"

I didn't want Brooke to be disappointed in me for thinking up something cruel, so I decided to turn this into something positive. "Yeah, that's what I'd do, all right."

"Guys," Brooke cried out a short time later, "look at how the light plays on the water downstream. Let's go get a better look."

Amber and I were abandoned as the others climbed down the trail alongside the falls. We moved a short ways away from the falls so we could talk without having to shout. "They say that if you kiss on this spot during a full moon, then, if you happen to be in a singing group, it will be a big success. Would you like to find out if that's true?"

She laughed. "To be perfectly honest, I'm not sure success would be worth the price."

"Hey, we're talking huge success here."

She punched me on the arm lightly. "My gosh, Greg, that is the cheesiest line I've ever heard. No wonder you can't get a girl to keep seeing you. You go out a couple times, but then it ends. Why don't you stick with one of them for a while?"

"I think you probably know the answer to that question." I put my arms around her.

She had that worried look again. "Greg, c'mon. We've gone over this a hundred times."

Finally, I gave into a desire I'd had for months and kissed her.

When she broke free, she was mad. "You had no right to

171

do that, Greg, no right at all. I thought we had an agreement."

"Right, some agreement," I muttered. "You get everything you want and I get nothing. You don't want a friend. You want a puppy dog. Well, I can't do that anymore."

"I can't stand it when you're like this." She started to leave.

"Wait. Don't go."

"I can't be with you alone, Greg. I don't trust you anymore. You really went too far that time."

I followed her up the path. "You're not going to tell Brandon, are you?" I asked.

"I think I should, don't you?"

"It's not like you're married to him. You don't have to tell him everything that happens between us, do you?"

"What is wrong with you? Don't you have any integrity?"

"I do—but—just not with you."

"You can't have it both ways, Greg," Amber said. "I can't be your best friend, your singing partner, practically your sister, and your steady girl too. It won't work that way and you know it. I can't believe you would kiss me when you knew that's not what I wanted."

"What *do* you want?"

"I want things to stay just the way they've been."

"I want more than that," I said.

"Then what you want can never be. I'm sorry to tell you that, but it's the truth."

I swore in front of her. It was the first time I'd ever done that. I must have picked it up from Ryan. Except he'd stopped. And I'd picked it up. I felt awful. "I'm sorry. That just slipped out."

"I'm finding out all sorts of things about you tonight, aren't I?" she said.

I'd had it with her. "I'm not going to let you ruin this night for me."

"I wish I could say the same thing, but it's too late for that. You've already ruined my night."

For me the midnight picnic and the ride back home were torture. Ryan took his usual seat on the right front seat. Amber retreated as far to the back as she could manage. Brooke and Jonathan sat in the second seat and talked about college.

I didn't say anything until Brooke leaned forward and quietly asked me what I was thinking about.

"Nothing," I grumbled. "My mind is a complete blank."

She whispered in my ear. "I saw you and Amber back there. You were way out of line, Greg. I really think you need to apologize to Amber."

"I tried, but it didn't do any good."

"Try again. The way I look at it, if you two don't get this worked out, Fast Forward is finished."

"I hate to apologize."

"I know, but sometimes you have to do things you don't want to."

When we got to Amber's house, I walked her to the door. "I'm sorry, Amber, for what I did," I said.

"I accept your apology, but don't let it happen again. I mean it, Greg."

I remember thinking then that all my friends knew my flaws. Except for one person—Jennifer. I remember when she told me I was her hero. I'd never been anyone's hero before, and the way things were going, I wasn't likely to be anyone's hero in the near future.

"There's just one more thing," I said, embarrassed to be saying this to Amber. "Don't tell Jennifer about what happened tonight. Okay?"

Amber seemed surprised. "Okay, I won't, but why?"

"I guess maybe I don't want her to know how messed up I am."

"I won't tell her."

"Thanks. I am sorry."

"You should be. Good night, Greg."

*   *   *   *

I'd had it with just being Amber's friend while she focused her affection on Brandon. I decided to start looking for a girl I could go out with. I didn't need much. Just a girl who adored me even when I was in a foul mood. Someone who'd wait around on weekends until Fast Forward was done practicing or performing. Someone I could call on a moment's notice, tell her I was coming by, and she'd be there when I pulled into her driveway, so I wouldn't even have to go inside and talk to her mom and dad. Someone who wouldn't ask me to explain myself. Someone who would never say I was being unreasonable. Someone who could read my thoughts. Someone who could bake bread better than Amber and who'd let me sit in her kitchen and watch her bring the bread hot out of the oven. Someone who'd love to hear me sing. Also, I needed a girl with a two-syllable name so I could finish the love song I'd written especially for her.

I didn't care what she looked like either, except that when she and Amber were in a room together, nobody would pay any attention to Amber. Maybe a girl who looked like Sharon Stone, but if she did, I'd want her to be on the seminary council with Brooke.

I wasn't fussy. All I wanted was a girl that'd make Amber crazy with jealousy.

*   *   *   *

I didn't find what I was looking for, but instead I found Camille Armstrong. I'm embarrassed to even say how we met. It's not something I'm proud of because it went against everything I stood for in high school. I liked to believe that I

174

was the master of my destiny, completely independent of my parents.

This is how Camille and I got together. My dad was in the temple. He works there every Wednesday night. He started talking with another temple worker who had a daughter named Camille. She couldn't seem to find a boy her age who lived the standards of the Church.

"She should meet my son," my dad said.

They talked for a while, and then her dad asked, "Do you think you could get your son to call my daughter?"

My dad thought about it. "Probably not."

So they arranged a two-family get-together.

One night not long after that, I came home for supper and saw three strangers in our living room. My dad motioned for me to come into the room. "Greg, these are the Armstrongs, and this is their daughter, Camille."

"Hi there."

"Brother Armstrong and I work in the temple together, but we hardly see each other any other time. So I invited him and his family over for supper."

"Oh," I said.

Camille looked as embarrassed as I felt.

After a few minutes of boring adult conversation, my dad turned to me and said, "Why don't you show Camille our computer?"

"What for?" I asked. "It's just a computer."

"Camille is very smart," her dad said.

Camille scowled at her dad. It made me like her a lot more than if she'd been all bubbly and brighteyed. I realized she was as bummed out about this as I was.

No use me punishing her too. She had no control over her parents either. "Come on," I said. "I'm sure we can find something to do."

We went in my dad's office and sat down in front of the computer.

"I'm sorry, but we don't have any games on this thing," I said. "I tried to get some on it, but my dad kept saying 'It's not a toy.' So I really don't know what he wants me to show you."

"It doesn't matter."

"Have you ever used a spreadsheet?" I asked.

"No."

"I'll show you that then."

"Sure."

We both sat in front of the computer. "Put your hand on the mouse, and I'll guide you through," I said.

I was sitting on her right side. She put her right hand on the mouse. I put my right hand on top of hers. She was surprised by the physical contact but not unhappy the way Amber would have been. "Is this what they call *hands-on learning?*" she asked with a smile.

"Something like that," I said, giving her my Young Santa Claus laugh. It seemed to put her at ease, just like Amber said it would.

As I moved her hand, which was on the mouse, from one icon to the other, my cheek kept brushing up against her long blonde hair. Before very long, we were both blushing, but neither one of us said anything.

Amber had taught me to pay attention to the color of a girl's eyes. I looked into Camille's beautiful blue eyes and said softly, "The thing about spreadsheets is that you can have things going on that aren't that obvious on the surface," I said. "Hidden things."

She turned to me. "Really? Hidden things?"

"Yes, that's right." I looked down just in time to notice that my fingers were caressing her hand.

She looked down at my hand and broke into a big grin. "I see what you mean."

"Computers are my life," I lied.

"I can see that."

I gave her another Young Santa Claus laugh.

"You have the most wonderful laugh," she said.

"Really? I've never noticed. I just find life fun and interesting."

"I can see that."

"How would you describe the color of your eyes?" I said.

"Blue."

"Oh, no, the word *blue* doesn't begin to do justice to how beautiful they are."

"Thank you."

Thanks, Amber, for giving me that line, I thought.

A short time later, my dad came in to see how we were getting along. That changed the mood drastically. I'm not sure why. I think it was because we'd each made up our mind that we were not going to go along with anything our dads might have schemed to try to bring us together. The presence of my dad made us realize we were having a good time. Which ruined all our plans.

After my dad left, I said, "Let's do an example to see how a spreadsheet can be used to add up a set of numbers. Just write down a set of numbers in this column."

"Any numbers?" she asked.

"Sure."

"All right. This is my phone number." She typed the number and then turned to me with a big smile.

I glanced at her phone number on the screen. "Actually, it'll be easier to add without the spaces."

She made the correction.

"And this is my locker combination at school." She entered three numbers in succession down the column.

"You shouldn't give that out to just anybody," I said.

"You're right. I've never given it to anyone before now."

"So does that mean if you end up missing some candy from your locker, you're going to come after me?" I asked.

"That's right." She smiled at me.

This was totally out of control. We were both playing the same game—flirting big-time while, on the surface, talking about something so boring that usually just the mention of the word *spreadsheet* makes people's eyes glaze over.

I felt like we needed to slow this down, so I showed her how to add up columns of numbers using a spreadsheet.

"I could get my coach to use this to run stats for each game."

"Coach?" I asked.

"Yes. I've played basketball for Sugar the past two years."

"Really? Do you know Amber Whittaker? She used to play for Madison."

"Yeah, sure. I've played against her."

"How did you do against her?"

"I had a really good night."

I smiled. "Really? Good for you."

*   *   *   *

Because I was a graduate of The Amber School of Knowing How to Treat a Girl, the next day I called Camille and told her I'd really enjoyed being with her. I could tell she was glad I'd called. She probably didn't expect me to call. And I wouldn't have, if it hadn't been for Amber. *Always call the next day*, she had told me.

While I was on the phone, I asked Camille if she'd like to go with me to a fireside on Sunday. That was a good move, also inspired by Amber. How can a girl turn down a guy who asks her to a fireside?

I felt like I had a secret weapon because I'd picked up so much information from Amber in our Saturday morning bread-making sessions.

At first I thought of this as just a way to test Amber's suggestions, but it was amazing to see Camille respond so well to the things I did. On our second date, I brought her a flower. (Amber's idea.) One morning I drove all the way to

178

Sugar City and put a little note in her locker. (Amber's suggestion.) When I came to pick her up, I always spent time talking with her folks. (Again, Amber.)

At first Camille was just the General Motors proving ground for Amber's theories of how a guy should treat a girl. Amber would give me a suggestion, I'd try it, and report back.

But then something happened I had not anticipated. Camille started treating me like I really was wonderful, and that made me try harder. I became even better around her. And then we developed feelings for each other, which made me treat her even better.

I think Camille fell in love with me first. It was a shock to me that anyone could actually like me when I was so messed up. The thing was, Camille didn't know I was messed up.

Camille didn't know how badly I treated people sometimes because that only happened at our practices where we had to be brutally honest with each other. The rest of the time I was not too bad of a person.

Camille didn't know I still had feelings for Amber. How could she? Amber was seeing Brandon exclusively. All I ever said to Camille about Amber was that we were singing together.

Camille didn't know that after Ryan had taught me about repentance, I'd gone to a teacher and confessed to him that I'd cheated on a quiz and then I'd gone to my bishop about it. Amber knew it, though.

Camille didn't know that at one time my dad and I had built huge walls between us. She didn't know it because he and I were getting along much better now.

Camille didn't know that once I had nearly run away from home with Amber, Brooke, Ryan, and Jonathan. How could I tell her about it? My folks didn't even know.

Camille also didn't know that many of the things I did

179

around her were inspired by Amber's suggestions—that, in some ways, I was Amber's creation.

Camille believed that I was good and kind and wonderful. Her faith in me helped me want to have those qualities.

It got to the point where I couldn't imagine ever knowingly hurting Camille.

*　　*　　*　　*

A few weeks after I first started going with Camille, Amber arranged to have Fast Forward perform for a school assembly at Eagle Rock Junior High School in Idaho Falls. It meant that we would miss an afternoon of classes, but we didn't mind. We talked our choir director into getting us excused.

As we began to set up in the auditorium of the school, it didn't seem the best place to perform. The stage was too far away from the audience, but there was nothing to do except try to make the best of it.

I must have been in a bad mood that day. "Are we getting paid for this?" I asked.

"No, we're not," Amber answered. "It won't hurt us to perform without getting paid."

"I wasn't complaining, okay? I just wanted to know."

"Oh, I almost forgot," Amber said. "They want us to say something about not drinking or smoking or using drugs," Amber said.

"And you're just telling us this now?" I asked.

"Sorry, I just remembered. It doesn't have to be much. I can say something if that's all right with everyone."

That was all right with us.

"Maybe we could have one of the guys say something too. How about you, Greg?"

"Don't expect much from me."

"I never do," Amber teased.

I was in no mood for this. "You know what? I don't feel like my day is complete until you start ripping on me."

She was surprised by my reaction. "Sorry, I was just kidding," Amber said.

"I don't want to talk," I said.

"Ryan, how about you?" Amber asked.

"I don't even like junior high kids." As soon as Ryan said this, he knew he'd left himself wide open. "Go ahead and say it," he said softly. He looked like he was living all over again the night Amber had grilled him about what he'd done to Nicole. But there had already been enough said on that topic. No one felt like getting on Ryan's case again.

Brooke to the rescue: "It might be better if we sing more and not be so preachy. Why not let Amber be the only one who talks."

We agreed.

"Can we have a prayer before we start?" Brooke said.

"Oh, yes, good idea," Amber said.

We had a prayer backstage. It was exactly what we needed.

The principal came down the aisle and onto the stage. He welcomed us and then added, "To tell you the truth, I'm not sure how this is going to go. During our last assembly we had a lot of rowdiness in the audience. If that happens this time, I may end up sending everyone back to their classrooms. But, from what I've heard, you're very good, so things will probably turn out fine." He turned to leave. "The students will be here in about five minutes, just after the bell rings."

I did a sound check on each of the microphones. We went over again the order of the songs we were going to sing. And then we went backstage to wait.

A loud bell rang throughout the school. A minute later we watched students pour into the auditorium.

The principal introduced us. "Today we have a singing

group called Fast Forward. They sing without a piano. That's called *a cappella*. They're in high school, and they're going to sing for you today."

There were a few audible groans. Some boys, in a gesture of hopelessness, slumped over and rested their foreheads on the back of the seat ahead of them. The girls just kept talking.

We began with "I Need You." At first, the kids were really indifferent. But as we sang, they gradually began paying attention. The boys sat up in their chairs and leaned forward. The girls quit talking. I'd never heard Amber sound so good. Her voice was free and full. She added more animation in her movements than I'd ever seen. By the time we finished our second number, the students were right with us.

We sang four songs, and then Amber took over. "Thank you so much," Amber said. "You're the best audience we've ever had. We're going to sing some more songs, but first there's something we want you to think about."

She took one step forward. "When we found out we would be coming here to sing for you, we decided we wanted to do something besides entertain you. It's only been three or four years since we were in junior high school and were going through some of the same things you are. We remember how tough it is to resist all the pressures."

Amber has this way of connecting with an audience. The way she handles a microphone and moves around on stage makes every person in the audience believe she's doing this just for them. Besides being gorgeous, she's tall and athletic looking, so it's hard not to be impressed by her. The kids—especially the girls—were really listening to what she had to say.

"What can help is to have friends you can lean on. That's what we've got in our group. We don't always get along perfectly, but we are best friends. And we support each other. I hope each of you has got someone like that in your life."

She smiled that great smile of hers and concluded, "I don't want to preach to you or anything like that. I just want to say that it's cool to do your best in school. And when somebody offers you drugs or a cigarette or a drink of alcohol, it *really is* all right to say no."

Our next song was "My Girl," so as soon as Amber finished talking, I started laying down a beat, sounding like a string bass. It was Ryan's solo. The audience got into the mood of the song, and, of course, the girls all fell in love with him.

Our next song was "Chain Gang." As we were singing it, I looked at the kids sitting in the first few rows and wondered how each of them was doing.

After a few more songs, the principal stood up in the back of the auditorium and pointed to his watch. The time had raced by.

"It's time for us to quit, but we have some tapes of some of the songs you heard today, if anyone wants 'em," I announced. "They're ten dollars, but for you guys we'll give 'em to you for five."

"We love you guys!" Amber called out, as the audience clapped.

The principal came onstage and announced. "Every body hurry and get to your next class." But getting to class was not what some students had in mind as they moved forward and up onto the stage and surrounded us. It was the first time anyone had ever asked us for our autographs. It was like we were famous. It was a great feeling.

The principal let us talk to the students for a long time, and then he asked them to get back to class. He waited until everyone was gone and then spoke to us. He shook our hands enthusiastically. "This has been the best assembly we've had this year. I've never seen our students so excited about anything. You guys should be doing this every day.

There must be grant money you could get from the state. Just think of all the good you could do."

"That'd be great," Amber said. "There's nothing I'd rather do than that."

"There's only one thing," I said. "We have missions we need to serve."

"Maybe after your missions then," the principal said. "I wish you all the best. Thanks so much for coming."

"Just think if we could go around giving assemblies," Amber said. "Every day a different town, all around the country, being together, singing every day. If I could have that, it's all I'd ever ask for the rest of my life. I wouldn't care about anything else."

"It would be great, but let's face it—it might not happen," Ryan said.

"Why wouldn't it happen?" Brooke said.

"Three of us will be gone for two years on our missions. A lot can happen in two years."

"Like what?" she asked.

"Well, for one thing, you and Amber will probably both be married by the time we get back," Jonathan said.

"Let's make a pact," Amber said.

"We can't do that," Ryan said.

"Why not?" Amber asked.

"It's not fair. None of us know what's going to happen in the next two years. We can say we'll try to get together after our missions, but we can't make a pact. We'll just have to see how things are when we get back."

A short time later we were on Highway 20, heading north. It's a four-lane highway that runs between Idaho Falls and Rexburg. On the other lane I saw Brandon's pickup going south. I knew he was heading to where we'd just come from because he wanted Amber to ride with him. I didn't know if he'd seen me or not, but I took the first exit to try to ditch him. It was selfish of me, I know, but I didn't want Amber to ride home with Brandon. He was with her so much of the time anyway. I didn't think it was fair of him to try to rob me of this time too.

"Where are we going?" Ryan asked.

"You guys want to go to swim in the hot springs at Heise?" I asked.

"We don't have any suits," Brooke said.

"I think they rent suits."

I was mainly trying to get over a hill so Brandon wouldn't be able to find me, even if he had seen my mini-van.

"I've never heard of them renting suits," Jonathan said. "Besides, we don't have any money."

We were now hidden from anyone on Highway 20. I slowed down and stopped. And then, just to stall for a little more time, I asked each one how much money they had. We didn't have enough money to go swimming.

"I don't think anyone except you wants to go swimming anyway," Amber said. "I need to get back."

"Why?"

"Brandon's folks invited me to go to a concert at Ricks," she said.

"Don't worry. I'll get you there on time," I said.

Instead of going back to Highway 20, I decided to take some county roads home, ones that Brandon would never think we'd be on.

That would have been the end of it, but then Amber started telling Brooke how wonderful Brandon was. That put me in a bad mood. I don't know why. She and I talked about him on Saturday mornings, but that was different. Her questions on Saturdays were like, "What should I do when this happens?" But this was different. Sometimes I tried to kid myself that Brandon didn't mean much to her, but the way she was talking to Brooke, I could tell she liked him a lot.

Even though the conversation drifted to what it would be

185

like to be able to give programs at schools every day, I was still in a sour mood.

"I can't get enough of singing with you guys," Amber said. "It's all I think about."

That shouldn't have set me off, but it did. "Amber, do you know why you're so crazy about this and the rest of us aren't?" I asked. "It's because you sing lead and we sing backup. Our job is to make you look good. So then you soak up all the glory. Well, that's fine. I don't mind that, but you'll have to excuse us if we're not caught up in this as much as you are. Has it ever occurred to you we might not want to spend the rest of our lives standing in your shadow, making you look good? You are one of the most selfish people I've ever met."

"That's it—stop the car!" Amber cried out.

"What are you talking about?" I snapped.

"Just stop. I mean it. Right now."

I pulled over and stopped. Amber opened the sliding door of the minivan.

"What are you doing?" I asked.

"I'm going to walk home," Amber said.

"Are you crazy? You can't walk home. We're twenty miles from Rexburg."

"I can't be around you anymore today, Greg. I hate it when you get this way."

"Come on, Amber. Be reasonable," Brooke said. "It'll be dark before long. And it's way too far. You can't walk all the way home."

"I'm not going to stay in here and have Greg shoot me down all the time. I can only take so much of that."

"Fine. Get out, walk home, see if I care," I grumbled.

Amber stepped out of the van. "Thanks for the ride," she said sarcastically, and then she slammed the van door shut. I sped off.

"Greg, stop. I mean it," Brooke called out from the back.

186

I kept driving.

"You can't leave her out here all by herself," Brooke said.

"It was her choice."

"Let me out, too, then," Brooke said. "I'm not going to let her walk alone at night along this highway."

"I'll go with you, just in case," Ryan said.

"Me, too," Jonathan said.

"Let us all out," Brooke said.

"What is wrong with you people?" I complained, pulling to the side of the road and stopping the minivan.

"We'll walk with her unless you go and apologize to her," Brooke said.

"Why do I always have to be the one who apologizes?"

"Just say you're sorry," Brooke suggested.

"Sorry for what?"

"She'll fill in the blanks," Jonathan said.

"I hate this. I hate girls," I raged. "I hate the way they twist everything you say. I hate it that they're so emotional and take everything so personal. They just wait to take anything you say the wrong way. I really do hate that."

"You're not perfect either, you know," Brooke said.

"But you and Amber are, right?" I shot back.

"Nobody's perfect," Brooke said.

"You got that right, sister."

"Go back and apologize or we'll never get home," Brooke said.

"I hate this. You know I hate this," I grumbled as I opened my door and then slammed it as hard as I could. I started walking back to find Amber.

Amber stopped walking toward me when she saw me.

"I'm sorry," I called out.

"Don't give me that. Greg. I know you too well. You're not sorry. Not really."

It was true. I wasn't sorry. I decided to change the subject. "I can't let you walk home."

187

"I'm not going to ride with you, Greg."

"Am I that bad?" I asked.

"Yes. You're awful sometimes."

"Really?" I said.

"Really."

"I didn't know that," I said.

"I know you don't, but you are," she said.

I looked at her. Most of the time I tried to ignore how beautiful she was.

"Why are you looking at me that way?" she asked.

"No reason."

"There's always a reason for everything you do, Greg, so don't give me that."

"I was just thinking you're a lot better looking now," I said.

"Are you saying I was bad looking once, but now not so much?"

"Why do you have to twist everything I say into something it's not?" I asked.

"Why can't you ever say what you mean?" she complained.

"Man, you are such a pain in the rear end," I said.

"Don't you go saying *rear end* in front of me!"

"Everything has a front end and also a rear end. I mean that's not really new information to you, is it?"

"You are so crude," she said.

"A car has a front end and a rear end. A train has a front end and a rear end."

"I get the idea, okay? I'm so glad to find out what you're really like."

"Why?"

"Because I used to think I liked you, but now I know that was a big mistake," she said.

"Well, let me tell you something. I'm so glad I'm not

188

Brandon. He's like a little dog that you've got jumping through hoops. You'd never get me doing that."

"That's because it's impossible for you to ever admit you made a mistake," she said.

She brushed past me going toward the minivan.

"Where are you going?" I asked.

"I'm going home."

"I won't let you walk home alone."

She turned to face me. "Oh, really? And how are you going to stop me?"

She was right. There was little I could do. "Okay, look. You drive home, and I'll walk."

"You'd do that?" she asked.

"It'll be better if I'm the one walking instead of you."

She stopped walking but kept her back to me. I could hear her sniffling.

"Are you bawling?" I asked.

"No."

"Don't lie."

"All right, maybe a little."

"How come?"

"I don't know."

It was almost dark. We were standing on the side of the highway. There was no other traffic. Up the road and around a curve was the minivan, its motor still running.

"Greg?" she said.

"Yes."

"Sometimes I wonder if maybe we should be more than just friends," she said.

"You do?"

"Sometimes I do."

"What about Brandon?" I asked.

"I like him and everything, but he and I can't talk about everything like you and I can. I'll quit going with him if you'll quit going with Camille."

"All right, it's a deal."

"Really?" she asked.

"Sure, no problem. So does that mean we're going together now?"

"I guess it does," she said.

"What a great day." I put my arm around her waist as we walked down the highway.

"Tell me how you're going to break up with Camille," Amber said.

I didn't mind her asking because this was what we did every Saturday morning anyway. *How do you do this? How do you say this? What should you do in this case?* It was a fair question. How was I going to break up with Camille? "Can I do it with a note?" I asked.

"No."

"Over the phone?"

"No, you have to do it face-to-face," she said.

"Why?"

"She's been very good for you, Greg. I think you owe her that kind of respect, don't you?"

"What would I say?" I wondered if Amber noticed me slipping from What *will* I say? to What *would* I say? The thought of hurting Camille was very painful to me.

"I guess you'd have to tell her the truth," Amber said.

"And what would that be?"

"I don't know. You tell me."

Camille had been the best thing that had ever happened to me. To break up with her now would be difficult. She trusted me so much. She thought so highly of me. She helped me see myself in a better light than I could ever do without her. "I'm not sure I can break up with her now," I said.

"I understand," Amber said, pulling away from me. "My gosh, we've made a real mess of this, haven't we?"

I put my arm around her. I wasn't going to kiss her, but

190

she, more than me, made it happen. I felt like a traitor to Camille. "This isn't right," I said.

"No, but it's not wrong either."

"No, it isn't wrong, but it isn't right either," I said.

"I've been such a fool," she said.

"I know, me too."

We kissed again. Who was I kidding? All I'd ever wanted was to be with Amber. "All right, you win. I'll break up with Camille."

"Just like that?" she asked.

"Yeah, sure. Why not?"

"You like her, though, don't you?"

"Yeah, she's okay, but I'd rather go with you."

"For how long?"

"Until I go on my mission, I guess."

"You think we'll last that long?" she asked.

"Sure, why not?"

"We don't always agree on everything," she said.

"We'll work things out."

"What if we break up?" Amber asked.

"We'll get back together in a few days."

"What would happen to Fast Forward if we broke up permanently?" she asked.

"I don't know."

"I do. Fast Forward would end if you and I broke up," she said.

"We're not going to break up."

"But if we did, then we'd quit singing together. I don't know if I could handle that."

I could feel the battle being lost, so I kissed her again—longer and with more passion.

She was mad at me when we pulled apart. "What was that all about?" she asked.

"What a dumb question," I said.

"It's not a dumb question. This last kiss was different

191

than the first two. The first one was about friendship, the second was about love, but the third was different. It was like you were thinking *If I give her my best kiss, she'll be putty in my hand and quit asking so many questions.*"

"Yeah, so? It worked, didn't it?" I asked.

"Not at all."

"You're lying. It got to you."

"I can't stand it when you're like this," she said.

"You know the trouble with you?" I asked. "You're not willing to admit how much you need me."

"I need *you?*" she asked. "You're the one like a puppy dog at my heels all the time. I can't even turn around without you bumping into me."

She walked a short distance away and then turned to look at me. After what seemed like a long time, she said quietly, "You know this isn't going to work, don't you? We can't even kiss without getting into an argument. If we start going with each other, Fast Forward is doomed. I couldn't take that. Let's promise we'll do whatever we can to keep the group together."

I was bitter about our priorities. "You don't want a love that lasts. You just want Fast Forward to be eternal, right?" I said.

"Yes, that's what I want. It's the only thing that seems important to me now. Everything else is boring and senseless."

"Let's go home," I said. She walked beside me and reached out for my hand.

"It was great while it lasted, wasn't it?" she asked. "How long did we go together? Five minutes?"

"A world record for us," I said. "Do you think we'll ever get it right?"

"I don't know. I hope so. Let's promise not to tell anyone else about this, okay?"

"Okay."

A minute later I opened the side door of the minivan, waited for Amber to climb in, and then shut it. In a few minutes we were on our way again.

It had been a long day.

She broke up with Brandon a month later, but I continued going with Camille.

In music and in life, timing is everything.

12

Wearing my cap and gown, I sat and waited for the commencement speaker to finish up, so I, along with the rest of our graduating class, could walk across the stage to pick up an empty diploma cover and the note saying they'd mail us our diplomas later.

My mom and dad were in the audience. My dad had bought a new camera for the occasion. I knew he'd be one of those who'd stand without embarrassment right in front of the stage to take pictures as the envelope is handed out.

I glanced around to see if I could get Brooke's attention, but she was listening to the commencement speaker. Amber, being a Whittaker and therefore sitting on the last row, was too far away for me to signal.

Camille was in the audience with my mom and dad. She'd graduated from Sugar earlier in the day. She'd been accepted to Ricks.

Brooke and Amber would be attending Ricks too. I was going to work for my dad until leaving on my mission right after spud harvest.

The speaker said that commencement was not an end but a beginning. *Duh, like we haven't figured that out by now,* I thought. I had a bad attitude because Fast Forward wasn't singing for commencement. We'd tried out but hadn't been selected. I guess they didn't pick us because we weren't as sloppy sentimental as the girl they'd chosen. She'd written an original song, one of those syrupy ballads that's sung once for graduation ceremonies and is immediately forgotten.

This is so cheesy, I thought as I listened to the girl sing her very sincere but totally awful song. *We could have done a lot better.*

I turned to locate my folks in the audience. My dad didn't look comfortable wearing a suit. When he wore a suit, it was either for a wedding or a funeral or church. The thought occurred to me that I had one more spud harvest to work with my dad before leaving on my mission. It didn't seem fair that just before it was time for me to leave, we were finally getting along.

I wasn't sure what to do that night after graduation. Camille's parents were having a reception for her at their house in Sugar, and she had asked me to be there. Even though Camille and I were talking about getting married after my mission, I still wanted to spend at least some time that night with Ryan, Jonathan, Amber, and Brooke.

None of us in Fast Forward knew for sure what the future would hold, but we wanted to continue singing together as long as possible. I was planning to go on my mission in December, and Ryan would go in March and Jonathan in April.

The plan we finally came up with for graduation night was that we'd meet at Amber's house at midnight. That would give me time to be with Camille. And then we'd go out to the sand dunes for baked potatoes and toppings.

I was about a half hour late getting to Amber's place. Amber met me at the door. "You've got lipstick on your face," she said quietly enough so nobody else would hear.

"Thanks." I excused myself and went into the bathroom to wipe it off. When I came out, I said, "You guys all ready?"

"We've been waiting for you," Jonathan said.

"Yeah, sorry. I couldn't get away."

Amber grinned at me. "Apparently not."

We left a few minutes later.

The place we usually went to was taken by some seniors who were getting drunk, so we trudged over a few more ridges until we were out of earshot.

It was awkward for us. We were starting to do that thing where you say, "This is probably the last time we'll do this."

We started a fire and sat around talking while it burned down. Then we dropped the potatoes in their foil wrappings onto the coals. It would take a while before they'd be ready, but we had plenty of time.

Brooke was the first to say it. "I love you guys."

We all stared into the fire and muttered something like, "Me too."

"Amber, say that thing you're always telling us," I said.

She looked over at me and smiled. "Oh, you mean, 'Act your age, Greg'?"

"No, the other."

"This is my dream."

"Yeah, right. That's the one."

"Let's promise we'll all get together after you guys get home from your missions," Amber said.

"You make us promise that every time we come here," Ryan said.

"Please."

"We'll get together after we get back from our missions," I said dutifully.

Brooke came to me for a hug. "You've been so good for me." And then she made the rounds. Ryan was the next one to be hugged. "I'm so proud of you, Ryan. You've really made some big changes in your life."

"You've helped me a lot," he said.

Next, Brooke knelt down by Jonathan. "You're the greatest, Jonathan."

He smiled. "I am, aren't I?"

Brooke hugged Jonathan from behind, and then Amber joined in. Amber looked back at Ryan and me. "You guys, get over here," she said. We went over and joined in the group hug.

No one said anything. We just held on as our high school time slipped away like the sand we were standing on. I started to wonder if I'd been wrong about that girl's song at graduation. It had been sloppy sentimental, but that's the way graduations mostly are.

We ate and talked until the sky turned from black to a dull gray. And then we started back.

Just before we got to the van, we topped a dune and looked down at the kegger still going on below us. People were standing around a fire, drinking beer and talking.

"Isn't that Nicole?" Amber said.

It was Nicole, all right. She had a plastic cup in her hand, and she was talking to some guy.

"I need to go talk to her," Ryan said. He trudged down the slope, and we sat down and waited. We were close enough to hear what went on.

Ryan walked up to Nicole. "Can I talk to you, Nicole?"

"Sure, have a beer and we'll talk." Her speech was slightly slurred.

"I don't drink anymore."

"You used to."

"I've changed since then."

She made a wide sweeping gesture. "Me too. Ask anybody here. They'll tell you how much I've changed."

"Let me take you home. You don't belong here."

She laughed. "Are you kidding? This is the only place I *do* belong."

"You could turn your life around."

197

"Sorry, not interested. You know the trouble with you? You're too uptight. Have a beer. C'mon, just one, for old time's sake."

He shook his head. "I've done a lot of changing."

"Really?" She took a sip from her cup.

"Yes. I'm planning on going on a mission."

"Well, that's certainly a convenient religion you got there, Ryan. You mess with me, say you're sorry, and then announce to the whole world that you're going on a mission. Man, you are such a hypocrite. You want to know something? I liked you better before you got religion."

"If you'd just let me help you . . ."

She threw the beer in her cup in his face and then swore at him.

Ryan turned and started up the slope to where we were waiting.

Nicole saw us. "Are those your singing buddies, Ryan? Would you like me to tell them what you're really like?"

As Ryan walked up the ridge to where we were waiting, Nicole yelled at the top of her voice, accusing him of far worse things than he'd ever admitted to us. If what she was saying was true, then Ryan really had seduced her when she was fourteen.

Ryan met us on top of the ridge. He looked like he was about to cry. "She's lying. I told you guys everything. There isn't anything else. Please, you've got to believe me."

Once we finally convinced him we believed him, he began to agonize about Nicole's attitude. "Why won't she listen to me?" he asked. "Why won't she even try to change?"

Brooke looked at Ryan's stricken face and said softly, "Let it go, Ryan, you've done all you can."

We continued on our way to the road.

We got home around five.

High school was over.

13

I slept until noon the next day. I would have slept longer, but I heard voices at my door, and then my mom opened the door and said, "Greg, Camille is here."

"Hey, sleepyhead, are you going to snooze all day?" Camille said, standing next to my mom, both of them radiating that awful sense of superiority so common to people who like to get up early.

"Come in the kitchen when you're dressed," my mom said.

I got up and pulled on a pair of jeans and a sweatshirt. Then I stumbled to the bathroom, splashed some water on my face, brushed my teeth to get rid of morning breath, tried to do something with my hair, and then went into the kitchen.

The three of us talked for a while, and then my mom excused herself to make some phone calls.

"You can't be this tired because of me," Camille said. "Did you do something after you left me?"

I hadn't told her my plans. "Yeah, actually . . . Fast Forward went to the sand dunes."

"Really? What time did you get home?"

"It was pretty late."

"It's okay," she said confidentially. "You can tell me. I won't ground you."

"It was about five-thirty by the time I got home."

She smiled, but I could tell she was hurt that I'd abandoned her to go with my friends. "The way you guys are so close makes me want to take up singing."

"Then you and I would have to break up," I said.

"We still might be closer, though."

"How's that?"

"You come to me for some things, but for everything else, you go to them. You've got everything in neat little compartments, don't you?"

"What are you talking about?"

"Are you ever going to open up to me like you do to them?" she asked.

"I open up to you all the time."

"I wish that were true, Greg, but it's not." She paused. "We're adults officially now, right? So maybe I can ask some of the hard questions I've been holding back. Like . . . how do you feel about Amber?"

"She's a good friend."

"Last night we went in our backyard and sat on our bench swing and you held me in your arms and told me you loved me. And then you excused yourself and spent the next . . . what? . . . five hours with Amber. Did you pour your heart out to her? Did you tell her of your hopes and dreams for the future?"

"What do you want me to do, refuse to talk to her from now on? I can't do that. I talk to Jonathan. I talk to Ryan. I also talk to Brooke and Amber."

"Great—the only problem is you don't talk to me."

"We talk all the time."

"Do we? I'm sorry, but I feel like I'm getting the short end of the stick here. Do you ever think about Amber when you're holding me?"

200

I paused and then said no. The answer was right, but it was the hesitation that did me in.

She didn't believe me. "C'mon, Greg, be honest."

"All right. I used to do that when we first started going together, but I don't do it anymore."

Even as close as she was to tears, she still managed a smile. "I'm so glad that at least you know my name now. That's real progress, isn't it?"

"Don't do this to me, Camille. You're the one I want to marry after I get back from my mission, not Amber."

"You say that, but I still feel like you're holding back a part of yourself for her."

"That's not true," I said.

"Then why didn't you spend more time with me last night? Or why didn't you take me along with you to the sand dunes?"

"All right, I should've done that. I can see that now, but the reason I didn't take you is not because I have anything to hide."

"Here's another hard question for you," she said. "Suppose that after your mission, we actually do get married. Will you still be wanting to sing with Fast Forward?"

This whole thing was like walking through a mine field. "I don't know."

"You *know*, Greg. You just won't tell me. How can we have any kind of a serious relationship if you won't open up to me?"

"All right, I'll answer your question. We have talked about getting together after our missions and singing. And I would do that even if you and I were married."

"I can understand that. Don't get me wrong, Greg. I'm not trying to take you away from Fast Forward. I just want you to be more honest and open with me. If you can't do that, then I don't see how we could ever possibly have a future together."

"I'll try, but you'll have to help me."

"I'll do all I can to help you." She paused. "I really do care a great deal for you, Greg."

"I know. Me too." I decided to risk saying how I felt at that moment. "Can I say something else?"

"Yes, of course."

"Can you let me get a few more hours of sleep? And then maybe we could get together tonight."

"Of course. You see, that wasn't so hard, was it?"

I smiled. "No, it was pretty easy, actually."

I walked her out to her car and then came back and sprawled across my bed. Just before I fell asleep again, I wondered why the commencement speaker hadn't warned the senior boys that we'd be spending the rest of our lives being told to open up to some woman. But if we ever started doing that, like they asked us to, then we'd spend the rest of our time apologizing for not saying exactly what they wanted to hear.

Even though I was a high school graduate, I still needed Amber for advice on how to deal with girls. Later in the day, I went over to her house and told her what Camille had said to me. I asked her what I should do. She gave me some suggestions. I tried them and they seemed to work.

*   *   *   *

With missions fast approaching, Fast Forward tried to crowd two years' worth of performing into one summer. We sang for every conceivable activity. We sang at a dog show. We sang at a rodeo, out in the middle of the arena; we had to watch our step just getting out there. We sang at just about every wedding reception in the county. We sang "The Lion Sleeps Tonight" at the Idaho Falls zoo when they got a new lion. We sang at a restaurant in West Yellowstone three times. We strolled along the streets in Jackson Hole and sang. We sang in Salt Lake City for the 24th of July.

And every time we sang, we set up a card table and sold our demo tape afterward. Most of the time we made more money doing that than what they paid us to sing for them.

Near the middle of July, Alisa, Jonathan's friend from California, came to see him. Jonathan had been back to see her a couple of times since they'd first met, but this was the first time she'd come to Idaho.

At first I didn't care for her. I'm not sure why. To me, it seemed like she felt she knew it all. Maybe that's because I figured that with her being from California, she'd think there was nothing we could do that'd impress her.

Another thing I didn't like about Alisa was the mysterious hold she seemed to have on Jonathan. Okay, she wasn't bad-looking. She had this pale complexion and a high forehead and a kind of Mona Lisa smile. She was sophisticated-looking. It was hard to picture her eating a sloppy Joe and having some of it get on her chin. It was like she was above things that other people have to worry about.

I was pretty sure she had a low opinion of me. I remember after one practice, we were all at Jonathan's house just sitting around eating pizza. "I don't think Alisa has heard your 7-Up impersonation," Amber said, grinning at me. She probably thought that if I did it, Alisa would think even less of me than she already did. So, of course, I did it. It's not that big a deal. I can make the sound of opening up a bottle of 7-Up and pouring it into a glass.

When I did it, I looked at Alisa. She was giving me one of those looks that say, *I suppose he thinks this is very clever.*

That made me mad, so I decided to confront her. When Jonathan left to go get some more ice, I sat down next to Alisa. "You think you're better than me, don't you?" I said.

"No, why would you say that?"

"The way you look down on me all the time."

"I'm not looking down on you. If you want to know the

truth, I lost a contact on the plane, so I can only see out of one eye. Maybe that's what you're noticing."

Amber saw me with Alisa and came over to rescue her. "Don't mind Greg. He's like this with everyone."

"Go away, Amber. This is between me and Alisa," I said.

"I'm okay, really," Alisa said to Amber. "He doesn't scare me."

"You be careful what you say, Greg," Amber warned me as she walked away.

"I don't care much for Amber," I said.

"Really? That's not what I would have guessed," Alisa said.

"Based on what?"

"The way you look at her."

"People tell me that all the time, but I really don't know what they're talking about."

"When she comes in the room, you watch her every move," Alisa said. "She's a beautiful girl, isn't she?"

"Yeah, she is. Of course, she's gotten better-looking too. Take her eye makeup, for example. I suggested she go to a lighter shade. It's made a big improvement."

"She asks your advice about things like that?"

"She asks my advice about everything. I'm the same way with her."

"You must be very good friends then," she said.

"That's what we are all right . . . very good friends."

"You sound a little disappointed it's not more than that."

"Me, disappointed? No, not at all. That's how it has to be," I said. I'm sure I sounded a little melancholy.

"But you're going with another girl, aren't you?" Alisa asked.

"Excuse me, but is this any of your business?" I said.

"Not really. I was just hoping we could be friends, that's all."

"Speaking of friends, let's talk about Jonathan. He and I

have been friends a long time. I wouldn't want him to get hurt. So be careful, okay?"

"I'll be very careful," she said.

"I don't understand how it is between you and him."

"I don't either. It's like we knew each other before we were born."

"I really hate it when people say things like that," I grumbled.

"Why?"

"I only trust what's here and now, not some touchy-feely impression from the preexistence."

"Well, you asked, and I told you. What else can I do?" she said.

"Nothing, I guess. You probably think I'm hopeless, don't you?"

"Not at all," she said. "You're very important to Jonathan. I'd like to be your friend, too."

"All right, let's work for that. Look, I'm sorry if I offended you."

"You didn't offend me. I'm tougher than I look. Is it okay if I come to your practices?"

I should have said no because I'd said no to everyone else who had ever asked to come to our practices. But Alisa was different, and I was beginning to like her. "I guess so, as long as you don't say anything."

"What if I have a suggestion sometime about how you could improve a song?"

She was really pushing it now. "You can make the suggestion, but I might tell you I think your suggestion is a dumb idea."

"So, in other words, you'll treat me like you treat everyone else in the group?"

"Well, yeah, I guess you could say that."

"Sounds fair to me." We ceremoniously shook hands.

Amber saw me walking away from Alisa. "So what'd you do, Greg, cut her off at the knees?"

"No, but I'm thinking of doing that to you."

"If you'd have cut me off at the knees when we first met, then we'd have been about the same height, right?"

"I'm taller than you now," I said.

"No way."

"Turn around."

She turned around. I could feel my back against hers. I knew that with some girls, if I tried to stand with them back to back like that, they'd keep edging forward so I'd never have good contact. But with Amber I could feel her pushing back on me. I wasn't exactly sure what that meant. Maybe it was just that she was just very relaxed around me.

At any rate, I reached up and put my hand on her head and started patting her hair down.

She started laughing. "Excuse me, but what are you doing?"

"I just want this to be fair. You've been cheating all this time. Hair doesn't count when it comes to height."

She has such a great laugh. "I can't believe this. Are you done yet?"

"Not yet, Shorty."

"Shorty?" she howled. "You're calling *me* Shorty?"

"Okay, I'm done," I said. We turned around to face each other. "I'm this much taller than you," I said, holding my thumb and forefinger maybe an inch apart. "The reason people don't notice it is because your hair sticks up too high. So, if you'll just let me cut your hair on top . . ."

She put up her hand up to keep me away. "Stay away from me, Greg, I mean it!" She was laughing as she said it.

"I've got an idea. Let's dance."

"There's no music."

"No problem. We can dance to my singing,"

"Oh gosh, no thanks."

"What's wrong with my singing?" I asked.

"Nothing. It's just that you're such a perfectionist—you'd keep doing the song and making me dance with you over and over until we got it all right."

"Would that be so bad?" I asked.

"Camille might not approve."

"Oh, yeah, right," I said.

Unfortunately Alisa saw this. That was too bad because it probably reinforced her notion that Amber and I had something going between us besides friendship.

The thing Amber and I were beginning to experience is that if you push a friendship hard enough it begins to look like something more than that to people who don't really know what's going on.

*   *   *   *

Alisa was the only outsider we ever let come to our practices. Not that we were shy. We just didn't want others seeing how blunt we could be to each other. Like most families, we didn't always get along. When something wasn't working, I'd stop us and say something that to outsiders might sound mean. All right, maybe it was mean, but what was so wrong with wanting us to sound as good as we possibly could?

I didn't mind Alisa at our practices, though. For one thing, she never said much. And for another, the hurtful things we had said to each other didn't seem to faze her.

I remember, though, the first time she made a suggestion. "That chord is wrong." Everyone turned to see what'd I do.

"What?" I asked.

"The chord's wrong. It should be a minor third."

I'm not sure I even knew what a minor third was. "Says who?"

"Here, I'll show you." She had Ryan change his pitch by half a step. "That's the way it's supposed to be."

I knew Amber was watching to see if I'd bite Alisa's head

off, but I didn't. How could I? She was right. It did sound better with a minor third, if that's what it's called.

It didn't seem to matter how big a group Jonathan and Alisa were in. When they were together, they treated us as strangers and focused their attention on each other, carrying on entire conversations in hushed tones that we couldn't hear.

They seemed to have in their relationship what I wanted but could never seem to get.

*　　*　　*　　*

Amber had the hardest time of any of us facing the end of Fast Forward. During a practice, one moment she would be upbeat and happy, and the next she'd be quiet and moody. "I don't want this to ever end," she said after we'd performed the second time at West Yellowstone.

"It has to end sometime," Brooke said.

"Why does it?" Amber asked.

"We have to grow up sometime."

"This is the only thing . . ." Amber couldn't finish her sentence.

"I know," Brooke said, putting her hand on Amber's shoulder.

*　　*　　*　　*

There are so many bases you need to touch before you go on a mission. People you need to thank. I got some of it done but not all. One Sunday after church I went to Brooke's home.

"Did I forget something?" she asked when she saw me at the door. "We're not singing for a fireside tonight, are we?"

"No, I just thought I'd come by and say hello."

"Come in."

She picked up scattered segments of the Sunday news-paper as we walked into her living room. "Sorry the place is kind of a mess."

"It doesn't matter."

We sat down. Looking at her, I realized how much she meant to me. "You were really a great Peter Pan," I said.

"That was a long time ago."

"Is it true that Peter Pan can fly?" I asked.

"Yes, that's true."

"Anywhere in the world?" I asked.

"Yes, anywhere," she said.

"When I'm having a tough day on my mission, will you fly to me and cheer me up, the way you've been doing since Fast Forward got together?"

"I wish I could, but they clipped my wings. But I'll write you—once a month for sure—even more if you want me to."

"I've got to tell you something." I paused. "I just wish that someday I can be as good a person as you."

"Greg, you're the greatest!"

"No, I'm not. You're the one who's kept us together."

"I'm sure that's not true," Brooke said.

"It is, though. You're the nicest person I've ever known. I just wanted to tell you that once before I leave on my mission." I loved her adorable pixie face. "Can I have a picture of you that I can take on my mission?"

She laughed. "Sure, I'll give you a hundred. Give them to all your companions who are about to come home." She got serious again. "I want to write something on it first. I'll give it you tomorrow night."

I stood up. "I need to go now. Thanks for everything, Brooke."

We held each other for a long time, even when her dad came in and sat down to read the newspaper. I didn't care.

*　　*　　*　　*

I received my mission call in the mail during spud harvest in October. My mom called me on our cellular phone during the middle of the day.

209

"Guess what came in the mail today?" my mom said excitedly.

"Are you sure?"

"I'm sure. When do you want to open it?"

"After work."

"When will that be?"

"Around eleven tonight. Can you call Camille and everybody in Fast Forward and ask them to come over to be with us when I open it?"

It was a cloudy day. We were afraid it was going to rain, so we worked as hard as we could to try to get as much of the crop into the potato cellar as we could. I was driving truck again. I could never stay at the sorting area long enough to say much to my dad, but we talked on the cellular about my mission call.

"Are you excited?" he asked.

"Yeah, I really am."

"I'm excited for you."

We stopped at ten that night and drove in and showered. My dad changed into his suit. I told him he didn't need to do that, but he said that something as important as a call from the Lord deserved our best. So I changed into one of the suits we'd bought for my mission. It was the first time I'd worn it.

My dad and I had some leftover supper together in the kitchen before anyone else showed up. He said the prayer on the food and then asked for a special blessing on me.

"Thanks," I said.

He put his hand on my arm. "All I've ever wanted was for you to be happy."

"I know that now. Thanks."

There was one more thing I wanted to happen. "Dad, do you suppose we could camp out at least once before I leave on my mission? I mean, even if there's snow on the ground."

"Would you like to do that?" he asked.

"Yeah, I would."

"We'll do it then. As soon as we get done with spud harvest."

"Thanks."

The doorbell rang. It was my friends, who'd come to watch me open my mission call.

*   *   *   *

I'll never forget that scene. I was sitting on a chair out in the middle of our living room. Camille was standing at my side, her hand on my shoulder. Jonathan, Amber, and Brooke were on our living room sofa, with my dad and mom in chairs to my right. Ryan was the official photographer for the event, so he was all over the place.

Slowly I opened the envelope.

"What mission is it?" Jonathan asked.

"Minnesota Minneapolis," I said.

"All right!" Jonathan cried out like I'd won the lottery. He was always the optimist about everything,

Camille, no doubt aware of Amber's presence, leaned down and gave me a hug. "Greg, you're going to be such a terrific missionary," she said. There were handshakes and hugs all around, and I couldn't stop grinning. It was great.

Mom brought out a cake she had baked, and while we were eating, she said, "What are you planning for your farewell?"

"I definitely want Fast Forward to sing 'God Be with You Till We Meet Again,'" I said.

"We'd be happy to do that," Brooke said.

"That's just a hymn, isn't it?" Camille asked.

"Yeah, sure," Brooke said.

"Will you be singing it the way it is in the hymn book?" Camille asked.

"Probably so," Brooke said.

"If that's the case, could I sing with you guys?" Camille asked.

"No," Amber said quickly.

"Why not?" I asked.

"Because she's not a part of Fast Forward," Amber said. "It might be the last time we sing together. I think we should keep it just us."

"That's fine. I don't want to intrude," Camille said.

"Good, then it's settled," Amber said.

"All right," I said, "but in addition to Fast Forward singing, I'd also like Camille to sing a duet with me."

"Fine," Amber said tersely.

* * * *

The last time I saw Amber before my mission, was the morning I went with my folks to the MTC in Provo. She came over to say good-bye. It was around seven in the morning. She pulled up as we were loading my things into the minivan.

I'd been set apart by my stake president and was wearing my missionary suit.

Amber was in jeans and a sweatshirt. "I just came to say good-bye," she said.

We were keeping our distance. My mom and dad came out of the house. It was time to go. I had to be in the MTC at two that afternoon.

"Thanks for coming," I said.

I thought about shaking her hand, but I wasn't that sure I could do that without holding her close to me, which would have broken missionary rules. I wanted to be a good missionary. I'd been looking forward to this ever since I could remember.

"I just wanted to thank you for everything you've done for me," she said.

"I didn't do anything."

"You were my best friend. I'll always remember the good times we've shared."

"Me too."

"I wrote you a note," she said, handing me a light blue envelope.

My dad looked at his watch. "We need to go if we're going to get there on time," he said.

"I know."

My mom got in back, so I could ride in front, next to my dad.

With a car door between us, Amber came closer. She put out her hand. She had tears in her eyes.

I touched her hand lightly, and then my dad started the car and we moved slowly away. "Write me," I called out as her hand slipped away from mine.

"You know I will," she called out.

And then we pulled away and I was on my own.

Here is the note Amber wrote me the day I left on my mission.

Dear Greg,

I just wanted to write and thank you for being such a good friend. You've always been the one I went to when I had a problem. I'm not sure what I'm going to do now.

The one thing I regret is that I took you for granted so much of the time. You were always there for me when I needed you. I'm not sure if I'll ever have a friend like you ever again in my life.

I know you'll be a good missionary. I'll be sure and write.

Love,

Amber

*　　*　　*　　*

By the end of April, Ryan, Jonathan, and I were all on our missions. Amber, Camille, and Brooke were going to Ricks College. Brooke had volunteered to keep us all

213

informed. She wrote us once a month. And when she received a letter from any one of us, she copied it and sent it to the rest.

Camille lasted until my twentieth month. That's when she wrote to tell me she was engaged.

The first few months, Amber wrote me twice a month, but then it gradually tapered off. By the time I'd been out a year and a half, she'd quit writing.

I guess that's when she met Michael.

14

I had a difficult time at the beginning of my first semester at Ricks. Part of it was trying to adjust to life after a mission. I felt like I'd lost my purpose in life. I was so conditioned to having a companion and constantly being involved in teaching the gospel that I felt guilty most of the time—like I was being lazy and irresponsible.

Also, my best friends from high school were gone. Amber was back at BYU with Michael, planning their wedding. Brooke was in Pocatello at ISU, waiting for Ryan to get off his mission. Ryan and Jonathan were still on their missions. And, of course, Camille had fallen in love and gotten married just before I finished my mission.

I was not the same either. Because of my mission, I was more goal directed, more serious, more confident that my prayers were heard.

I don't know if I ever would have called Jennifer on my own after running into her in the grocery store the night after I came home from my mission. But, as it turned out, I didn't need to. I saw her in the bookstore the first week after classes started.

She seemed happy to see me. "Want to buy me an ice

cream cone?" she asked after we'd made it through the checkout counter.

We ended up in a booth in the Nordic Landing.

"I hope you don't mind me saying this, but you look kind of lost," she said.

"I'm just trying to get adjusted, that's all."

"You're not going to spend the rest of your life wishing things had turned out different between you and Amber, are you?"

"No, I'm okay with that. Really."

"Good, I'm glad to hear it. What is it then?"

"I don't know. Nothing, really," I said.

"Do you ever wish you were back on your mission?"

"Almost every day."

"I know your mission was a great time in your life, but it's over now. This is your mission now, Greg."

"You mean eating ice cream with you?"

"That's right."

"What a great mission."

"Of course it is." After saying it, though, she yawned.

I felt even more out of it than usual. "Oh my gosh, I'm boring you, aren't I?" I asked. "I'm really sorry."

"No, not at all. I'm just tired, that's all. I do custodial work at the Romney Building. We start work around four in the morning, so I have to get up around three-thirty. The good news is I'm all done for the day at seven. So if I do anything on a weekday, I have to be home by about nine-thirty so I can get enough sleep."

"You get up that early to work? I'm impressed."

"Don't be. It's just something I have to do if I want to go to college. So far I'm paying my own way, just like Amber."

"Are you seeing anyone now?" I asked.

"Oh, you know. Sometimes I'll go out with somebody from my campus ward."

216

"I'd like to start seeing you once in a while, if that's all right."

"Yeah, sure, no problem. You want to start getting together for lunch?" she asked.

"That'd be great."

She pulled out her planner. "Let's look at our schedules."

We found we could get together for lunch. She said she usually brought her lunch to save money, so we could either eat on campus or go home for lunch.

We started seeing each other every day and sometimes on the weekends too. But even when I was with Jennifer, Amber was there with me too because Amber had been the one who taught me how to treat a girl. In my mind I often heard Amber's voice from the past advising me what to do. Once I showed up at the Romney Building just before they closed it for the night. I taped a note on the bathroom mirror in one of the rest rooms Jennifer would be cleaning the next morning. Maybe it wasn't that great of an idea because it meant she had to clean the tape off the mirror, but at four in the morning, she enjoyed seeing it. And where did I learn about writing notes of appreciation to a girl? From Amber.

I'm sure that Amber never thought that someday she'd help me win over her younger sister.

There was something else going on that I was too embarrassed to admit to Jennifer. The two Whittaker girls didn't come from a rich family. Because Jennifer was the youngest, she had inherited some of Amber's things. That meant that, once in a while, Jennifer would wear a church dress that used to be Amber's. That would bring back a flood of memories. And on the phone, I couldn't tell the difference between Amber's and Jennifer's voices. Also, they looked enough alike that at a dance with dim lighting it was like dancing with Amber.

*　　*　　*　　*

I'm not sure who I kissed the first time I kissed Jennifer. Jennifer was in one of Amber's dresses and was wearing Amber's perfume from high school. So she sounded, looked, and smelled like Amber.

The next day I felt guilty. Fantasizing that I was with Amber wasn't fair to Jennifer.

The easiest thing, of course, would have been just to stop seeing her without having to explain anything. *How are you going to break up with her?* I remember Amber asking me in high school when we talked about my breaking up with Camille.

Can I do it with a note? I had asked.

No.

How about over the phone?

No, you have to do it face-to-face. She's been very good for you, Greg. I think you owe her that kind of respect, don't you?

Amber had been right. I needed to talk to Jennifer about what was going on.

A day later, while we were at lunch, I brought it up. "About last night . . . ," I said after we'd finished eating.

"Yes?"

"Sometimes you remind me of Amber. That's nice in a way, but the thing is, I can never be sure if I'm reacting to you or to something about you that reminds me of her. Last night you were wearing one of the dresses she used to wear. And you were wearing her perfume. You have the same color hair as Amber. When you talk, sometimes I can't tell the difference between your voices. So it gets confusing for me sometimes."

"Oh, gosh, I'm sorry. I didn't mean to do that to you. I have clothes of my own. I can wear them around you. I can change perfume, too."

We finished eating and cleaned up before going back to

218

campus. She seemed troubled. Finally, in the car on our way back, she said, "I have a confession to make. I knew it was Amber's dress and perfume."

"What?"

"I wanted to be close to you."

"Oh." Now we were both embarrassed.

"You know what? I think maybe we'd better start over again," she said.

"Yeah, maybe so. Maybe we could just work on being good friends for a while."

We agreed to do that.

*   *   *   *

Ryan returned home from his mission in March. Along with his family, Brooke and Jennifer and I met him at the Idaho Falls airport. We had a sign that read *Welcome Home, Ryan!* And we had a couple of helium-filled balloons. As he walked into the terminal, we cheered and started singing, "He'll be coming 'round the mountain when he comes."

Ryan hugged his mom first and then his dad, but the hug I noticed most of all was the one he gave his sister, Jamie. In the two years he'd been gone on his mission, she'd forgiven him of what had happened between him and Nicole.

After he got through hugging his family, he started on us. He hugged me and then shook hands with Brooke and Jennifer.

To Jennifer, he said, "You've done something to your hair, haven't you?"

"This is Jennifer," I said. "Amber's younger sister."

Ryan turned red. "Sorry. My gosh, you look a lot like Amber."

Jennifer glanced at me and smiled. "I've been told that before."

It was fascinating to see how much Ryan had changed.

He'd obviously been a good missionary. The last few months he'd served as assistant to his mission president. Not that it means anything. I was a good elder, too, but I was never a mission assistant. So that proves my point, right?

With Ryan home, we were excited for Jonathan to return. The closer it got, the more we talked about starting up Fast Forward again. Jennifer offered to take Amber's place. It wasn't that we had a long line of people applying for the job. And Jennifer could sing—just not as well as Amber.

A month later, a couple of days before Jonathan got home, Ryan and I had this dumb idea for a sign. We bought some poster board and wrote *Welcome Home, Greg,* as though it had been used for me. And then we crossed out my name and wrote in Ryan's name. And then, finally, we crossed out Ryan's name and wrote in Jonathan's. We wanted it to look like we were too cheap to buy another poster. The next day we bought some helium balloons, but we asked the lady to fill them only about halfway. So instead of floating, they just bobbed around on the floor. We were pretty sure Jonathan would appreciate the humor, although his aunts and uncles might not.

I can't remember why, but for some reason Jennifer couldn't make it to the airport to welcome Jonathan home.

While we were waiting for Jonathan's flight, I noticed that Alisa was there from California. We talked for a while, and then I asked, "Is it awkward waiting here for Jonathan when you're not sure the two of you are still going to feel the same way about each other?"

She smiled. "Yes, it is, actually."

"Hey, don't worry. If he ignores you, I'll tell him you're my date."

She smiled "All right, it's a deal."

"I hope things work out for you both."

"Thanks," she said. "If they do, don't ever think that I'm going to take him away from you. He'll always be your best friend no matter what happens between him and me. I'll always encourage him to sing with Fast Forward, if that's what he wants to do."

I sat with her while we waited. Finally they announced the arrival of Jonathan's plane. His mom and sisters bunched up around where he'd be coming, with Ryan, Brooke, Alisa, and me behind them.

And then he was there—my friend Jonathan! I was so happy to see him. I'd missed his great smile. He looked good, except he'd lost some weight, which he certainly didn't need to do.

I held up the sign so he'd see it as he came into the terminal. He read it and started to laugh.

We let his family have first crack at him—his mom, his two sisters, an aunt and uncle from Boise, and his grandmother. Then it was our turn. He and I did a bear hug.

"Whose idea was the sign?" he asked me.

"Ryan and I worked on it," I said.

"It was great."

Brooke was next in line. "Well, are you going to hug me or not?" she asked.

Jonathan smiled. "Oh, look, my *sister* Brooke!" he announced for the benefit of any General Authority who might have been looking on, and then he gave her a big hug.

Ryan and Jonathan hugged, and then Jonathan saw Alisa. "Oh my gosh!" he said. They just looked at each other. Jonathan wasn't sure what to do. Even though he'd just hugged Brooke, Alisa was in a much different category.

Alisa saved the day. "Welcome home, Elder," she said, sticking out her hand and giving him a big smile.

Relieved, Jonathan gave her a missionary handshake.

"If you want, I can hug him for you," Brooke offered. "I'm his sister, you know."

Alisa smiled. "That's okay. I can wait until he's released."

It was such a big relief for me to have Jonathan back. With him home, I quit feeling like I was alone and drifting.

Alisa stayed a week. The three of us spent a lot of time together. I could see what was going on between her and Jonathan, and it was all right with me. She really had a lot of great ideas—about music, about starting Fast Forward again, and about other things.

Even before Alisa left, Fast Forward got together to practice. It wasn't that bad, really, even without Amber. Jennifer sang Amber's part. She'd listened to the tape so often she had Amber's parts memorized, so we didn't have to teach her much. She wasn't as strong vocally as Amber, but she fit in with us and she learned fast.

After Alisa left, we started practicing every night.

I had come a long way since high school. I was more in control of what I said. But somehow, at a practice, all that seemed to fly out the window. I wanted everything to be perfect, and when it wasn't, I'd get mad.

Jennifer had never seen me at a practice when I blew up. But she did one night the week after Alisa left. "Stop, stop, stop," I cried out. "What is going on here? Brooke, you missed your note. What is wrong with you? I mean, we've only done this song five thousand times."

Brooke was surprised at my reaction. "I thought we were just doing this for fun," she said.

"You think it's fun to sound awful?" I asked.

"You don't have to make such a big deal out of it, Greg," Jennifer said.

"If I don't say something, who will? I mean, you guys seem to think that everything's great if we hit maybe half the notes in a song. Well, I can't work that way. Either we do it right, or we don't do it at all."

222

"You don't have to jump down our throats just because of one missed note," Jennifer said.

"That's just the way I am. If you don't like it, then leave."

"Don't mind him," Brooke said to Jennifer. "He gets this way at practices."

Jennifer came over to me. "You can't go around treating people like dirt, so quit it right now. Who do you think you are, anyway?"

"Just back off, okay? You're always on my case about something," I complained.

"That must be Amber you're thinking of. I'm her sister, Jennifer."

She was right. She'd caught me. "I need a break," I said, leaving to go out to my car.

Always before, Amber would come out to talk me into coming back to the practice, but this time nobody came out. And, in fact, they just went on singing without me.

So after a few minutes I went back inside and joined them.

On the way home, Jennifer let me have it. She told me again that I couldn't go around walking over people like that.

She was right, of course. After I got home, I called and apologized to everybody.

*   *   *   *

The second week in April, one week after Jonathan got home, Jennifer became *The Mystery Lady*. "How important am I to you?" she asked in her driveway after I'd taken her home from a practice.

"I like you a lot."

"Is that all?"

"What do you want me to say?" I asked.

That made her mad. "Just forget it, okay?" She opened the door to get out.

223

I followed her up to her front door. "What'd I do wrong now?"

"Nothing. Just forget it. Can't I be unreasonable once in a while too? Or is that totally reserved for you?"

"Why are you so mad at me?" I asked.

"I'm not mad at you."

"You're mad about something. Maybe you should talk about it."

"Maybe you should just mind your own business!" She slammed the door in my face on her way in.

I tried to talk to her on the phone when I got home, but when I called, her mom said she'd already gone to bed.

The next morning I got up early and went to the Romney Building. I arrived there a little after five o'clock. There was a cleaning cart outside one of the men's rest rooms. I walked in and there she was. She was working in one of the stalls. She saw my feet. "We're closed for cleaning."

"Jennifer, we need to talk."

She came out to see me. "I can't stop working."

"That's okay. Can I help?"

"Most guys aren't very good at this. They take a couple of swipes with a cloth and call it good. I used to have a guy help me, but he wasn't worth much. I kept having to go over what he'd done. These rooms have to be spotless."

"Give me something I can do then."

She thought about it. "Do the counters and the sinks."

She showed me what to do. We worked for a few minutes with mostly just small talk.

"I'm sorry about last night," she said as we made our way to the next rest room.

"Is it something I said?" I asked.

"No, not at all. It's just something I need to tell you, that's all. I found out about it yesterday."

"What is it?"

"Amber broke up with Michael a couple of days ago."

After a long pause, I asked, "What happened?"

"I don't know. She didn't say much, except that it didn't work out. After her finals she's coming home to work and save money. She's decided to go on a mission in the fall. The reason I didn't tell you is because . . . " She stopped and shook her head. "I'm sorry. I don't think I can talk about this now."

"Jennifer," I said softly.

She put up her hand. "Just go away, Greg. I really don't want to talk to you now."

"Nothing's changed between us," I said.

"No, you're wrong. Everything's changed, and you know it."

She was right. Everything had changed.

"Do you have Amber's phone number and address?" I asked.

She blinked back her tears, grabbed a scrap of paper from her cart, and wrote the information down.

"I'm going to go see her," I said.

She smiled through glistening eyes. "Yes, of course. That's exactly what you should do. Give her my love."

I drove home and told my mom what had happened and that I was going to Provo to see Amber. My dad was working, so I talked to him on his cellular phone. He needed to know I wouldn't be around to help him.

I arrived in Provo around noon. Although I'd never attended BYU, I'd been at the MTC, so I was able to find my way to the Wilkinson Center. I called her apartment and got a roommate to give me her class schedule. I was waiting in the hall when she got out of class at one o'clock. She was with two other girls.

She stopped when she saw me. "Greg? What are you doing here?"

"I came to see you."

"Why?"

"I just wanted to know how you were doing, that's all," I said.

"I'm fine."

"You sure?"

"Yes, of course. You came down here just to see me?" Amber asked.

"Yeah, pretty much."

"That is so nice of you to do that," she said.

We were looking into each other's eyes in a way we had never done before. Don't get me wrong. It wasn't true love. That had never been our style. It was more like we both realized what good friends we had been all this time.

"Who is this guy, anyway?" one of her friends whispered.

Amber was embarrassed that she'd forgotten to introduce me. "Oh, this is Greg Foster. We're old friends."

"I can see that," one of the girls said with a big smile.

"Actually, Greg is seeing my sister Jennifer now."

"Oh." The girl's smile disappeared.

"How's Jennifer doing these days?" Amber asked.

"Real good."

"I understand she's singing with you guys," Amber said.

"That's right. She does a good job. She's not as good as you were, though."

Amber smiled. "That's kind of you to say, but I'm sure it isn't true."

I had the feeling we were playing this scene for Amber's two friends, and I didn't like it. "Maybe we could have you sing with us this summer."

"Thanks, but I think I'll be too busy getting ready for my mission. I might need to work two jobs to save up enough money. Besides, you've got Jennifer now."

Everyone had loyalties. Amber and Jennifer had loyalties to each other. I had loyalties to Jennifer. She'd been good to me. How could I hurt her feelings?

226

I had the feeling that Amber, Jennifer, and I were like a train. No matter what other paths we might consider taking, we were always forced to follow the track.

"Can I spend some time with you this afternoon?" I asked.

"I've got a class at three, but I guess I'm free until then."

"Maybe we could have lunch together then."

"That would be good. Where do you want to go?" she said.

Anywhere as long as we could ditch her friends. "Off campus."

*   *   *   *

We got something from Subway and then drove up Provo Canyon to Canyon Glen Park. We sat at a picnic table and ate and then walked along a bike path that parallels the Provo River.

"Jennifer told me you and Michael broke up," I said.

"Yes, that's right."

"What happened?"

"The closer we got to getting married, the more nervous I got. I kept having the feeling that Michael didn't want a wife as much as he wanted someone to stand next to him and look good. I wanted to work after we were married, but Michael didn't want me to. He said there was no need for me to ever work. I told him that once we had kids, I wouldn't want to work, but before that, I didn't see anything wrong with me working. His folks were building this house for Michael and me right next to their house. I started to feel like I was going to be spending my whole life straightening up bath towels and watching someone clean our pool. I'm no China doll. I've always worked. I just can't sit around and do nothing."

"That doesn't seem like something you two couldn't work out," I said.

227

"I agree. We should have been able to work it out, but he wouldn't budge. He wanted me to do all the compromising. That's not what you need in a marriage. Remember in high school when we didn't agree with each other? Well, it got ugly at times, but at least we talked it out until we came to some kind of agreement." She paused. "Michael has been spoiled all his life. He's always gotten his way. I'm not used to caving in and just going along with what someone tells me to do." She sighed. "Finally I decided maybe this wasn't right for me after all. So I told him. He took it very well. Almost too well. I'm wondering if maybe he was thinking the same thing. Anyway, it's over now."

She was wearing a peach-colored cotton button shirt. It was a great color for her. Her hair took on copper tones as the sunlight hit it.

"With Michael out of my life, I've decided to go on a mission," Amber said.

"That's what Jennifer said. You'll be a good missionary."

"I hope so. I'll probably go in the fall. I'll be home right after finals. And then I'll work and save up money until I leave on my mission."

"That's really good."

"Is there any chance that you and Jennifer will get married while I'm gone on my mission?" she asked.

"I suppose that could happen. She's been very good for me."

"I don't suppose you two could rush things a little so I can be at your wedding?"

"I don't think so. We're kind of at a standstill right now."

"What's the problem?"

I sighed. "The problem is she looks a lot like you. Sometimes I get confused who I'm with." I paused. "So we need to work that out."

We sat by the side of the river. I don't think we'd ever been able to talk so easily as we did that afternoon. Nothing

228

earth-shattering. Just two old friends getting together again. The afternoon breeze made a soft whispering sound through the trees, and there was the smell of cottonwood trees.

I was struck once again with how well we knew each other. There was nothing we had to hide from each other because we'd been such good friends in high school. We'd both seen each other at our worst and also at our best.

After we ate, we practiced skipping rocks across the water. The record was six skips, which I did. She teased me by saying I'd cheated because I always had the flatter rock. To prove that wasn't the reason, I found her the smoothest, flattest rock there could be and challenged her to break my record. She smiled and said she didn't need to compete with me because she already felt good about herself. "I'll just keep the rock as a souvenir," she said.

"Do you know why it's so smooth?" I asked.

"Of course. The water rubbed it smooth."

"That's like us. I'm the rock and you're the water. You got rid of my rough spots. Do you have any idea how much I learned from you?"

"I learned from you too, Greg. I think we're more like two rocks, polishing each other."

We made our way up the bike path. This was a time to celebrate our friendship.

"Greg, I've got to tell you something," she said. "I've never met any other guy I could talk to as easily as I can talk to you."

"I know. Me either with girls. I've missed that."

"I have too."

We talked about our testimonies, how they had grown, what we had learned from life. We talked about our folks, how much more we appreciated them now than we had when we were younger.

We talked about our friends—Ryan, Jonathan, and Brooke and how they had each grown and changed.

We talked about ideas. She had recently taken a class on the poet Robert Frost, and she quoted one of his poems from memory: "Stopping by Woods on a Snowy Evening."

I knew it was getting late and that we didn't have much time left. "How about if you look at the river, and I look at you?"

She smiled at the request but did what I asked. While she studied the river and the trees and the shadows against the far bank, she let me look at her wonderful face. The surprising thing was that there were few if any romantic thoughts running through my mind. It was more like taking a measure of how far she'd come since high school. There was a gentle beauty in her face that had not been there two years before. There was kindness and refinement and confidence.

She was self-conscious about my looking at her. "So, what do you think you see?" she asked.

"A beautiful woman."

She smiled. "Thank you. You've turned out pretty well yourself."

"I had a good teacher," I said.

"Me too. You're a part of me. I guess you always will be, no matter what happens." She stood up. "This has been wonderful, Greg, but what time is it? I need to make sure I get back in plenty of time. We always have a quiz at the beginning of class."

For one brief instant before we started back, we looked into each other's eyes, and we, just briefly, acknowledged that there was something more than just a good friendship. But we could hardly dwell on that—she was going on a mission and I was dating her sister.

I got her back to campus on time. "Maybe I'll see you around sometime when you get home," I said.

"I'm sure you will. Whenever Fast Forward sings, I'll be in the audience clapping the loudest."

There wasn't much else to say. Except good-bye. Once again.

As I watched her hurry off to class, I said to myself, *I love you, Amber. I don't want you to go on a mission. I want to marry you.*

It was a start. At least I'd admitted it to myself.

Before I left Provo, I stopped and bought a card. I thanked Amber for a wonderful afternoon. I mailed it as I was leaving town. I knew she'd appreciate the card. After all, she was the one who taught me to do things like that.

*   *   *   *

Before our missions, when Jonathan and I needed to talk, we went camping, but now, after our missions, we went to the temple.

We went to the Idaho Falls Temple the next day. On our way to Idaho Falls, I told him that Amber was coming back to get ready to go on a mission.

"What are you going to do?" he asked.

"What can I do? Is it right for me to stop her from serving a mission? My mission was the best thing that ever happened to me. How can I stand in her way? And if I do, what about Jennifer? I don't want to hurt her feelings. She's been so good to me."

"So, what *are* you going to do?" Jonathan asked.

"I don't know. I was hoping I could get some direction today in the temple."

It's hard to explain what it means to go to the temple. There's such a feeling of peace. Just being there with Jonathan comforted me. I said a lot of silent prayers that things would work out.

In the celestial room of the temple, Jonathan and I talked in soft tones about our missions. We had gone out to change the world, but by the time we'd been out a year, we had realized it is very hard to change the world. And so we'd ended up teaching and baptizing a few people. But after we were home, we realized that *we* were the ones who had changed the most.

On our way home, I still didn't know how it was going to work out. But I did feel that Heavenly Father was aware of my situation and would help me.

*   *   *   *

"Ladies and gentlemen, back for the first time in two years, Rexburg's own singing group. Let's give a big hand to Fast Forward!"

It was June, and we were back singing again, this time for the Sons of Norway annual picnic. The audience was polite, although some talked or ate through our concert, but that's what you'd expect at a picnic. A few glared at us because we were interrupting their conversations, and a few listened to the new sound of Fast Forward.

Amber was leaning against a tree, watching us perform. She seemed genuinely happy that Jennifer was having the same kind of experience she'd had. After we finished, Amber came up and told us what a good job we'd done.

We all decided to go to the sand dunes to cook some hot dogs. It would be kind of a reunion. We talked Amber into coming with us.

Usually Jennifer sat in the front with me when the group was going somewhere. I wondered if she'd do that with Amber along. Or if Amber would sit in the front.

They decided to sit by each other, clear in the back.

At the sand dunes, sitting by the fire across from Amber, I tried not to pay a lot of attention to her because I didn't want to hurt Jennifer's feelings, but a couple of times Jennifer caught me staring at Amber. Amber must have known I was looking at her, but she never made eye contact. So, it was a little tricky.

Amber finally had it with me looking at her. She met my

gaze boldly and said, "I'm so excited about my mission. I can hardly wait to go."

I decided to enjoy the moment and not worry about the future. Amber was going on a mission and there was probably nothing I could do to stop that from happening. Maybe after she was gone, I would marry someone else. Maybe even her younger sister.

We ended up singing songs from girls camp. Amber, Brooke, and Jennifer taught them to us. After they'd run out of songs, they asked the guys to teach them songs from Scouting. We told them that Scouts didn't sing.

We stayed later than we should have. On the way home, Brooke and Ryan sat in the back seat of the minivan, talking privately to each other, not really seeming to notice that we were there. Jonathan sat with Jennifer and told her all about Alisa.

Amber sat in front with me. She asked me about my mission. The more I talked about what I'd learned, the better I felt. My mission had been the best thing that had ever happened to me. I realized it would be the same for Amber. By the time we pulled into her driveway, I didn't feel so bad about her going on a mission.

I walked Amber and Jennifer to the door and said good night.

It was a good night after all.

15

Just after supper on the fifth of July, Jennifer called. "Greg, hurry up and get over here! I have some really good news. I just found out today. Gosh, I'm so excited."

I went right over.

Clear back in January, Jennifer and I had worked out a way for me to pick her up without my having to actually go inside. The idea was that Jennifer would watch for me and come out of the house. That way, I wouldn't have to confront her dad. He enjoyed watching me squirm. "You're here for Amber?" he asked me once at the door.

"No, Jennifer, actually."

"Really? My little girl, Jennifer?" he asked. I wasn't as intimidated by Mr. Whittaker as I was before my mission, but Jennifer didn't appreciate the way he teased me. So we worked out a system.

But this time, when I pulled up, it was Amber, not Jennifer, who flew out of the house. She ran over to my side of the car. I rolled down my window. "Talk her out of leaving, Greg. There's no reason for her to leave."

"What?"

A second later Jennifer ran out and jumped in the car. "Let's go. Good-bye, Amber."

"Talk some sense into her," Amber said to me as I was backing out of their driveway.

I really need to get away from this family, I thought.

Jennifer and I drove away. "What's going on?" I asked.

"I got a job. I'm going to be working for the rest of the summer at Badger Creek Leadership Camp. I'll be working with youth groups. It's what I've always dreamed of doing. One of the girls got sick and had to quit. They had my application and called me today. Isn't that great?"

I was stunned. "You're leaving?"

"Yes, I'm going there tomorrow morning. I'm so excited."

"But what about Fast Forward?"

She tossed off the question as if it weren't important. "You'll have to get someone else. Ask Amber. Maybe she can fill in."

My mind was racing. I wasn't sure what was happening. "Is there any other reason why you took this job?" I asked.

"That's strange. Amber asked me the same question. There isn't. It's just a great job."

"Is this about Amber and me?" I asked.

"No, of course not." She paused. "But I do think you two need some time together. Don't you?"

"I don't know."

"Trust me—you do. Whatever happens, Greg, it's all right with me. I mean, it really is." She stopped. "I'm okay with this. My dad gave me a father's blessing, and that's helped me a lot. It's going to be all right, Greg. Whatever happens."

"Amber's going on a mission."

"I know, but she won't be gone forever. We'll just have to see what happens."

We drove around for an hour, and then I took her home. At the door she kissed me on the cheek and then went inside.

It was much later that I found out that shortly after Amber had come home, Jennifer had spent hours trying to

235

find any job that would take her away for the rest of the summer.

Jennifer did this for Amber and me. So Amber and I could be together before she left on her mission. So we could see where we stood.

She did it for us. It still chokes me up.

*　　*　　*　　*

With Jennifer out of the picture, Amber started singing with us again.

Amber and I were strangely reserved around each other. Amber may have felt a loyalty to Jennifer, or else it was because she was getting ready for her mission. At any rate, the only time she and I spent together was singing with Fast Forward.

We would get together every night after work to practice. And sometimes on Saturday we would be together from noon until two or three in the morning, depending on where we traveled to perform.

Singing with Fast Forward wasn't the same as it had been in high school. We were older, and, hopefully, wiser. We knew by then that instant success is seldom instant. We treated the summer as a gift that might never be repeated. This might be our last chance to ever be together.

Amber and Brooke had taken voice lessons while the guys had been on missions. They were both much better singers than they'd been in high school. They also knew a lot of musical terms the guys were ignorant of. Terms like *sforzando,* for example.

"I think we need a *sforzando* here," Amber said one night during a practice.

At first there was just a puzzled silence. And then I said, "Let's see. Isn't that one of the new Volkswagens?"

"No, actually it's a hot dog with chili," Ryan added.

236

"You guys are all wrong," Jonathan said. "Bubba Sforzando is a linebacker for the Buffalo Bills."

Eventually Amber told us what it meant. She was right. It was what we needed.

*   *   *   *

Everyone had someone now, except me and Amber. But she didn't count because she was going on a mission. Brooke and Ryan had gone beyond being just good friends. Jonathan and Alisa, although apart much of the time, were now talking about getting married.

The more time I spent with Amber, though, even while talking about serving a mission, the more I realized how seriously in love I was with her. I didn't see how I could stand to be separated from her for eighteen months. But I kept thinking, *If she really wants to serve a mission, who am I to stand in her way?*

Once, after a practice, I asked Brooke, "Does Amber ever talk about me?"

"Well, yeah, sure. I guess so."

"What does she say?" I asked.

"I don't know. Just the usual."

"Mainly about the group?"

"Yeah, mainly. Why are you asking?" she asked.

"Oh, no reason."

"Come on, Greg. I know you better than that."

"It's just that I like her better than I used to," I admitted.

"How much better?" she asked.

"A lot better. And in a different way."

"Are you in love with her?" she asked.

Strangely enough, I had to think about it. Not because I didn't love Amber, but because I felt even admitting it was a lost cause—that she and I would always be out of sync. Just before my mission, she was serious about me. And now it

237

was my turn. I couldn't see that we'd ever get it right. "What difference does it make?" I said. "She's going on a mission."

"Just answer the question," Brooke continued. "Are you in love with her?"

"Yes, very much. I don't want her to go on a mission. I want her to marry me."

"Does she know that?" Brooke asked.

"No."

"Well, are you going to tell her or not?" Brooke asked.

"What good would it do? She's going on a mission anyway."

"You have to tell her how you feel," Brooke said.

"What about Jennifer? She's been a good friend. I'm sure Amber doesn't want to do anything that would hurt Jennifer."

Brooke shook her head. "This is crazy. Everybody's walking around on tippy-toes. If you love Amber enough to marry her, you've got to tell her. Is that such a hard concept?"

"All she talks about is going on a mission. How can I stand in her way?" I asked.

"You don't have to plan out her whole life. But you do need to tell her how you feel. And if you want to marry her, then you have to ask her."

"Why?" I asked. "So she can shoot me down like she always does?"

"What if she's thinking, *If he was really interested in me, he'd say something.* Tell her how you feel, Greg. You have to do it, and you have to do it right away."

"I'm not sure how to do it."

"It's not that hard. You just say—*I love you, and I want to marry you.*"

"She'll laugh at me," I said.

"Not when she knows you're serious." Brooke paused. "You'd better start talking. She'll be turning in her mission papers real soon."

When I tried to reach Amber the next day after work, her

238

dad answered the phone. "Jennifer's gone. She'll be away all summer," he said once he recognized my voice.

"I'm calling for Amber."

"Amber?" he asked after a long silence. I was sure he was doing this on purpose.

"Yes, Amber."

"You know what? I'm grateful we don't have any more daughters at home. I get confused."

"Can I please talk to Amber?" I asked.

"She's not home. She's having her mission interview with our bishop."

I asked him to have her call me.

Amber called me at nine. She was excited. She was almost finished with her mission papers. She told me she had scheduled an interview with her stake president for Sunday. "With any luck," she said, "I'll be sending in my papers on Monday."

I had a sinking feeling. I was already too late. "You'll be a good missionary."

"I hope so."

A minute later I called Brooke and told her what'd happened. "How can I stand in her way?" I asked.

"You want me to come over there and knock some sense into your head? She needs to know how you feel. Tell her."

I decided Brooke was right. I had to tell Amber. But I didn't have much time. Once she sent in her papers, it was almost a done deal. I had to do something, and I had to do it fast. And it had to be something that her bishop and stake president would recognize as a valid reason for her not to serve a mission.

I called my stake president. He told me that if Amber had immediate prospects for marriage, Amber's stake president might advise her to delay her mission until that was resolved.

Like if somebody had proposed to her, for example.

239

The next day I bought an engagement ring. It cost me eight hundred dollars. I put a hundred dollars down and agreed to pay the rest in installments. It was going to take me a couple of years to pay it off. But it'd be worth it if Amber said yes.

At the practice that night, during a break, I approached Amber. "I was wondering if you'd like to go with me to Mesa Falls after this is over."

"You mean everybody?"

"No, just you and me."

She looked confused. "What for?"

"I don't know. Just to see it."

"I've seen it lots of times."

I decided that if I needed to beg, I'd do it. "Amber, please, just this once, go with me to Mesa Falls."

She noticed my change in attitude. "Well, sure, okay."

At first on the way up, we didn't talk much. I had some music playing. It was a blend of music and the sound of ocean waves. I looked over at her. Her eyes were closed, but she was moving to the music.

She was wearing an off-white polo shirt and a baseball cap she wore occasionally.

I felt like my whole future depended on this night. I was too nervous to talk. But Amber didn't seem to notice.

She was the best friend I'd ever had. If I didn't marry her, all that would end someday. I knew there was a danger in what I was planning to do that night, and that I might end up losing her even as a friend. But I had to tell her how I felt, because if I didn't, she'd leave on her mission, and maybe we'd never get together again.

The music stopped. She opened her eyes and looked over at me. "Makes you wish we were going to the beach for a midnight swim, doesn't it?" she said.

"I'd like that very much."

"This is really weird, being here without everybody else," she said. "I keep wondering why everybody in the back is so quiet."

"We should have been doing this all along."

"Why?" she asked.

I didn't know what to say. If she had a clue about how I felt about her, she wasn't letting on. "I don't know," I finally said.

"Jennifer called last night. She loves her job. She said to tell you hello."

"She's a cute kid," I said.

"Have you taken a good look at her lately? She's no kid."

"You're right."

"Do you like her?" Amber asked.

"Yes, very much—as a friend."

"She'll be back in the fall. I'm sure she'll want to sing with you guys after I'm on my mission."

"I suppose."

"I am enjoying singing again, though. Sometimes I wish we could just go on the way it is now for the rest of our lives."

"I've wished that too."

She must have decided to change the subject. "Jennifer told me your mom got a cat while you were gone, but that you don't like cats. So how is that working now?"

"He sleeps on my bed at night," I grumbled.

She seemed surprised. "Really? So you two are pals now, right?"

"Not really. I hate it that he sleeps on my bed."

"Why do you let him do it then?"

"He comes in my room late at night when I'm asleep. That's why I don't like cats. They're too sneaky."

"My gosh, Greg, he's a cat. What do you want him to do, make an appointment?"

241

"You're right," I said.

"We don't have that much time together before I leave on my mission. I'm so excited about going. That's all I can think about. It's not just the idea of telling people about the Church, but, also, it'll be such a change. The last few weeks I've felt like I was on a plateau. I think it's good to be constantly challenged. You know, having new experiences, doing new things. Do you ever feel that way?"

"I've felt that way too," I said. "I'm ready for some new experiences."

"What kind of experiences are you thinking of?" she asked.

I felt my face getting warm. What I was thinking was that I wanted to be married to her. "Oh, you know . . . something I've never experienced before."

"That is so weird—both of us feeling the same way."

By the time we got to the parking lot at Mesa Falls, it was eleven-thirty. The only other time I'd been there at night was during a full moon, but we had no such luck that night. Fortunately, I had a flashlight in my pickup. It helped us make our way along the trail leading to the falls.

I tried to hold Amber's hand, but she wouldn't have it. "I can see okay, really."

We made our way down the path that led to the lookout by the falls. We didn't say much until we walked down to the vantage point directly over the falls.

"I have something for you!" I shouted, trying to be heard above the roar of the falls.

"What?"

I pulled a ring box from my pocket and shined my flashlight on it and handed it to her. It felt like when I was in grade school and brought a Christmas present to my first-grade teacher and watched while she opened it, all the time worrying she wouldn't like it.

Amber's reaction completely caught me off guard. She

burst out laughing. "I remember this!" Our faces were practically touching because it was so noisy next to the falls.

"Remember what?" I shouted back, shining the flashlight so I could see her.

"It's a joke, right? You talked about it one time when we came here. Let's see, how did that go? Oh, yeah, you go to give this to a girl and then you pretend to stumble and drop the box over the falls. And then you tell the girl it must be fate and to forget the whole thing. I kept wondering why you wanted to bring me up here. Now I know. You wanted to do this, right? So you got yourself an empty ring box, did you? This is just perfect! What a great gag!"

"Well . . . no . . . actually . . ."

"Now it all makes sense! Well, I can do one better than that!" She moved next to the railing and waved the box over the edge of the falls.

"Don't drop it!" I yelled. As I lunged to grab the ring box, I must have scared her, or else I bumped her too hard, because the ring box slipped out of her hand. I watched it disappear into the misty darkness below.

Eight hundred dollars down a very large drain.

She noticed my horrified expression. "What?"

I didn't want her to know what had happened. I tried to smile, but I'm sure it ended up looking like a grimace. "Nothing. It was a great joke, wasn't it? Let's go home."

I turned to leave, but I felt sick. Amber caught up with me and grabbed the flashlight and shined it in my face. "What was in the box, Greg?"

I couldn't say the words. But she could tell something was wrong by my expression.

"Oh my gosh! There wasn't a ring in the box, was there?" she cried out.

It was impossible to hide it from her. "Well, yeah."

We walked back to where we'd been standing and shined the flashlight down through the mist to the churning water below. She put her hand to her face. "Oh, no," she moaned. "Oh, Greg, what can I say?"

"It wasn't your fault, Amber. It was me. I knocked it out of your hand."

We walked up the trail to a bench and sat down. We were far enough away from the falls that we didn't have to yell at each other anymore.

"I'm so sorry. I'm so terribly sorry," she said.

"Don't worry about it. Really, it's okay. Besides, it was my fault."

"Let's go look for it now," she said.

"Even if we could get down to the bottom of the falls, we wouldn't be able to see anything in the dark. I'll come back in the morning and see if I can find it. It'll probably turn up."

She stood up. "I feel just awful. Can we go now?"

We didn't make it to the car. About halfway to the parking lot, she had to sit down on a bench.

"You okay?" I asked.

"I feel like I'm going to be sick."

"I felt that way at first, but now I'm okay."

She wiped her eyes. "What kind of a ring was it?" she asked.

"It was an engagement ring," I said, embarrassed to admit how badly I'd messed this up.

"Why would you bring an engagement ring up here?" she asked.

"I was going to ask you to marry me."

"Seriously, why did you bring the ring?" she asked.

"That's the reason."

"That can't be it. This isn't funny anymore, Greg. Be serious."

"I am serious. I think we should get married."

"To each other?" she asked.

"Yes."

She sounded like she was in shock. "So I'd be your wife . . . and you'd be my husband, right?"

"Oh, c'mon, Amber. Is that really such a stretch? We've known each other practically all our lives."

"I always wondered what people meant when they talked about being blindsided. Now I know. How much did the ring cost?"

"Not much."

"Tell me the truth, Greg," she warned. "How much?"

"Eight hundred dollars."

"Oh my gosh . . . Look, I'll pay you back."

"No, no, it's all right. It's all my fault. It was a dumb idea to give it to you here."

"What time do you want to go looking for it in the morning?" she asked.

"Maybe six o'clock. That'll give me a couple of hours before I have to be to work."

"Let me help. I don't have to be to work until nine," she said.

We returned to the parking lot and started back to Rexburg.

I tried to be logical. "If it stays in the box, then it'll just float downstream and it might end up getting washed up on the bank somewhere. But if it comes out of the box, then it'll sink down and be buried by the sand on the bottom. We'll just have to see what happens."

We didn't talk much on our way home. At her door, she said, "I can't even begin to tell you how bad I feel about this."

"It's okay. Really. It was totally my fault anyway."

I held her hand for a second, said good night, and then left. Then I went home and tried to sleep. It wasn't easy, though. And even when I fell asleep, I kept dreaming about the ring. I dreamed a fish ate it and a fisherman caught the fish and brought the ring over to me. And then I dreamed

245

that Jennifer was near the bottom of the falls and she caught it but wouldn't give it back to me.

The next morning, Amber came out as soon as I pulled into her driveway. "How'd you sleep last night?" she asked.

"Not very well. How about you?"

"The same. I kept thinking about what we can do to get your ring back. How about if we contact the radio stations and the newspaper and see if they'll advertise what happened?"

After a long pause, I said, "All right."

"You seem reluctant."

"People are going to make fun of us."

"What do we care as long as it helps you get your ring back."

My ring? She might have felt horrible about dropping the ring, but she still didn't get it. It was as though she hadn't even thought about my wanting to marry her.

It's not easy to get near the base of the falls. We had to make our way slowly down a steep path just below the falls and then work our way upstream. But then the walls of the canyon closed in on us. With all the noise and mist and the river churning through the gorge, it was a scary place to be. It was easy to see there was no way we were going to find that little ring box. It could be anywhere—ten miles downstream or resting on the bottom.

I gave up looking long before she did. At one place we came to a shallow area. "It could be here," she said. She took off her shoes and socks and rolled up her pant legs and stepped into the water and searched for the ring. I sat on the bank and watched.

After a few minutes she looked at me. "Why aren't you helping?"

"I don't care about the ring."

"Why wouldn't you care about it? It cost you eight hundred dollars."

"I care about you, not some dumb ring. If I had to throw a hundred rings over these falls to make you see how much you mean to me, I'd gladly do it."

Amber has this thing she does just before she starts to cry. It must be a carryover from when she was very young. Her upper lip comes up, and for a second you can see her teeth, so it's almost like she's smiling, but then the tears come. That's what she did then. And then she waded to the bank and sat beside me. I put my arm around her.

I loaned her my sweatshirt to use as a towel to dry off her feet before she put her shoes on again.

We stayed there, not saying much, until the sun made its way to where we were sitting and that reminded us that it was getting late. I looked at my watch. We both needed to get back for work.

Just before we drove away, I said, "It probably floated downstream and somebody will find it." I said it, not because I believed it, but because I didn't want Amber to feel so bad.

"You think so?"

"Sure I do."

On the way back to Rexburg, she said she had a headache. She thought it might have been because she hadn't eaten anything, So when we got to town, we went through the drive-through at McDonald's. We decided to eat in the parking lot.

Before, when my plan was to propose to Amber near the falls, I had in mind to get down on my knees and formally ask for her hand in marriage. But the loss of the ring had wiped me out. Even so, I needed to propose to her before she had her mission interview with her stake president. He needed to know she had a serious offer of marriage.

So, there, while she was chewing her Egg McMuffin, I turned to her and said, "Amber, will you marry me?"

247

I must not have said it loud enough. "Excuse me. What did you say?"

"Will you marry me?"

She put down her Egg McMuffin and rubbed her forehead. "Is there any aspirin in the glove box?" she asked.

"No."

"Just because I feel bad about the ring doesn't mean I have to marry you, does it?" She said it in a little girl's voice. It made me wonder that if I'd said yes, if she would have obediently agreed to marry me. It was tempting, of course, but I didn't want her to marry me just because she felt guilty about the ring or felt sorry for me.

"No, of course not. Forget the ring. The ring is water under the bridge." I stopped, realizing that probably wasn't the best way to say it.

She started rummaging through the glove box. "Are you sure you don't have any aspirin? It doesn't even have to be aspirin. Tylenol . . . Excedrin . . . Ibuprofen . . . anything."

"I'm sure I don't have anything. Look, don't worry about the ring. Let's just talk about us."

She didn't say anything for a while. I thought maybe it was because she was so overcome with emotion. Maybe, all this time, she'd been holding back in telling me how she felt about me. Maybe this was all it would take.

Maybe not. She reached for the door. "Somebody inside McDonald's has got to have some aspirin."

I felt some responsibility for her headache. "I'll go with you."

We went from table to table asking customers if they had any aspirin. Finally we found a nice grandmotherly-type woman who had some in her purse.

We thanked the woman and returned to the car. "I'll feel better real soon," Amber said.

"Good."

"You're really serious about wanting me to marry you?" she asked.

"Yes, of course."

She was bent over, resting her head on her hand. "I just can't understand you sometimes," she said. "We've gotten along so well. This will probably ruin everything."

"How's that?"

"Because we've always been best friends, but by the time this is over, I don't know what we'll be."

"We'll still be good friends . . . but we'll be married. The only difference will be that . . . well . . . we'll sleep in the same bed at night."

She turned her head to look at me. "Greg, that is so like you, to bring something like that up. Do we have to talk about that? I'm not feeling very well anyway."

Talk about a guy's self-esteem taking a big hit. "Why not talk about it?"

"Because we're friends. Friends should stay friends. They definitely should not get married and spend time . . . in the same bed." She made an expression like someone had just given her a lemon.

I had to smile. "Actually, I wouldn't mind."

"This just hasn't been my week, has it? First I throw an eight-hundred-dollar ring over Mesa Falls, and then I find out you have a dirty mind."

"It's not dirty if you're married. My mom and dad taught me that."

"Really? Well, apparently your family home evening lessons were a lot different from ours." She turned away so I wouldn't notice, but I could tell she was smiling.

"I learned it from watching the way they treated each other. It could be the same for us if we were married."

"Why are you hitting me with this all of a sudden?" she asked.

"Because you've had your interview with your bishop

already, and you're scheduled to meet with your stake president. That's why I had to hurry. Tell your stake president I just proposed to you and that I want to get married right away and that I can't stand to wait for you to serve a mission."

"You want me to tell my stake president that you have absolutely no self-control and can't wait until after my mission for us to get married?"

She was making me mad. "That's right. Tell him that."

"That is so pathetic." She shook her head. "So, basically, the reason you decided to propose is because you wanted to get your offer on the table before I met with my stake president. Is that it?"

"That's only part of the reason."

"What's the other part?" she asked.

"The other part is that I realized I needed to tell you how I feel about you now. Amber, I've loved you ever since that first time we got together to sing. That's been part of our problem. Because you never felt the same way about me, there's been this tension between us. That's why we've had such a hard time getting along. My love for you has just gotten stronger since then. I'm totally serious about wanting to marry you. I love you."

She seemed a little surprised that I had stumbled on the right answer. "But is it fair for you to ask me to change all my plans to serve a mission?"

"Maybe it isn't fair, but this isn't something I just came up with. I've always cared about you. You don't even know this, but I've kept a picture of you on my bulletin board since we were in high school. I look at it almost every day."

"What picture is that?"

"It's from the newspaper, when the girls basketball team took state."

She scowled. "Is that the picture that shows me with my

mouth open and my armpit out there for all the world to see?"

"I don't focus on the armpit. To me the armpit is just part of the whole package. The way I look at it, if a girl has arms, she's got to have armpits too."

Amber shook her head and suppressed a smile. "You haven't had anyone coaching you what to say, have you?"

"No."

"I can tell. I could have helped you—if it hadn't been about me."

I needed to do better. I tried to imagine what Amber or Brooke would tell me to say. "The truth is, I don't think I can stand not being with you for the rest of my life."

"Really?" she said softly, touching my hand. "Maybe if you'd told me this before you gave me the ring, I wouldn't have thrown it over the falls."

"I wanted to get your attention."

"Well, you certainly did that. Are you really serious about not wanting me to go on a mission?"

"Yes, of course. I feel like I've been waiting for you since we were in high school. I don't want to wait anymore."

That made her mad. "Oh, I see—whatever Greg wants, Greg gets. Is that it?"

"Guys are supposed to serve missions. For girls it's an option."

"What makes you such an expert all of a sudden?" she asked.

"I phoned my stake president. Look, I know this has caught you by surprise. You don't have to give me an answer right away."

She sighed. "All right, fair enough. Maybe if we could go on a date. I mean a real date."

"How about tonight?"

"All right, tonight, but only if my headache goes away by then."

I took Amber home, then went looking for my dad. We were supposed to be working, but we ended up sitting in his pickup talking. The more we talked, the more I realized how much I was like him. Except for one thing. He'd learned from being married. "There's one thing about your wife, when you have one, that you always need to remember," he said.

"What's that?"

"When she's mad at you, she's right."

"How can she always be right?"

"It doesn't matter if she's right or not. Whatever she says, you need to treat it like she was right. You might win an argument with her, but if she still feels the same way, it's not really going to matter. Don't expect her to do all the changing. The only person you can change is you. Even now, listen hard when Amber gets after you. She's probably right."

I asked my dad for a father's blessing. He didn't want to give it in his work clothes. We quit work a little early and then went home. We got cleaned up, and then he came into my room and laid his hands on my head and gave me a blessing.

It was just what I needed.

16

In preparation for our big date, I washed and waxed the minivan. I even bought a new shirt and tie. Also, like a lawyer facing a tough case, I wrote down ten reasons why Amber should marry me. When I showed them to my mom, she wasn't impressed.

"All she needs to know is that you love her."

I had hoped Amber would come out when she saw me pull up, so I wouldn't have to go in and face her dad. But either because this was an official date, or because Amber wanted to watch me squirm, she made me walk up and ring the bell.

Mr. Whittaker answered the door. "Greg, how nice to see you. Amber isn't quite ready, but come in anyway." He wasn't his usual sarcastic self. I figured Amber's mom must have put the leash on her husband.

Amber's mom greeted me with even more than her ordinary warmth.

The three of us sat down. "I understand you've proposed to Amber," Mr. Whittaker said. "Are you sure you've got the right one? Amber's the tall one, you know."

Mrs. Whittaker shot a disapproving glance at her husband.

"Yes, that's right. It's Amber I want to marry," I said.

"You mean after her mission, right?" he asked.

I cleared my throat. "Actually, I'm trying to talk her into not going on a mission."

"Why don't you want her to serve a mission?" Mr. Whittaker asked.

"Because I'm ready to get married now."

"Doesn't that seem a little selfish of you?"

I turned to Amber's mom. "Sister Whittaker, did you serve a mission?"

"No, I didn't."

"Thank you." I turned to Mr. Whittaker and smiled. "I rest my case."

I caught just a hint of a smile from him.

Amber must have decided I'd suffered enough. She came into the living room, and we said our good-byes and left.

Amber looked absolutely beautiful. She was wearing a flowery summer dress. Her hair was done up on top, which was a nice change because it helped highlight her long, slender, and very appealing neck.

"You look real nice," I said as we drove away. It was, of course, the understatement of the century. "You smell good, too." She was wearing some kind of nice fragrance.

"Thanks," she said politely. "So do you."

She looked so beautiful that, at the restaurant, it was hard at first for me to keep a conversation going. I'd glance down at my menu, come up with something to say, look up at her and forget it all.

It was hard to believe I'd grown up with this beautiful woman, that I knew her when she used to cut holes in the knees of her jeans, and that once I'd seen her put a slice of pepperoni over one eye so she'd look like a pirate. Could this be the same person? It didn't seem possible. "I really don't know how to act with you tonight," I said.

"I know. Me either. Why do you suppose that is?"

"It's because we're trying to shift gears," I said.

"That's it, all right," she said.

I reached across the table to hold her hand. "I've been thinking about you all day. I'm ninety-five percent certain that I'm hopelessly in love with you."

She fought back a smile. "What about the other five percent?"

"It's an escape percentage. You've got to have it in case things don't turn out."

"I can see you've made a real study of this," she said.

"Yeah, pretty much."

"I've been thinking about us too," she said. "I really think we should try to keep the mission issue separate."

"I see. You want no linkage then between the marriage issue and the mission issue?" I asked.

"That's right, no linkage. First we decide whether or not we should get married. If we do decide to get married, then the next issue is whether or not I should serve a mission."

"Can I ask a question? Why are we talking like a couple of lawyers?" I asked.

"Because we're trying to be careful," she said.

"Yes, of course. So no linkage. I can agree to that. In a way it's like a basketball tournament. The first thing is we've got to get through the quarterfinals. That could be trying to decide if we're going to get married. If we get through that, then we go to the semifinals. That'll be when we decide if you should go on a mission before we get married. And then there's the championship game. That will be when we actually get married." I turned the place mat over and drew the kind of brackets they use for tournaments. "So, right now we're here." I tapped my pen on the paper. "At the quarterfinals."

She smiled. "Excuse me, but should I call you *Coach*?"

"Sorry. I guess I got a little carried away."

"Not at all. I enjoyed it."

The waiter brought us menus and told us the specials of the day and then left.

"I talked to Jennifer today," Amber said. "I told her everything."

"How did she take it?"

"She sounded really happy. She said she wasn't surprised. I told her I haven't decided yet what to do. Oh, she told me to tell you she hopes you find the ring."

We looked at the menus for a while. "Have you decided what you're going to have yet?" I asked.

"I'm thinking of having the baked salmon with rice pilaf."

Fish? I thought. *Why would anyone want to eat fish? And how can anyone in Idaho eat rice with a clear conscience?*

"Really?" I said.

"Why? Is there something wrong with that?"

"No, it's just that I've never known you to order fish before."

"I didn't used to like fish, but now I do," she said.

"Did you pick that up from Michael?" I asked.

"Yes, I did, as a matter of fact."

"I thought so."

"Michael was good for me in many ways."

"How would it be different if Michael were here instead of me?"

"Well, for one thing, we'd both have the baked salmon."

"Anything else?"

"Michael is an avid reader. He loves to talk about world events. It was fascinating to talk to him. He knows so much."

"Really?" I asked.

"Yes."

If she wanted world events, I'd give her world events. "I read today where the Red Wings might fire their manager."

"Really? How interesting." She paused. "What sport do they play?"

"Hockey."

"Michael didn't care much for sports. He was more into global economic issues."

"Oh," I said, feeling foolish all over again.

"Relax, Greg. You don't have to be Michael. Just be yourself."

"Sure. You know what I can't understand? How Michael could stand to let you get away. If I were him, I'd have done anything to get you back."

The waiter came to get our order. Amber still wasn't sure what she wanted. She asked me to order first.

"I'll have the baked salmon and rice pilaf," I said.

Amber smiled at me. "I'll have the same thing," she told the waiter.

"You see? I can change," I said proudly after the waiter left.

She smiled. "I'm impressed."

By the time we finished our salads, we had started to treat each other like we usually did—like old friends. We talked about easy, comfortable things. There was plenty to talk about. Jonathan and Alisa were engaged. Ryan and Brooke seemed to be heading that way.

One important thing I learned that night is this: *Never order salmon and rice pilaf if you're very hungry.*

Over dessert, Amber leaned over and asked, "This is a little awkward to talk about, but we're in new territory, so I think we need to set down some ground rules. Are we going to kiss each other tonight?"

I did not want to seem too enthusiastic about the idea, for fear of scaring her away. "Gosh, I don't know. What do you think about that?"

"I think it's a definite possibility," she said. "But where?"

"On the lips?"

She smiled. "Actually, I meant that in the geographical sense."

"Oh, sorry. How about in your driveway?"

"I don't know if that's such a good idea. My dad is puzzled enough by all this already. First it's *you and me* and then it's *you and Jennifer* and now it's *you and me* again. I don't want him to get too confused. So maybe not my drive-way."

"Where would you suggest we go then?" I asked.

"I really don't know."

"This is just going to be a good-night kiss, right?" I asked. "I mean we're not talking about some marathon session, are we?"

She scowled. "What do you think?"

"Sorry."

"This is so weird," she said. "It's almost clinical. Let's just drop the subject, okay? If it happens, it happens. Where it happens isn't important. Whatever you do, though, please promise you won't take me to Mesa Falls."

After we ate, we drove to Ricks and walked around the gardens, looking at the flowers and shrubs, and as it got darker, bending down to read their names in the fading light of the day.

"Maybe someday we'll have a rose garden," I said.

"I'd like that very much."

"I can see us, at dusk, working in a garden," I said.

"I can see that too. Will we have vegetables in our gar-den?"

"I'm sure we will," I said.

"And will we can or freeze them for the winter?"

"Yes, we'll do that."

"I knew that's what you'd say," she said.

"Is that bad?" I asked.

"No, not at all. It's just that . . ."

"What?"

She seemed on the verge of tears, which made no sense at all. "Is something wrong?" I asked.

She reached for my hand. "No, not really. I just realized

something. I've always gone for flashy guys. Brandon was that way, and so was Michael. You're not like that, though. You're steady and dependable. Even when we sing, you're the one who gives us a background beat. You set the musical foundation for everything the rest of us do. I've always been waiting for my prince in shining armor to come. And yet, all this time, you've been right here next to me, always my friend, always trying to help me any way you could."

"What does this have to do with having a garden?"

"I couldn't see Brandon or Michael ever working in a garden, or helping me can beans, or changing a messy diaper, or any of those things I've seen my dad do in his marriage. But I can see you doing those things."

"So what are you saying?"

"I'm saying that you'll make a great husband and father someday."

"*Your* husband?" I asked hopefully.

"I don't know yet, but, hey, at least this is a start, right?"

"Let me ask you a question," I said. "Some people think that if they find the right person to marry, they won't have any problems in their marriage. Do you feel that way?"

"Not really. I think that no matter who a person marries, they're going to face problems."

"I agree. So the main difference between a successful marriage and one that fails is the ability of the husband and wife to work out their problems. Would you agree with that?"

"Yes, of course."

"We've got it made then. I'm pretty sure we could work out our problems if we were married, because we've been doing that ever since we've known each other."

"You're probably right. I just haven't thought of you that way before, that's all."

"I know you haven't. Mostly we've been really good friends. And I want that to continue. The truth is that if we both marry someone else, we won't be able to be best

259

friends anymore. I won't be able to call you when I have a problem, and you won't be able to call me. So if we want to stay good friends, the only way that can happen is if we get married."

"I would miss not having you as my best friend," she said.

"Then you have to marry me. That's all there is to it."

"You're very a persuasive guy when you want to be."

At nine o'clock we went to the movie *Mr. Holland's Opus*. On our way out of the theater, I said, "I want to be a Mr. Holland someday."

"You will."

We got into my mom's minivan. "I'll take you home now."

"Yes, of course." We both knew what that meant. Just before we arrived at her house, she said, "I'm getting a real panicky feeling right now."

"You are? Well, that's okay. We don't have to . . . you know . . . kiss."

She breathed a sigh of relief. "Thanks. I'm just not ready for that."

"No problem."

At the door, she said, "Thank you. I had a wonderful time."

"So did I."

"I'm sorry about the other," she said.

"The other?"

"The kissing part. It's just such a big change for us, that's all. I'll think about it and tell you when I'm ready."

"Look, don't worry about it."

"Well, I think it's important that if we do get engaged, we kiss each other at least once."

We hugged each other and said good night.

      *   *   *   *

At two-thirty in the morning, there was a gentle tapping on my second-story bedroom window. "Greg?" a voice called out.

I went to the window and opened it. "Amber! How did you get up here?"

"I climbed the tree. I've thought about it. I'm ready now."

"Ready for what?" I asked.

"For us to have a good-night kiss."

"Now?"

"Yes. Right away. I can't guarantee how I'll feel in the morning."

"Just a minute," I said. It was dark in my room, but I groped around until I found a pair of trousers and pulled them on over my pajama bottoms. I was just putting on my shoes when my mom knocked, then opened my bedroom door. She was tying the sash on her robe.

"Is there somebody out there on the roof? I thought I heard talking," she said.

"Yes. It's Amber."

"Amber? What does she want?"

"Well, actually, she wants me to give her a good-night kiss."

"Now?"

"Yes."

"Why?"

"We're trying to see if we can switch gears."

The light was shining into my room from the hall. My mom looked worried. "Don't switch too many gears."

"I know. We'll be careful."

"Is Amber actually standing on the roof?" she asked.

"Yes."

"Well, invite her in."

261

I went to the window. "My mom says you should come in."

Amber crawled sheepishly through the window and into my bedroom.

"Can I fix you anything?" Mom asked.

"No thanks. I'll just be here for a minute . . . and then I'll be on my way." It was dark, but I think Amber's face was red.

All the talking woke my dad up. Wearing his pajamas, he came into my bedroom. "Is something wrong? Why is everybody up?"

"I need to talk to you privately," my mom said to my dad, pushing him out into the hall. My mom tried to be quiet, but Amber and I could hear what they were saying, "Amber came over because she wants Greg to kiss her."

"Why?"

"Greg says they're changing gears."

"What does that mean?"

"They're trying to see if they're in love with each other."

"Let me get this straight—Amber came over here at this time of night just to have him kiss her?"

"Yes."

"Wasn't he out with her tonight? Why didn't they take care of it then? He's got a full day of work tomorrow. I don't want him falling asleep on the job."

"This won't take long. I think it's just one kiss."

It was too embarrassing to listen to that any longer. Taking Amber's hand, I said, "Let's get out of here." We walked past my parents, down the stairs, and out the front door.

Once we escaped, Amber said, "If anyone ever asks for my most embarrassing moment, this will be it. Your mom and dad probably think I'm some hot, passionate, love-starved woman."

262

"I'm sure they don't." I paused. "But while we're talking about it, do you think there's any possibility you might be?"

"Might be what?"

"A 'hot, passionate, love-starved woman.'"

She punched me in the stomach, but it didn't really hurt.

We walked to her car. "Let me tell you how this happened tonight," she began. "I went to bed like a good little girl, but then I started thinking about what good friends we've been, and then all of a sudden I started to think about you in a different way, a much different way, actually. So that was a big change for me. And now I really want to be kissed, if that's all right with you."

"Do you have any mints or anything?" I asked.

"No, why?"

"I just got up. I probably have morning mouth."

"It's not morning," she said.

"I know, but I've been asleep."

"Breathe on me," she said.

I did.

"You're fine."

"Good. I brushed before I went to bed, but that was a couple of hours ago."

"Did you floss?" she asked.

"No, why?"

"It's very important to floss," she said.

"I can go floss now if that's really important to you."

"No, that's fine. You can start tomorrow."

"I will. Thank you." I started to move in for the kiss.

"Wait." She put her hand out to stop me from getting any closer.

"What?"

"If we break up someday, promise me you won't go around saying I climbed on your roof in the middle of the night and begged you to kiss me."

"You have my word."

263

"I suppose it doesn't matter—nobody'd believe you anyway. Greg, something is happening to me. I don't know what it is. It's not like me to need anybody. When I thought about coming over here, I wasn't going to do it at first because it seemed like a sign of weakness for me to want you to hold me. But then I realized that if we do get married, then maybe feelings like this are okay, because probably that's the way it is when two people are married. They have to go to each other to fulfill their needs—their emotional needs, and, I suppose, their physical needs too. You want to know something? I didn't know I had physical needs until tonight. And then something happened, and now here I am. Say something nice to me first, though."

Actually, I had one or two nice things to say from the list I'd worked on that I hadn't used on our date. This was number four: "If you and I had just met, I'm sure I'd fall in love with you because of how wonderful you are now. Anyone would love you the way you are now."

"Thank you, Greg."

"But, the thing is, we've known each other so long. And if there's still a seventeen-year-old inside that mind of yours, I love that seventeen-year-old. And I love the part of you I knew when we were eighteen and so on, through all the other years we've been best friends. That's why my love for you is deeper than any other guy you'll ever meet."

"Oh, Greg, that is so sweet."

Our first postmission kiss was slow and gentle and unhurried.

"Amber, will you marry me?" I asked.

Her head was resting on my shoulder. "This is really not a good time to ask that."

"Why not?"

"Because you know I'll say yes," she said.

"That's why I asked."

"What if I decide I want to marry you, but that I'd like to go on a mission first?" she asked.

Good question. Was it fair for me to stand in her way if she wanted to serve a mission? "I don't know what to say."

"Just tell me how you feel," she asked.

"If you go away . . . I think it will break my heart."

"Oh, Greg," she said.

Okay, I realize that guys don't usually go around talking like that. Most guys, if their heart got broken, would think about taking it to Sears to see if it was still under warranty.

I knew my heart wasn't really going to break if she left me for a year and a half. I'd get through it somehow. But I also knew I'd be miserable the whole time and that I'd pull into myself and turn glum and I wouldn't smile much. My world turns to gray when Amber's not around. How could I stand to have us separated one more time?

I had grown up to be a man. But being a man is trickier than it looks. It doesn't just mean you can overhaul an engine or can lift things that are heavy or that you can change a flat tire. It means you respect women, and, when you're talking to a woman, you try to say things in such a way that she'll know what you're thinking. And right then I was thinking I didn't want Amber to ever leave me.

She got all misty-eyed. "Greg, that is the sweetest thing any guy has ever said to me."

"I hope so."

"This is so confusing," she said. "All right, I'll talk to my stake president and see what he says."

"Of course, talk to him, but, also, talk to your heart and see what it says."

"Oh, Greg, I love you." She kissed me again and then suddenly pulled away.

"What's wrong?" I asked.

"Is that your dad at the window?"

We waved to my dad and then we kissed again.

"Looks like we finally changed gears," I whispered in her ear.

"Looks that way."

*　　*　　*　　*

Amber met with her stake president after work the next day. I went with her, met him, and then waited in the hall while he talked to her in his office.

A few minutes later, on her way out, Amber told me he wanted to talk with me privately.

I went in and sat down across the desk from him. "I understand you've proposed to Amber," he said.

"That's right. I love her a great deal. I'm hoping we can be married in the Idaho Falls Temple before school starts in the fall."

"She's had her heart set on serving a mission, so this is a hard decision for her," he said.

"I'm sure it is." I sighed. "You're probably wondering why I don't want to wait for her to serve a mission before we get married. I'm sure some guys can do that, but I'm not sure if I can. I don't want to risk losing her. I know that sounds selfish, and maybe it is, but I'm in love with her, and I want to be with her, every day for the rest of my life, and then, even beyond that."

I was afraid he would lecture me on self-control and patience and learning to sacrifice. I knew all about those things. Actually, this was the first time in my life I'd ever let my heart call the shots.

With my head down, expecting the worst, I said, "I love her, President. I want to be with her from now on . . ." And then with a great deal of hesitation, I added, "But, as far as her mission goes, I'll do whatever you think is best."

There, I'd done it. I'd said the words I never wanted to say, and it felt awful. But if Amber's stake president felt inspired that she should serve a mission first, then I'd support that decision. But the thought of her leaving me for a year and a half was very hard to take.

He looked at me for a long time, maybe trying to decide if I was worthy of Amber. Finally he said, "If Amber's willing, and from my conversation with her I think she's starting to lean in that direction now, I'd suggest you two should continue your courtship. And if things work out for you both, then I would not be at all disappointed if you got married."

"Yes! Thank you, thank you!" I ran over and hugged the poor man.

Amber and I were so happy when we left the stake center. I drove to a grocery store. Amber came inside with me while I fed coin after coin into the gum machines. Just my luck—I kept getting gum. It took about five dollars before I finally got a plastic ring. I got down on my knees and placed it on her finger. "Amber, will you marry me?"

It was a little hard for both of us to stay completely serious with shoppers staring at us. "If I say yes, do I get to keep the gum, too?" she asked.

"Absolutely."

"I accept then."

I stood up, and with the shoppers at the checkout counter cheering us, we hugged and kissed once again.

*   *   *   *

Even before we told our folks, we wanted to tell Jennifer our news. So we drove out to see her. Badger Creek is a leadership training camp run by Ricks College where ordinary people are run through a horrible obstacle course. People pay money to be punished physically. Go figure.

"We have some news!" Amber said with a big cheesy grin as soon as we found Jennifer.

"Oh my gosh! Really? That sounds exciting. But don't tell

267

me yet. I'm just finishing my shift. Let me give you a tour around the place, and then we can talk."

Our tour ended up in front of what looked like a telephone pole, about twenty-five feet tall, except it didn't have any wires. There was a ladder leaning up against the pole. And then above the step ladder there were several one-foot lengths of two-by-fours nailed into the pole that could serve as a makeshift ladder. Two taller poles, rigged with cables, allowed a climber, fitted with a harness, to be safely belayed at all times.

"You want to try it?" Jennifer asked.

"Not really," I said.

"What exactly do you do?" Amber asked.

"Well, it's real easy. You use the ladder to climb partway up the pole, and after we take away the ladder, you use the two-by-four pieces to climb to the top. Then you stand up on top of the pole, turn around, and jump across and grab that trapeze. Then we lower you down."

"What if someone doesn't make it?" I asked.

"You'll have a harness around you attached to a rope. If you fall, we just lower you down. There's no danger at all. Who wants to try it?"

"I will," Amber said.

"Great," Jennifer said.

It took several minutes to get Amber rigged up in the harness.

"This is Kevin," Jennifer said with a big smile. "He'll be helping me."

The way Jennifer and Kevin smiled at each other it was obvious something was going on between them.

Finally everything was ready. Amber climbed up the ladder to the two-by-fours. They took the ladder away, and she crawled up the makeshift ladder until she reached the top. Without even pausing, she stood up on top of the pole, twenty-five feet in the air. When she lunged for the trapeze, she missed, but Kevin and Jennifer lowered her safely down to the ground.

"Okay, Greg, you're next," Jennifer said.

I looked at my watch. "No thanks. It's late, and, besides, we have something really important to tell you."

"Amber did it *and she's a girl*," Jennifer said to rub it in.

She knew I'd fall for that. "Fine, no problem. I'll do it," I said.

I should have just gone up the way Amber did, without stopping to think. But just before I reached the top of the pole, I paused to decide how I was going to stand up on top of the pole. That was not a good idea. It also was not a good idea to look down. I froze. *A person could die trying to do this,* I thought.

I didn't want it to be that obvious that I was scared to death. So I tried to buy some time. "Amber and I just got engaged," I said, clinging to the pole.

"Oh, my gosh!" Jennifer screamed. "That is so great!"

"We knew you'd be happy," I said, wondering how I'd look in the coffin.

Jennifer and Amber went crazy hugging each other. That was great, except Jennifer dropped the rope that was supposed to keep me from killing myself.

Finally Jennifer got back into a belay position with Kevin to help her.

Everyone was waiting for me to do something.

"Is there some reason why you're not moving?" Jennifer asked.

"No, no reason at all," I said.

"Well, hurry up then."

It was awful. Now I was *sure* I was going to die.

Jennifer seemed unconcerned about my impending death. "So when's the wedding date?" she asked Amber.

"We haven't talked about it."

"Where are you going to have the reception?" Jennifer asked.

"You got any ideas?" Amber asked.

"Well, it depends on how much you want to spend," Jennifer said.

"Excuse me, does anyone care about me up here?" I asked.

Jennifer glanced up at me. "Just jump, Greg. Don't be such a wimp."

Wimp, was I? I stood up, turned around, and leaped for the trapeze. And, of course, missed.

But I didn't die. They lowered me down safely, just like Jennifer said they would.

Once I got down, Jennifer and Amber walked off together, leaving me there with only Kevin. He helped me get my harness off.

"Women," I muttered.

"I know, I know," he said.

* * * *

After we left Badger Creek we returned to Rexburg to tell Amber's mom and dad our news.

When we walked into the house, Mr. Whittaker took one look at our silly grins. "What's going on?" he asked.

"Dad," I said, rushing to give him a big hug. I held on for dear life.

"Oh my gosh." He turned to his wife. "I kept telling you we needed to move, but would you do it? No. Now look what's happening."

"Sir, I'd like to ask your permission to marry Amber," I said.

I expected him to say something awful to embarrass me, but he didn't. He shook my hand. "If I had to pick a husband for Amber, you'd be the one I'd choose. I've always felt that way about you."

I was shocked. "You have?"

"Yes, that's why I was always so friendly when you dropped by."

"What are we doing now, rewriting history?"

It was the first time I'd ever seen him break into a real smile. "Something like that. But don't be too hard on me. In twenty years you see if you don't treat the boys who come around for your daughters just the way I treated you."

He had a point, all right.

*   *   *   *

My mom and dad took the news just the way I knew they would, with my mom all teary-eyed, hugging her future new daughter, and my dad telling Amber he had always hoped we'd get together someday.

It was wonderful except for one thing. "Is that your cat?" Amber asked, as Sylvester climbed up on the couch next to her.

"Yes, that's Sylvester," I said. "I'll take him outside."

"Don't do that." She reached out for him, and he came to her and plopped down on her lap. She stroked his fur. He closed his eyes in sweet contentment.

"I just love cats," Amber said. "We will have a cat some-day, won't we, Greg?"

My mother gave me a big smile. It was, I'm sure now, her revenge for all the bad things I'd ever said about Sylvester.

"Whatever you say, dear," I said, against my better judgment.

17

It was another night around a campfire at the sand dunes. Except this time we were sitting as couples: Amber and me, Ryan and Brooke, Jonathan and Alisa, who was visiting from California for a few days.

We were all happy. We were all broke. And we were all engaged. Amber and I had talked our folks into an August 23 date. It wasn't much time to prepare, but, like I said to Amber, "I'll do whatever it takes to get ready for this. I'll lick the stamps. I'll address the envelopes. I'll do whatever you want me to do."

Amber, her mom, and I were working hard to get everything ready in time.

After us, the next in the holding pattern was Ryan and Brooke. Brooke's family was having a family reunion at the end of August, and they could have all her aunts and uncles there if they had the wedding on August 31.

With Alisa and Jonathan, it was turning out to be a little more difficult to arrange schedules for relatives and friends in two different states. They were going to get married in the San Diego Temple the day before Thanksgiving.

We were going to be together fall semester because all of us would be at Ricks. But in January, Ryan and Brooke were planning to move to Pocatello, so Brooke could finish up at ISU. Jonathan and Alisa were talking about moving to California. Jonathan could work for one of her uncles while attending a community college there.

So we, that is, Fast Forward, had just a few months left. Unless.

"What if we could get a job singing every night?" Brooke asked.

"Around here? Forget it."

"C'mon, we've got to know somebody who can help us," Brooke said.

We doused the wood and drove to Ryan's house and sat down in front of his computer and came up with a list of everyone we knew who might be able to help us.

The next day we all had people to call. We asked each of them to buy a copy of our tape and send it to someone they knew who might be able to help us.

We called about thirty people. Most of them said they'd help us.

We sent them a copy of the tape we'd made in high school.

And then we waited.

*   *   *   *

Amber and I were married in the Idaho Falls Temple on August 23. There's a lot about that day I can't remember. I can't remember much of what the temple president said by way of advice. I do remember, though, how right it seemed for both of our families and our close friends to be in the sealing room together.

In a way, I guess Amber and I had been preparing for that day all our lives. It was graduation day for both of us.

In all our preparations we hadn't given much thought to what kind of a day it would be. I suppose we pictured it being sunny, but it wasn't. It rained most of the day. The photographer wasn't able to get any shots of us outside the temple, but, other than that, it didn't make much difference. And having grown up as the son of a farmer, I knew that rain brought life to the land so why not to the beginning of our life together as husband and wife.

Because we never did find the ring that went over Mesa Falls, we had finally given up and gotten another one. Amber said she didn't care that it wasn't as expensive because all that really mattered was that we loved each other.

In the sealing room where we were married, there were two large mirrors on opposite walls. Before the actual ceremony began, the temple president had us stand and look at our reflections in one of the mirrors. We saw what seemed like hundreds of reflections of ourselves. He said the many reflections might represent all our ancestors in the past all the way to Adam and Eve. And then he had us turn around to face the other wall. Again, we saw endless images of ourselves in the mirror. He said that these images might represent our children and their children, stretching forward into time.

"Here you are," he said, "in the present, forming the link between your ancestors and your posterity. Both the past and the future are focused beautifully on the here and now of the significant vows you are about to make. Surely, your ancestors in the past, and your future children, still in the spirit world, all join with you this day in the celebration of the eternal vows you are about to make."

It made me realize that this was more than just two people who loved each other, pledging their love for each other. Our wedding, as do all temple weddings, would have eternal consequences.

I can't describe how wonderful it was for Amber and me to kneel across the altar and look in each other's eyes and be married for time and eternity.

Our reception was held that night in Rexburg in her

ward's cultural hall. For the program, Fast Forward sang a new song Jonathan had written for us.

*   *   *   *

We spent the first night of our married life in my uncle's cabin near Island Park. The next day I woke up at ten-thirty. The sun was pouring into the cabin. I looked to my right and there was Amber, asleep beside me in our honey-moon bed.

Outside I could hear birds. A slight breeze rattled one window. We were bathed in sunshine, together in bed, bride and groom. On the night table next to the bed lay the half-burned candle from the night before, and on the floor was the boom box I'd brought so we could listen to music. They both had helped to make our first night together even more wonderful.

At that moment I could not imagine ever being any happier than I was right then. I was lying on my side looking at Amber as she slept, something I had, of course, never done before. She was so dazzlingly beautiful in the light of our first morning together.

After a few minutes, I decided I couldn't wait for her any longer, so I touched her cheek. She woke up, looked over at me, and smiled. "Excuse me, but are you supposed to be here in my bed?" she asked.

"Actually, as a matter of fact, I am."

"How nice for me," she purred.

"For me, too." The perfume of the night before was still very much with her.

"What do you want to do today?" she asked.

"Whatever you want."

"I'd like to take a hike," she said.

"All right."

Amber turned and gave me a kiss. "Here's to all the girls from high school who told me they didn't see any harm in

275

going all the way before they were married, as long as the guy and the girl loved each other. Their first time couldn't have been as wonderful as our first time."

"Yes, we definitely have the last laugh now," I said.

"Yes, we do, and that's a fact."

"Excuse me, but have I ever kissed your left eyebrow?" I whispered.

"Actually . . . I don't believe you have."

I kissed her left eyebrow. "There," I said.

"Come to think of it, I don't believe you've ever kissed my right eyebrow either." She was nearly giggling. "It probably feels left out."

Eventually we got ready for that hike of ours. The phone rang just before we were about to leave. "Who did you give the phone number here to?" Amber asked.

"Nobody."

"Are you sure?"

"Yes."

Amber was upset with me. "This is our honeymoon. We shouldn't be bothered by anybody. This is our time to be together."

"I didn't give out the number to anyone," I said. "It's probably just a wrong number. Besides, it could be for you."

"I don't even know the number."

"We won't answer it then," I said.

"Fine." We started to leave. "What if it's an emergency, though?" she asked.

"You want to answer it?"

"I'm not sure. What if it's just Ryan? It'd be just like him."

"Do you want me to answer it?" I asked.

"Yes, go ahead. In case it's an emergency."

I picked up the phone. "Hello." I turned to Amber. "It's Jonathan."

Amber grabbed the phone. "Hello, Jonathan. Look, I

know you're wondering about something. Yes, we did have a wonderful night together."

I put my ear close to hear their conversation.

Jonathan cleared his throat. "Actually, I didn't call about that."

Amber's face began to turn red. We both knew Jonathan would tease her about this for a long time. "Why did you call then?" she asked.

"Last night I got a call from a producer in California. Brandon Eliason's dad sent him our tape. He'll be in Boise next week and wants us to audition for him. If he likes us, he'll book us in Holiday Inns in Southern California beginning in January. He says he thinks he can keep us busy for at least six months. He thinks it might just give us the break we need."

It didn't seem right that Brandon Eliason, the guy Amber had gone with her senior year of high school, should be the one to get us our big break. But it made sense. Brandon's family had come from California. Brandon's dad was rich and knew a lot of influential people. From a philosophical point if view, I realized I should be glad Amber had gone out with Brandon her senior year. I should be, but I'm not. I haven't reached that state of perfection yet.

Anyway, because of Brandon's dad, we now had a chance.

"Oh my gosh," Amber said, sitting down on the bed.

"This is my dream," she said softly.

*   *   *   *

We've been on the road now for three months. We do two shows a night. We're working on a CD with some original songs. We still have great expectations about our future.

In high school the five of us were best friends, and we had a dream.

Dreams never die. But with time, though, they do grow and change.

Last night Amber told me we're going to have a baby.

That's another one of our many dreams.

Books by Jack Weyland

Brenda at the Prom

Charly

First Day of Forever

If Talent Were Pizza, You'd Be a Supreme

Kimberly

Last of the Big-Time Spenders

Michelle and Debra

A New Dawn

Nicole

Night on Lone Wolf Mountain

On the Run

PepperTide

Punch and Cookies Forever

The Reunion

Sam

Sara, Whenever I Hear Your Name

A Small Light in the Darkness

Stephanie

The Understudy